A DICTIONARY OF
WELLERISMS

A DICTIONARY OF
WELLERISMS

WOLFGANG MIEDER

STEWART A. KINGSBURY

New York   Oxford

OXFORD UNIVERSITY PRESS

1994

Oxford University Press

Oxford   New York   Toronto
Delhi   Bombay   Calcutta   Madras   Karachi
Kuala Lumpur   Singapore   Hong Kong   Tokyo
Nairobi   Dar es Salaam   Cape Town
Melbourne   Auckland   Madrid
and associated companies in
Berlin   Ibadan

Published by Oxford University Press, Inc.,
200 Madison Avenue, New York, New York 10016

LIBRARY OF CONGRESS CATALOGING-IN-PUBLICATION DATA
A Dictionary of wellerisms / [edited by]
Wolfgang Mieder, Stewart A. Kingsbury
p.   cm.
Includes bibliographical references and indexes.
ISBN 0-19-508318-0
I. Mieder, Wolfgang.   II. Kingsbury, Stewart A.
PN6271.D52   1994
398.9'21'0207--dc20   93-11275

Printing (last digit): 9 8 7 6 5 4 3 2 1

PRINTED IN THE UNITED STATES OF AMERICA
on acid-free paper

CONTENTS

PREFACE

This dictionary is the first book-length collection of wellerisms in the English language, containing all British and American wellerisms recorded in earlier published collections of proverbial texts as well as many new texts found through extensive field research. While many of the 1,516 wellerisms collected in this book were first published in literary and humorous magazines in the nineteenth century in Great Britain and North America, there are also numerous texts drawn from twentieth-century literature and from the Margaret M. Bryant collection of proverbial speech.

The Bryant collection is the result of painstaking field research carried out in the United States and parts of Canada by dozens of scholars for the American Dialect Society from the 1940s to the end of the 1970s. This great endeavor yielded approximately 150,000 citation slips, now stored at the library of the University of Missouri–Columbia. Quite a few unique wellerisms are included in this vast archive, ample proof that wellerisms continue to be in oral use among English speakers, and they are published here for the first time. Many others that appear in the archive have, of course, been registered before, but the fact that they were collected from folk speech is an indication of their tenacity as traditional expressions of folk humor.

Although major collections of wellerisms in some of the European languages are readily available and although small collections of wellerisms in English have been published before, in both England and the United States, no one has heretofore attempted a comprehensive collection of the rich British and American materials. This book therefore represents the first attempt to present all English-language wellerisms and their variants together in a single volume. In compiling it, we have attempted to document each wellerism by indicating its geographical origin, by giving its date of origin, and by providing, whenever possible, other information on the earliest known source, whether written or oral, in Great Britain, the United States, or, in several instances,

Canada. Further, for each wellerism we have listed precise references to its registration in one or more published secondary sources and/or the Bryant archive. The result is, we trust, an inclusive and well-documented collection of wellerisms, useful to the scholar of proverbial folk speech and appealing to the general reader interested in folk humor as such.

Oxford University Press (USA) generously supported our work on this book by giving us a grant for creation of a computerized database and by providing the expert editorial and technical help of Claude Conyers, Stephen Chasteen, and Catherine Guldner. Billie L. Schuller wrote software and designed and implemented the database for these rich materials. Our wives, Mildred Kingsbury and Barbara Mieder, helped with the verification of historical references. The interlibrary loan staffs of the University of Vermont and Northern Michigan University obtained numerous obscure sources for us, while Janet Sobieski of the Department of German and Russian and George B. Bryan of the Department of Theatre at the University of Vermont acted as supportive editorial assistants. We express our thanks and appreciation to all of them, knowing that this book owes its publication in considerable measure to their efforts.

We hope that *A Dictionary of Wellerisms* will be a valuable reference book for paremiologists (proverb scholars) and paremiographers (proverb collectors) as well as a useful research tool for folklorists, cultural historians, sociologists, anthropologists, linguists, literary scholars, and many others. However, scholarly honesty and humility oblige us to reiterate that this dictionary is but a first attempt to bring together in a single volume as many English-language wellerisms as possible. Although our collection will make the study of wellerisms much more accessible for regional, national, and international scholars and general readers, other such collections are needed in order to facilitate historical and comparative study of this fascinating genre on a global basis. It is our hope that we have laid the cornerstone for the study and enjoyment of the rich tradition of wellerisms in English, and it is our intention to continue collecting wellerisms from various media—print, electronic, and oral—with an eye to a second, substantially expanded edition of this book.

W.M.   S.A.K.

INTRODUCTION

The scholarly term *wellerism* did not appear in any dictionary until 1928, when it found its way into the tenth volume of James Murray's renowned *English Dictionary on Historical Principles* (Oxford, 1928). It is cited there as part of the title of Charles Kent's *Wellerisms from "Pickwick" and "Master Humphrey's Clock"* (London, 1886), which comprises numerous humorous selections from these works by Charles Dickens. Referring to the two main characters of these books, Sam Weller and his father, Tony Weller, Kent states that a "wellerism [is] a speech or expression employed by, or typical of, either of these characters" (p. 294).

The lexicographers of the gargantuan *Webster's Third International Dictionary of the English Language* (Springfield, Mass., 1963) also refer to these witty Dickensian characters and provide a somewhat more informative definition by explaining that a wellerism is "an expression of comparison comprising a usu[ally] well-known quotation followed by a facetious sequel (as 'every one to his own taste,' said the old woman as she kissed the cow)" (p. 2595). Finally, in the twentieth volume of the second edition of *The Oxford English Dictionary* (Oxford, 1989), one discovers that a wellerism is defined quite precisely as "a form of comparison in which a familiar saying or proverb is identified, often punningly, with what was said by someone in a specified but humorously inapposite situation" (p. 128).

The Oxford English Dictionary also provides the information that the term *wellerism* most likely was used for the first time in the *Boston Morning Globe* of 9 January 1839. Interestingly, James Tidwell also discovered the term in a Philadelphia publication, *Alexander's Weekly Messenger,* bearing the very same date as the Boston newspaper (Tidwell 1950:259). Whatever the provenance of the term, once the popular press began to use it as a headline over short lists of such humorous sayings, it caught on and became recognized internationally. During the nineteenth century, when American newspapers and magazines published numerous short lists of such texts, the somewhat jingoistic term *Yankeeism* was used on occasion, as, for example, in *Yankee Notions,* vol. 1 (1852), p. 78 (see Whiting 1945:4; Loomis 1949:3). This term was abandoned, however, once people realized that wellerisms were not restricted to American folk speech.

To define a wellerism is difficult because of the varied ways of formulating this type of text. Normally a wellerism consists of three parts: a statement (quite often a proverb, proverbial expression, quotation, exclamation, etc.), a speaker who makes this remark, and a phrase or clause that places the utterance in a new light or an incompatible setting. Most wellerisms follow this triadic structure, whose incongruity gives them a typically humorous, ironic, or satirical effect, as in the following examples (numbered according to their sequence in the body of texts).

> "It sure pays to fiddle your time away," said the violin player, as he drew down his $150 a week. (no. 422)
>
> "Overcome evil with good," as the preacher said when he knocked a rascal down with the Bible. (no. 511)
>
> "Let there be light," murmured the raven-haired beauty, as she drew forth the peroxide bottle. (no. 715)
>
> "Ruff," cried the dog as he sat on the cactus. (no. 1069)

There are, however, quite a few wellerisms that do not exhibit the third element of the characteristic triadic structure, as in the following examples.

> "The only trouble with my profession is that it is apt to be a rather confining one," as an ex-convict said. (no. 237)
>
> "I was taken by a morsel," says the fish. (no. 844)
>
> "I'm bored stiff," said the dead man. (no. 1262)

Such texts may have been reduced from longer originals that included the contextualizing situation, or they may well have been coined in this shortened format.

Some wellerisms reverse the normal triadic structure by first identifying the speaker, then giving the situation (often merely by identifying the addressee), and finally stating the quoted speech. The following examples illustrate this type of wellerism.

Said the sieve to the needle, "You've a hole in your head." (no. 606)

As the farmer said to the potato, "I'll plant you now and dig you later." (no. 954)

The ant said to the elephant, "Let's be sports and not step on each other." (no. 1258)

Finally, there are those expanded wellerisms that develop into short dialogues. Two examples follow.

"There's cheat in all trades but hours," observed the clock-dial. "You are a handsome punster," rejoined the bell. "Another word and I'll strike!" said the hammer." (no. 625)

"Do you see the point?" asked the needle of the cloth as it passed through it. "No, but I feel it," replied the cloth with a groan. (no. 965)

The joy and delight in creating one pun after another leads to such strings of wellerisms, in which the speaker of one text is challenged by another.

Because wellerisms are essentially based on the incongruity of combining a more or less straightforward assertion by a speaker with an unexpected or inappropriate situation (see Taylor 1931:217), the results are often witty puns that range from hilarious humor to rather macabre or grotesque satire. There is nothing sacrosanct for the coiner of wellerisms. Literally, anything goes. Yet wellerisms are not necessarily mere silly wordplay. Revelatory comments regarding social issues, political problems, and human nature in general are often hidden behind these short, formulaic phrases. Wellerisms thus frequently serve as indicators of the value system of the society in which they were coined and used, folkloric mirrors of everyday attitudes and popular culture.

Many wellerisms are certainly "politically incorrect" by today's standards of judgment, and this *Dictionary of Wellerisms* contains numerous texts from earlier times that reveal attitudes contrary to the more enlightened and tolerant views of contemporary society. They are included here not only for reasons of scholarly comprehensiveness but also because they indicate clearly how attitudes regarding race, gender, ethnicity, sexuality, obscenity, and so on have changed. In fact, it must be emphasized that the misogyny of wellerisms is very troublesome indeed. There is no doubt that wellerisms, like so many other folklore genres, are the products of a patriarchal society. They are blatantly anti-woman and show the worldview of historical periods during which respect for women was sorely missing.

Despite their abundance in Great Britain and the United States, wellerisms are anything but specifically British or American. (See the Bibliography at the back of this volume.) Swedish, Finnish, Dutch, and German scholars long ago confirmed that wellerisms have been popular in northern Europe for centuries, and at one time they believed that this form of folk speech did not exist in southern Europe. But this claim has long since been discredited, and there are now, for example, numerous collections of Italian wellerisms in many dialects. Wellerisms have also been recorded in the Baltic and Slavic languages, and there is an impressive amount of scholarship on African wellerisms as well. Newer research is showing that people seem to have reacted to proverbial wisdom in the form of wellerisms almost everywhere.

The origin and history of wellerisms are quite nebulous. It has been known for quite some time that wellerisms existed in classical antiquity. Both Friedrich Seiler (1924:1-23) and Archer Taylor (1931:203-208) have drawn attention to such ancient Greek wellerisms as "'All the women we need are inside,' said the bridegroom and closed the door on the bride," by Theocritus, and "'The water will tell you,' said the guide when the travelers asked him how deep the river was," by no one less than Plato. Quintilian cites "'It is not our burden,' said the ox, [looking] at the saddle" in classical Latin, and there are also numerous medieval Latin wellerisms, such as "'Something is better than nothing,' said the wolf when he swallowed the louse," from the eleventh century. Yet recent scholarship has discovered wellerisms even on the cuneiform tablets of the Sumerians, dating from approximately 2500 to 1100 B.C.E. (see Gordon 1958; Alster 1975:211-213). The structure of these early wellerisms differs slightly, usually with the situation before the statement, as, for example, in "The ass, after he had thrown off his packs, 'The burdens of former days are forgotten' [he said]." In addition, many African wellerisms use yet another structural pattern, placing the speaker before the statement and ignoring the situation altogether: "The dog says, 'It is the same teeth which I use to play that I also use to bite'" (see Ojoade 1980:67).

Wellerisms begin to appear with some regularity in European proverb collections of the sixteenth century, making it clear that many writers of the early modern age, including Martin Luther, enjoyed the humor of this expressive form. Given the temper of the times, marked by turbulent ecclesiastical and social reform, it is not surprising to find numerous wellerisms dealing with the devil and anticlericalism as well as with scatology and obscenity. Many wellerisms from this period appear to be reduced versions of longer fables, tall tales, and other folk narratives. The most obvious is "'The grapes are sour,' said the fox and couldn't reach them" (no. 1231), which is a mere remnant of an Aesopian fable. Other, longer narratives about the devil and about animals were crystallized into witty wellerisms. On occasion, however, the path from tale to wellerism might also have been reversed. It is possible that some wellerisms were lengthened into tall tales, giving the narrator the opportunity to spin a longer yarn. Much more research needs to be done on this fascinating interrelationship of wellerisms and folk narratives (see especially Siegfried Neumann 1968, 1969).

Investigating the origins of wellerisms in England, Bartlett Jere Whiting (1960:311) discovered the earliest text, dating from 731 C.E., in the works of the Venerable Bede: "Deus miserere animabus, dixit Osuald cadens in terram," translated by T. Miller as "'God have mercy on our people,' said Oswald, falling to the ground" (no. 821). Another early text, from medieval times, is "'To late y-war,' quoth Beautee, whan it paste" (no. 686), given by Geoffrey Chaucer in his *Troilus and Criseyde* (c.1385). Thereafter, from the sixteenth century onward, wellerisms can be found in many great works of English literature, including those of William Shakespeare, Ben Jonson, Nicholas Breton, Daniel Defoe, and Jonathan Swift. In America, Benjamin Franklin printed his only wellerism in August 1735 in *Poor Richard's Almanac*: "'Great wits jump [agree],' says the poet, and hit his head against the post" (no. 1507).

As might be expected, standard English proverb collections of the sixteenth and seventeenth centuries also started to record some wellerisms. John Heywood's *English Proverbs* (1546), David Ferguson's *Scottish Proverbs* (1641), James Howell's *English Proverbs* (1659), and John Ray's *English Proverbs* (1678) all include fine examples of the genre, as do, from the next century, James Kelly's *Scottish Proverbs* (1721) and Allan Ramsay's *Scots Proverbs* (1737). Many of the proverb collections of the eighteenth century were too moralistic and didactic in nature to pay much attention to the rather suspect spirit of wellerisms, but once the nineteenth century began, such humorous texts became quite common in proverb collections, literary works, and the burgeoning mass media.

When Charles Dickens entered the stage, he was thus by no means the innovator of a unique phraseological unit, as the first appearances of the word *wellerism* in 1839 might suggest. The traditional folklore genre of the wellerism was well established in England when Dickens began to publish his serialized *Posthumous Papers of the Pickwick Club* in April 1836. He might have known some wellerisms from oral currency, but it is also quite possible that he was influenced by Charles Beazley's musical farce entitled *The Boarding House* (1811). In this humorous play the character Simon Spatterdash uses about a dozen wellerisms. As chance would have it, the actor who played this character, Samuel Vale (1797-1848), gained some notoriety by continuing to quote such curious "comparisons," as wellerisms were usually referred to at the time, in theatrical taverns. In fact, there was even talk of the latest "Sam Valerism" from 1831 to 1836 (see Bede 1882:389). Perhaps Dickens drew on the name of Sam Vale to create his own Sam Weller, whose use of about forty such texts led to the new term *wellerism*.

The popularity of the fictional character Sam Weller can readily be seen from such subsequent dramatizations as George Thomas Moncrieff's *Sam Weller, or, The Pickwickians* (1837), Edward Stirling's *The Pickwick Club* (1837), and William Leman Rede's *The Peregrinations of Pickwick* (1837). Moncrieff's play was without doubt the most successful of the three, having opened at the Strand Theatre in London on 10 July 1837 and at New York's Park Theatre on 15 March 1838, with other performances later that year in New Orleans and Philadelphia (see Bryan and Mieder 1994). With Dickens's novel just published, three plays drawn from it making the rounds, and all of them featuring Sam Weller uttering witty comparisons, it should surprise no one that two American journalists came up with the term *wellerism* in January 1839. It was the natural outgrowth of what today would be called a "Sam Weller mania."

The wellerisms that Dickens included in his *Pickwick Papers* have been the subject of a number of literary and folkloristic investigations (see especially Williams 1966; Baer 1983). Suffice it to say that the servant Sam Weller uses his proverbial utterances to educate his master, Mr. Pickwick, in a manner quite similar to the way in which Sancho Panza employs proverbs to educate Don Quixote. Wellerisms are perfectly suited to teach by indirection in that they ascribe an enlightening, albeit humorous or ironic, remark to another person in quite a different context in order not to implicate the speaker in the truth or message of the statement. Wellerisms in the *Pickwick Papers* thus act as a sort of "safety valve" (Baer 1983:182) through which Sam Weller instructs Mr. Pickwick in the many social, political, and psychological disparities of the world. With a certain ironic detachment the wellerisms comment on such themes as marriage, politics, violence, class distinctions, and aggression. Dickens's wellerisms are a far cry from some of the funnier modern texts like jokes and puns based on the pure joy of word-play, and it is clear that Dickens used most of his wellerisms as satirical comments on social and political issues.

The creation of wellerisms for the mere fun of it, without any par-ticular literary context or social message, became fashionable toward the end of the 1830s in both England and the United States. Newspapers and magazines such as the British *Punch* and the American *Yankee Notions* and *California Golden Era*, to name but three, helped to bring about the so-called golden age of wellerisms, from 1840 to about 1880 (see Whit-ing 1945:4). American journalists in particular delighted in filling small spaces with the welleresque creations of local humorists from coast to coast. Scholars like C. Grant Loomis, James Tidwell, and Bartlett Jere Whiting have excerpted several hundred texts from such publications, and there can be no doubt that the nineteenth century was the heyday of the English-language wellerism.

This is not to say that wellerisms have had no place in twentieth-century humor, but it is perhaps fair to observe that the joke as a humor-ous genre has replaced to a major degree the formerly very popular wellerism. Nevertheless, the tradition is not completely dead. A modern Charles Dickens of sorts in the use of wellerisms, the writer of detective fiction Leslie Charteris (1907–1993) created a whole string of rather suggestive wellerisms based on an actress and a bishop in the 1930s, among them " 'This is my idea of a night out,' as the bishop said to the actress" (no. 876) and " 'But I'm not nearly satisfied yet,' as the actress said to the bishop" (no. 1084).

Such thematic, generative cycles of wellerisms are, however, noth-ing new either. The most productive has been a group of wellerisms based on a blind man as speaker, ranging from the short and simple " 'I see,' said the blind man" (no. 1130) to such longer forms as " 'I see,' said the blind man to his deaf wife, as he climbed the cherry tree to get an apple for his lame uncle" (no. 1155). The earliest recorded text of this cycle is found in John Heywood's *The Pardoner and the Frere* (1533) as "'Marry, that I would see!' quoth blind Hew" (no. 1103). Other variants include personal names, and such texts usually go back to some localized event involving a particular person (see Taylor 1959:287–289). As the actual contexts of such utterances were forgotten, the names were replaced by the more generic "blind man," giving inventive folk humorists the opportunity to add new punning situations not attached to any particular incident. (See the many variants registered herein as nos. 1103–1162.)

Another cycle, one that is quite internationally disseminated throughout Europe, is based on the proverb "Every little [bit] helps." The earliest known English variant is "'Every little helps,' quoth the wren when she pissed in the sea" (no. 730), recorded in 1605, and the most recent American variant is "'Every little bit helps,' said the ant as he peed in the ocean" (no. 747), recorded from oral speech in Idaho in 1966. Still another cycle, especially widespread and still current in the United States, is based on the proverb "Each to his own taste" or "Everyone to his own notion" (or "opinion" or "fancy"). In numerous recorded texts, this proverb is spoken variously by an old man, an old woman, a farmer, or some other person as he or she kisses a cow, a calf, a pig, or some other unlikely recipient of physical affection.

Although lists of wellerisms are no longer published in the popular press in Great Britain and the United States, they still compete, as a genre of verbal folklore, with jokes, one-liners, puns, and other forms of popular humor. The dozens of wellerisms collected from oral sources and recorded herein for the first time are ample proof of the survival of this genre in the contemporary world. Furthermore, diligent readers of this dictionary will discover many texts in which puns and wordplay arise from mass-media advertising, automotive and air travel, sports, and other contexts of modern society. These are clear indications that, although the popularity of wellerisms may have waned, it has not altogether faded.

HOW TO USE THIS BOOK

Turning now to the more pragmatic aspects of this dictionary, we offer the following guidelines to its organization and use.

ORDER OF ENTRIES. We have followed the standard lexicographical method of listing wellerisms in alphabetical order according to the most significant key word appearing in the first part of their normal triadic structure. Under each key word the texts are arranged chronologically. Thus, the wellerism "'That's a flame of mine,' as the bellows said to the fire" from 1858 is listed under the key word *flame,* followed by the two texts "'I've been to see an old flame,' remarked the young man, who had recently journeyed to see Vesuvius," recorded in 1892, and "'There's my flame,' said the fireman" from 1926 (nos. 440–442). For ease of cross-referencing and indexing, we have numbered the entries consecutively from 1 through 1516.

We admit that our selection of the "most significant" key word in the quoted statement of a wellerism may sometimes seem arbitrary. When faced with alternatives, we generally chose to put wellerisms under the key word that would result in a pair or group of similar texts or that would shed light on the meaning of the text(s) in view.

VARIANTS. Variants are listed as separate entries, thereby showing how single wellerisms develop over time into distinct texts. Thus, while the key word remains the same, all three parts of a given wellerism may undergo considerable change. See, for example, the two texts "'Every man to his own taste,' as the farmer said when he kissed the pig" (no. 1329) and "'Everyone to her own taste,' as the old woman said when she kissed the cow" (no. 1334).

DOCUMENTATION. Geographical origin of the earliest known written or oral source is indicated by the abbreviation GB (for Great Britain), US (for United States), or Can (for Canada). For American and Canadian written sources, an abbreviation of the name of the state or province in which publication occurred, when known, follows in parentheses. Wherever possible, we have also provided basic information on the author, title, and date of the earliest known written source for each wellerism.

We have, further, given references to the forty-nine secondary sources from which we have drawn our texts and on which we have based our documentation. (See the List of Sources at the back of the book.) After "Cited in," abbreviated references are listed in chronological order. In addition, we have made reference to the Margaret M. Bryant collection of proverbial speech for every wellerism that is recorded therein and have noted the state or states in which the wellerism was collected.

For example, under the headword *blush* the reader will find the following entry (no. 114):

"I blush for you," as the rouge pot said to the lady.
GB, *Punch,* vol. 3 (1842), p. 239; US (Mass.), *Yankee Notions,* vol. 1 (1852), p. 244. Cited in Loomis 2, p. 5; Loomis 3, p. 113; Mieder, p. 232. Recorded in Bryant (Calif., Minn., N.J.).

The reader can immediately determine that this wellerism was published in Great Britain as early as 1842 and in the United States (Massachusetts) as early as 1852. Since this is a relatively well-known wellerism, it has been cited in three scholarly publications, which we have identified simply as Loomis 2, Loomis 3, and Mieder. Upon consulting our List of Sources, the reader will discover that this wellerism is cited in C. Grant Loomis, "Traditional American Wordplay: Wellerisms or Yankeeisms," *Western Folklore* 8 (1949); C. Grant Loomis, "Wellerisms in *Punch,*" *Western Folklore* 14 (1955); and Wolfgang Mieder, *American Proverbs: A Study in Texts and Contexts* (Bern, 1989). Finally, we have indicated that this wellerism was recorded in the Margaret M. Bryant collection (c.1945–1980) from oral sources in California, Minnesota, and New Jersey.

We obviously could not list all the additional historical references that all secondary sources amass for each wellerism. The result would have been a much larger dictionary. Historically interested scholars will have easy access to most of the secondary sources we consulted and can therein easily research later references. Our dictionary will, however, give them an immediate idea of the first occurrence of a wellerism in British and/or American written sources as well as its recorded distribution in the United States and Canada based on the Margaret M. Bryant collection. Regarding those wellerisms from the Bryant collection that lack any other bibliographic notation, we can state only that they were current between the mid-1940s and the end of the 1970s and that they are here registered in print for the first time.

GLOSSES. In square brackets following documentation of texts, we have occasionally added glosses to clarify the meaning of wellerisms that might otherwise remain obscure to the general reader. These notes most often serve simply to explain meanings of archaic or obsolete words, dialect spellings, slang, colloquial expressions, and unusual idioms and terms. As additional aids to the reader, we have sometimes added notes on literary allusions, on folklore and local customs, on geographical locations, and on historical figures and events.

We must confess, however, that there are some wellerisms in this dictionary whose meanings remain unknown despite all attempts by scholars to explicate them, as references to certain local individuals or the context of the wordplay have become obscured over time. We would also note that—although we hope that our glosses will enable readers to understand and enjoy most of the wellerisms registered herein—only rarely have we attempted to explain the puns and wordplay that are characteristic of these texts. Let readers then beware: keep your wits at the ready.

BACK MATTER. At the back of the book, readers will find a complete list of the secondary sources we have consulted in compiling this volume as well as a comprehensive, international bibiliography of the literature on wellerisms. An index of speakers and an index of situations are also provided. Readers seeking guidance to a specific text are advised to consult both indexes, as the Index of Speakers identifies not only speakers but also addressees, thus overlapping in purpose the Index of Situations.

WELLERISMS

accommodations

1 "Very cheap, but most wretched accommodations," as the fellow said when they rode him on a rail.

US (Mass.), *Yankee Blade* (21 Jul. 1849). Cited in Loomis 2, p. 4.

account   [See also no. 249.]

2 "I cannot account for it!" exclaimed the defaulting cashier.

US (Calif.), *Daily Examiner,* vol. 34, no. 86 (1882), p. 4. Cited in Loomis 4, p. 232.

3 "I'm not doing this on my own account," said the forger, as he passed over the check.

US (Calif.), *The Pelican,* vol. 26, no. 5 (1921), p. 38. Cited in Loomis 4, p. 238.

ace

4 "Bate me an ace," quoth Bolton.

GB, RICHARD EDWARDS, *Damon and Pithias* (1570); US, 1931. Cited in Wilson, p. 32; Lean, p. 742; Taylor 1, p. 202. [*The Oxford English Dictionary,* 2d ed., notes that this text is "an obsolete expression of incredulity."]

acquaintance

5 "For better acquaintance sake," as Sir John Ramsay drank to his father, when he met him on his return after a long absence and invited him to a glass of wine.

GB, JAMES KELLY, *Scottish Proverbs* (1721). Cited in Lean, p. 744. [Sir John Ramsay (1580?-1626) was a favorite of James VI of Scotland, who as James I succeeded to the British throne in 1603.]

6 "I'll cut your acquaintance," as the sword said to the gentleman ven he vos a goin' to fight his friend.

US (Pa.), *Alexander's Weekly Messenger* (13 Nov. 1839), p. 5. Cited in Tidwell 2, p. 262.

affections

7 "My affections are wasted on you," he softly remarked to her, as he gently placed his arm where he thought it would do the most good.

US (Calif.), *The Wasp,* vol. 14, no. 454 (1883), p. 7. Cited in Loomis 4, p. 233.

affirmative

8   "It is decided in the affirmative," as the thief said when the jury returned a verdict of guilty.

US (Mass.), *Yankee Blade* (23 Apr. 1845). Cited in Loomis 2, p. 8. Recorded in Bryant (N.Y.).

affliction

9   "In view of my affliction, don't do that," pleaded a man whose friend had offered him a sip out of a pocket flask within sight of his wife.

US (Calif.), *The Wasp,* vol. 3, no. 152 (1879), p. 763. Cited in Loomis 4, p. 231.

after

10   "After you," as the teakettle said to the dog's tail.

GB, *Punch,* vol. 2 (1842), p. 198. Cited in Loomis 3, p. 112.

11   "After you," said the chaser to the whiskey.

US (Calif.), *The Pelican,* vol. 1, no. 1 (1903), p. 13. Cited in Loomis 4, p. 235.

age

12   "Old age is coming on me rapidly," as the urchin said when he was stealing apples from an old man's garden, and saw the owner coming.

US (Mass.), *Ballou's Dollar Magazine,* vol. 1 (1855), p. 400. Cited in Loomis 2, p. 4; Whiting 2, p. 9. Recorded in Bryant (N.Y., S.C.).

aha

13   "Aha!" she cried, as she waved her wooden leg and died.

US (Idaho), 1966. Cited in Anon, p. 34.

ahem

14   "Ahem!" as Dick Smith said, when he swallowed the dishcloth.

US, 1931. Cited in Taylor 1, p. 210.

all in

15   "I'm all in," said the burglar, as he wiggled through the window.

US (Calif.), *The Pelican,* vol. 16, no. 2 (1914). Cited in Loomis 4, p. 237.

16   "I feel all in," remarked the Frosh, as the water closed over his head.

US (Calif.), *The Pelican,* vol. 27, no. 5 (1922), p. 28. Cited in Loomis 4, p. 239. [*Frosh,* high-school or college freshman.]

all over

17   "That's me all over, Mabel!" snickered the man after he had been run over by the steam-roller.

US (Calif.), *The Pelican,* vol. 25, no. 6 (1920), p. 20. Cited in Loomis 4, p. 238.

18 "It's all over now," said the co-ed, as she finished powdering her face.
US (Calif.), *The Pelican,* vol. 27, no. 8 (1922), p. 13. Cited in Loomis 4, p. 240; Mieder, p. 234.

19 "That's me all over," said the bug as it was squashed against the windshield.
US, c.1945-1980. Recorded in Bryant (Ill.).

20 When the grasshopper hit the windshield, he said, "That's me all over."
US, c.1945-1980. Recorded in Bryant (Kans.).

21 "I've got it all over you," boasted the old man as he sneezed.
US (Kans.), 1959. Cited in Koch 2, p. 196. Recorded in Bryant (Kans.).

all right

22 "We'll be all right now," said the doctor, "if we don't run out of patients."
US (Kans.), 1959. Cited in Koch 2, p. 196. Recorded in Bryant (Kans.).

all up

23 "It's all up," he cried, as she crossed the floor ventilator.
US (Calif.), *The Pelican,* vol. 22, no. 5 (1918), p. 22. Cited in Loomis 4, p. 238.

am

24 "I am where I would be," as the loafer said ven he vas astride the rum cask.
US (Pa.), *Alexander's Weekly Messenger* (1839). Cited in Tidwell 2, p. 260.

answer

25 "A soft answer turneth away wrath," as the man said when he hurled a squash at his enemy's head.
US (Mass.), *Ballou's Dollar Magazine,* vol. 3 (1856), p. 300. Cited in Loomis 2, p. 9. Recorded in Bryant (N.J.).

antelope

26 "That's an antelope," observed the small boy when he heard that his mother's sister had run away with the coachman.
US (Calif.), *The Wasp,* vol. 3, no. 144 (1879), p. 629. Cited in Loomis 4, p. 231.

anticipations

27 "We won't indulge in such horrid anticipations," as the hen-pecked husband said when the parson told him he would be joined to his wife in another world, never to separate.
US (Mass.), *Ballou's Dollar Magazine,* vol. 9 (1859), p. 100. Cited in Loomis 2, p. 6. Recorded in Bryant (N.Y.).

apples

28 "See how we apples swim!" quoth the horse turd.

GB, JOHN WITHALS, *Dictionary* (1576); US, 1931. Cited in Wilson, p. 17; Lean, p. 748; Taylor 1, p. 209.

arse

29 "Here's to you all, arse o'er head," as the moor bride drank to her maidens.

GB, JAMES KELLY, *Scottish Proverbs* (1721). Cited in Lean, p. 745.

art

30 "The art that conceals art," as the thief remarked when he slid an expensive oil painting under his coat.

US (Calif.), *Daily Examiner,* vol. 35, no. 171 (1882). Cited in Loomis 4, p. 233.

articles

31 "Several excellent articles on our outside today," as the editor said when he donned a new suit of clothes.

US (Maine), *Yankee Blade* (3 Dec. 1842). Cited in Loomis 2, p. 4. Recorded in Bryant (N.Y., S.C.).

attachment

32 "I have a strong attachment for you," as the constable said to the debtor.

US (Maine), *Yankee Blade* (30 Jul. 1842). Cited in Loomis 2, p. 4. Recorded in Bryant (N.Y.).

awake

33 "I believe there is no one awake but you and me," as the cock said to the sun.

US (N.Y.), *Yankee Notions,* vol. 1 (1852), p. 67. Cited in Loomis 2, p. 4.

awl

34 "I give thee my awl," as the cobbler said to the old shoe.

US (N.Y.), *Yankee Notions,* vol. 1 (1852), p. 71. Cited in Whiting 2, p. 8; Loomis 2, p. 4. Recorded in Bryant (Ariz.).

babe

35 "The babe's in the wood," remarked Fogs, pointing at the infant in his cradle.

US (Calif.), *Daily Examiner,* vol. 35, no. 52 (1882), p. 4. Cited in Loomis 4, p. 232.

back

36 "A man can't help what happens behind his back," as the loafer said when he was kicked out of doors.

US (Pa.), *Alexander's Weekly Messenger* (1839). Cited in Tidwell 2, p. 260. Recorded in Bryant (N.Y.).

37 "I'll stand to your back," as the pickpocket said ven he stole the man's pocketbook.

US (Pa.), *Alexander's Weekly Messenger* (1839). Cited in Tidwell 2, p. 259.

38 "I hate to hear people talk behind one's back," as the robber said when the constable called, "Stop thief!"

US (N.Y.), *Wilkes' Spirit of the Times,* vol. 4 (1861), p. 23. Cited in Loomis 2, p. 5. Recorded in Bryant (Ill., N.Y.).

39 "A man can't help what is done behind his back," as the scamp said when kicked out of doors.

US (N.Y.), *Wilkes' Spirit of the Times,* vol. 5 (1861), p. 247. Cited in Loomis 2, p. 5. Recorded in Bryant (N.Y.).

backare

40 "Backare," quoth Mortimer to his sow.

GB, JOHN HEYWOOD, *English Proverbs* (1546); US, 1931. Cited in Wilson, p. 252; Lean, p. 742; Taylor 1, p. 202. [*Backare,* back off, stand back, give way.]

bag

41 "What's no i' the bag will be i' the broo," quoth the Hieland man when he dirked the haggis.

GB, ALLAN CUNNINGHAM, *Glossary to Burns* (1834). Cited in Lean, p. 752. [*Dirked,* stabbed with a dagger; *haggis,* Scottish meat dish, boiled in a bag made from an animal's stomach.]

banisters

42 "Here's the banisters, but I swear I can't find the stairs," as the drunken fellow said when he walked around the bed post.

US (Pa.), *Alexander's Weekly Messenger* (1839). Cited in Tidwell 2, p. 260.

bar

43 "Bar that," as the Sheriff's Officer said to his first floor window.

GB, *Punch,* vol. 1 (1841), p. 233. Cited in Loomis 3, p. 111.

44 "I have risen from the bar to the bench," said a lawyer, on quitting the profession and taking up shoemaking.

US (Mass.), *Yankee Notions,* vol. 5 (1868), p. 59. Cited in Loomis 2, p. 5. Recorded in Bryant (N.Y., S.C.).

bargain

45 "Let's clinch the bargain," as the bear said when he patted the man on the shoulder.

US (Mass.), *Yankee Blade* (26 Nov. 1845). Cited in Loomis 2, p. 5. Recorded in Bryant (N.Y.).

bark

46 "My bark is on the sea," as the dog said when he fell overboard.

US (Mass.), *Yankee Blade* (31 Jul. 1847). Cited in Loomis 2, p. 4. Recorded in Bryant (N.Y.).

base

47 "I'll change my base," as the counterfeiter said when he offered a bogus for a greenback.

US (N.Y.), *Wilkes' Spirit of the Times,* vol. 7 (1862), p. 327. Cited in Loomis 2, p. 4. Recorded in Bryant (N.Y.).

be

48 "This is that must needs be," quoth the good man when he made his wife pin the basket.

GB, ANON., *Marriage of Wit and Wisdom* (c.1590). Cited in Lean, p. 750. [*Pin the basket,* conclude the matter.]

49 "It wos to be, and wos," as the old lady said arter she'd married the footman.

GB, CHARLES DICKENS, *Pickwick Papers* (1836). Cited in Maass, p. 212; Baer, p. 178.

50 "Howsomever and at any rate, be that as it may," as the old lady said when she dropped her false teeth in the well.

US, MICHAEL GRAVES, *Bubblin's an' B'ilin's at the Center* (1934), p. 105. Cited in Whiting 2, p. 11.

bear

51 "He becomes fond of the bear meat, and considers other game as not worth a notion," as old Johnson said of the devil.

US, DAVID CROCKETT, *A Narrative of the Life of David Crockett, Written by Himself* (1834). Cited in Whiting 2, p. 7.

52 "I can't bear you," as the sea said to the leaky ship.

GB, *Punch,* vol. 1 (1842), p. 50; US (N.Y.), *Porter's Spirit of the Times,* vol. 4 (1858), p. 46. Cited in Loomis 2, p. 4; Loomis 3, p. 110.

53 "This is more than I can bear," murmured the maiden, as she donned her chorus girl's costume.

US (Calif.), *The Pelican,* vol. 31, no. 8 (1926), p. 36. Cited in Loomis 4, p. 242.

bear–cat

54 "That's what they call a bear-cat," said little Willie, as he finished shaving the family feline with pa's safety razor.

US (Calif.), *The Pelican,* vol. 26, no. 5 (1921), p. 46. Cited in Loomis 4, p. 238.

beat

55 "This can't be beat," as the farmer said when he pulled up a carrot.

US (Mass.), *Yankee Blade* (23 Apr. 1844). Cited in Loomis 2, p. 4. Recorded in Bryant (N.Y.).

56 "This beats me out," as the rye said when the fellow hammered it over the head with the flail.

US (Mass.), *Yankee Blade* (26 Aug. 1848), p. 48. Cited in Loomis 2, p. 5. Recorded in Bryant (N.Y.).

57 "It beats all," as the Yankee shoemaker said when he saw the pegging machine at work.

US (Mass.), *Cambridge Tribune* (16 Jun. 1881), p. 15. Cited in Whiting 2, p. 10.

58 "Beat you Daddy, I ate the bar," said the young termite to his father as they met in a local pub.

US (Kans.), 1959. Cited in Koch 1, p. 180. Recorded in Bryant (Kans.). [The reference is to "Beat Me, Daddy, Eight to the Bar," the title of a popular song written in 1940.]

beau

59 "I'm going to draw the beau into a knot," as the lady said when standing at the hymeneal altar.

US (Mass.), *Yankee Notions,* vol. 3 (1854), p. 235. Cited in Loomis 1, p. 305; Whiting 2, p. 9; Loomis 2, p. 5. Recorded in Bryant (N.Y., S.C.).

beauty

60 "There's beauty without paint," quoth the devil when he saw the black man.

GB, ANDREW HENDERSON, *Scottish Proverbs* (1832). Cited in Lean, p. 750.

bed

61 "Such a bed as this is a perfect luxury," as the pig said when he rolled amongst the tulips.

GB, *Punch,* vol. 3 (1842), p. 178. Cited in Loomis 3, p. 112.

62 "Come, get up, you have been in bed long enough," as the gardener said when he was pulling up carrots to send to market.

US (Mass.), *Ballou's Dollar Magazine,* vol. 12 (1860), p. 598. Cited in Loomis 2, p. 5. Recorded in Bryant (N.Y.).

bedding

63   "Saft beddin's gude for sair banes," quoth Howie when he streekit him on the midden stead.

GB, 1904. Cited in Lean, p. 748. [*Saft,* soft; *sair,* sore; *streekit,* stretched out, lay down; *midden stead,* dung hill.]

bedrock

64   "I guess I'm down to bedrock now," soliloquized the patriarch Jacob, as he pillowed his head on a heap of stones.

US (Calif.), *The Pelican,* vol. 2, no. 1 (1904), p. 10. Cited in Loomis 4, p. 235.

bee

65   "Ah, sure enough . . . that mout be a bee," as the old woman said when she killed a wasp.

US, AUGUSTUS LONGSTREET, *Major Jones' Georgia Scenes* (1835). Cited in Whiting 2, p. 7. Recorded in Bryant (N.Y.).

66   "You've got a bee in your bonnet," as the hive said when the old lady came to look at the honey.

US (Wash.), *The Empire* (28 Mar. 1889), p. 3. Cited in Hines, p. 23; Mieder, p. 233.

67   "But it might be a bee for all that," as the old woman said when she looked in the hornets' nest for honey.

US, c.1945-1980. Recorded in Bryant (N.Y.).

beginning

68   "You know a bad beginning makes a good endin'," as the old woman said.

US, AUGUSTUS LONGSTREET, *Major Jones' Georgia Scenes* (1848). Cited in Taylor and Whiting, p. 23; Whiting 2, p. 7.

69   "All beginnings are hard," said the thief and stole the anvil.

US, 1948. Cited in Taylor 2, p. 316. Recorded in Bryant (Miss.).

70   "All beginnings are heavy," said the thief and stole the anvil.

US, 1948. Cited in Taylor 2, p. 316.

behind

71   "I've got thousands of dollars behind me," said the bunko artist, as he leaned up against the bank.

US (Calif.), *The Pelican,* vol. 27, no. 8 (1921), p. 10. Cited in Loomis 4, p. 2. [*Bunko artist,* swindler, con artist.]

72   "A little behind in my work," said the butcher as he backed into the meat grinder.

US (Tex.), 1956. Cited in Hendricks, p. 356; Koch 2, p. 196; Mieder, p. 237. Recorded in Bryant (Kans., Tex.).

behold

73 As one blind man said to another, "Let's behold ourselves."
GB, THOMAS SHELTON, trans., Miguel de Cervantes, *Don Quixote* (1612). Cited in Taylor 4, p. 288.

below

74 "Man wants but little here below," remarked the new arrival in Hades, as he hurriedly removed his overcoat.
US (Calif.), *The Pelican,* vol. 26, no. 5 (1921), p. 42. Cited in Loomis 4, p. 238.

bender

75 "I think I'll go on a bender," said the fly, as he started to crawl around a pretzel.
US (Calif.), *The Pelican,* vol. 40, no. 4 (1933), p. 9. Cited in Loomis 4, p. 244.

beside

76 "You look as if you were beside yourself," as the wag said to the fellow who stood by the side of his ass.
US (N.Y.), *Wilkes' Spirit of the Times,* vol. 4 (1861), p. 87. Cited in Loomis 2, p. 5; Mieder, p. 232.

best

77 "There's nae a best among them," as the fellow said by the fox cubs.
GB, WILLIAM HAZLITT, *English Proverbs* (1869). Cited in Lean, p. 750.

better

78 "Wal, here it comes, for better or for wus," as the minister said to Uncle Josh when he married him to Aunt Sally Fox, at the age of sixty-five.
US (N.Y.), *Spirit of the Times,* vol. 10 (1840), p. 229. Cited in Whiting 2, p. 10.

better half

79 "Oh, for a better half!" said the sorrowing widower when he found a counterfeit fifty-cent piece among his coins.
US (Calif.), *Daily Examiner,* vol. 34, no. 135 (1882), p. 4. Cited in Loomis 4, p. 232.

bettering

80 "The hope of bettering myself to be sure," as the old woman said when she leapt over the bridge at Kingston.
GB, WALTER SCOTT, *Kenilworth* (1821). Cited in Williams, p. 93.

beware

81 "Beware," as the potter said to the lump of clay. "I'll be burnt first," saucily replied the mud.
US (Mass.), *Yankee Blade* (22 Jan. 1845). Cited in Loomis 2, p. 5. Recorded in Bryant (N.Y.).

biers

82 "Two biers," ordered the gangster, as he gloated over his double kill.
US (Calif.), *The Pelican,* vol. 44, no. 3 (1937), p. 10. Cited in Loomis 4, p. 244.

big

83 "They won't be big now," said the elephant as his ears were clipped.
US, c.1945-1980. Recorded in Bryant (N.Y., S.C.).

bigger

84 "Not bigger: darn me, if 'tis, than the lettle end--o' nothing--sharpened," as the Irishman said.
GB, JOHN NEAL, *Brother Jonathan,* vol. 1 (1825). Cited in Whiting 2, p. 6.

bile

85 "Too much bile in my stomach," as the teakettle said when hanging over a hot fire.
US (N.Y.), *Spirit of the Times,* vol. 10 (1840), p. 221. Cited in Whiting 2, p. 7. Recorded in Bryant (Ariz.).

bill

86 "Take the bill down," said Sam emphatically. "I'm let to a single gentleman, and the terms is agreed upon."
GB, CHARLES DICKENS, *Pickwick Papers* (1836). Cited in Williams, p. 89.

87 "For further particulars see small bills," as the man said ven he was tried for counterfeiting shin plasters.
US (Pa.), *Alexander's Weekly Messenger* (1839). Cited in Tidwell 2, p. 261. [*Shin plasters,* paper tokens issued by rural stores as small change.]

88 "I wish to introduce a bill for the prevention of worms," as the red headed woodpecker said to the apple tree.
US (Maine), *Yankee Blade* (20 Aug. 1842). Cited in Loomis 2, p. 5. Recorded in Bryant (N.Y.).

89 "Stick no bills here," as Quilp said, scratching his leg and addressing himself to the mosquito.
US (Maine), *Yankee Blade* (10 Sep. 1842). Cited in Loomis 2, p. 5. Recorded in Bryant (N.Y.).

90 "I wish to introduce a bill into your honorable body," as the flea said to the senator.
US (Mass.), *Yankee Blade* (10 Apr. 1844). Cited in Loomis 2, p. 5. Recorded in Bryant (N.Y.).

91 "I hate doctors' bills," as the man said when he caught the family physician kissing his wife.
US (N.Y.), *Yankee Notions,* vol. 15 (1866), p. 4. Cited in Loomis 2, p. 6. Recorded in Bryant (N.Y.).

bird

92 "Thou art a bitter bird," said the raven to the starling.
GB, JOHN RAY, *English Proverbs* (1678). Cited in Lean, p. 750.

bit

93 "I'll try another bit," as the jockey said when his horse ran away with him.
GB, *Punch,* vol. 2 (1842), p. 161. Cited in Loomis 3, p. 112.

bite

94 "If you bite me, I'll bite you," as the pepper-pod said to the boy.
US (N.Y.), *Yankee Notions*, vol. 1 (1852), p. 78. Cited in Loomis 2, p. 5; Whiting 2, p. 8. Recorded in Bryant (Ariz., N.Y.).

95 "I'll take a bite, too," as the wolf said when he came across a man eating his dinner.
US (N.Y.), *Yankee Notions,* vol. 11 (1861), p. 25. Cited in Loomis 2, p. 5. Recorded in Bryant (Ariz., N.Y.).

blayed-out

96 "Come, that's blayed-out," as the Dutchman said to a fellow who made a lunge at him with an open knife.
US (Pa.), *Philadelphia Item* (4 Aug. 1881), p. 8. Cited in Whiting 2, p. 10.

blind

97 "Please help the blind," remarked the dealer in a cheap poker game.
US (Calif.), *The Wasp,* vol. 11, no. 377 (1883), p. 11. Cited in Loomis 4, p. 233.

block

98 As one ear said to the other, "I see we live on the same block."
US, c.1945-1980. Recorded in Bryant (Kans.).

blood

99 "Good blood will always show itself!" as the old lady said when she was struck by the redness of her nose.
US (N.Y.), *Yankee Notions,* vol. 14 (1865), p. 343. Cited in Loomis 2, p. 5. Recorded in Bryant (N.Y.).

100 "Blood will tell," quoth Macbeth, as he tried to scrub it off.
US (Calif.), *The Pelican,* vol. 13, no. 1 (1912). Cited in Loomis 4, p. 236; Mieder, p. 235.

101 "You make my blood boil," said the lobster indignantly to the hot water.
US (Calif.), *The Pelican,* vol. 30, no. 6 (1925), p. 42. Cited in Loomis 4, p. 241; Mieder, p. 235.

blow

102 "Blow for blow," as Conan said to the devil.

GB, WALTER SCOTT, *Waverly* (1814). Cited in Lean, p. 742. [Conan, a hero of Gaelic legend, made a vow never to take a blow without returning it.]

103 "You'll blow me," as the mutton said to the fly ven he vanted to stay all night with him.

US (Pa.), *Alexander's Weekly Messenger* (1839). Cited in Tidwell 2, p. 259.

104 "Come, let me blow you off," said the cyclone to the farm-house.

US (Calif.), *The Argonaut*, vol. 32, no. 7 (1893), p. 12. Cited in Loomis 4, p. 234.

105 "It's a hard blow," he remarked, as he reached for his nitroglycerine.

US (Calif.), *The Pelican*, vol. 16, no. 2 (1914). Cited in Loomis 4, p. 237.

blowed

106 "You be blow'd," as the fly said to the shin of beef in the dog days.

GB, *Punch*, vol. 2 (1842), p. 20. Cited in Loomis 3, p. 111. Recorded in Bryant (N.Y.). [*Blow'd*, spoiled by deposit of insect eggs; damned.]

107 "I'm blowed if I do," as the bugle said when asked to give a tune.

US (Mass.), *Ballou's Dollar Magazine*, vol. 4 (1856), p. 400. Cited in Loomis 2, p. 5. Recorded in Bryant (N.Y.).

108 "Oh, you be blowed!" as the bluebottle vulgarly said to the veal.

US (N.Y.), *Wilkes' Spirit of the Times*, vol. 5 (1861), p. 247. Cited in Loomis 2, p. 5. [See note at no. 106.]

blow out

109 "Ven ve next meets, I'm blessed if ve don't have a blow out," as the young frog said to the old 'un, ven he vanted to be a little bigger.

US (Pa.), *Alexander's Weekly Messenger* (1837). Cited in Tidwell 2, p. 258.

110 "Now, give us a good blow out," as the organ said to the bellows.

GB, *Punch*, vol. 2 (1842), p. 112. Cited in Loomis 3, p. 112.

blue

111 "I feel blue," he exclaimed, as a policeman caught him in his arms.

US (Calif.), *The Pelican*, vol. 16, no. 2 (1914). Cited in Loomis 4, p. 237.

112 "Oh, how blue I am," mourned the poet, as his fountain pen spattered upon him.

US (Calif.), *The Pelican*, vol. 25, no. 8 (1920), p. 20. Cited in Loomis 4, p. 238.

blush

113 "You make me blush," as the lobster cried out to the saucepan.

US (Pa.), *The Casket*, vol. 5 (1830), p. 377. Cited in Loomis 5, p. 51; Tidwell 2, p. 258.

114   "I blush for you," as the rouge pot said to the lady.

GB, *Punch,* vol. 3 (1842), p. 239; US (Mass.), *Yankee Notions,* vol. 1 (1852), p. 244. Cited in Loomis 2, p. 5; Loomis 3, p. 113; Mieder, p. 232. Recorded in Bryant (Calif., Minn., N.J.).

boarding out

115   "I'm boarding out tonight," as the loafer said when he curled up for the night on a pile of lumber.

US (N.Y.), *Yankee Notions,* vol. 1 (1852), p. 9. Cited in Whiting 2, p. 7; Loomis 2, p. 6. Recorded in Bryant (N.Y.).

boards

116   "I can't pass my boards," said the constipated mosquito.

US, c.1945-1980. Recorded in Bryant (Kans.).

bones

117   "I shall make no bones about it, anyway," smiled the convicted murderer when he learned his body was to be burned in quick lime.

US (Calif.), *The Pelican,* vol. 3, no. 1 (1905), p. 12. Cited in Loomis 4, p. 236.

bosom

118   "Come rest on this bosom," as the Atlantic said to the "Big Ship" ven she was going out of the Capes.

US (Pa.), *Alexander's Weekly Messenger* (1839). Cited in Tidwell 2, p. 259.

119   "Come rest in this bosom," as the turkey said to the stuffing.

US (Mass.), *Yankee Notions,* vol. 1 (1852), p. 76. Cited in Loomis 2,p. 6. Recorded in Bryant (N.Y.).

120   "Oh, come to this bosom," as the tipsy fellow said when he hugged a lamp post.

US (N.Y.), *Yankee Notions,* vol. 2 (1853), p. 208. Cited in Loomis 2, p. 6. Recorded in Bryant (N.Y.).

bottom

121   "I believe in getting to the bottom of things," as the schoolmarm said when she laid the refractory pupil over her knee.

US (Calif.), *California Golden Era,* vol. 18, no. 20 (1870), p. 7. Cited in Loomis 2, p. 6. Recorded in Bryant (N.Y.).

122   "We've got to get to the bottom of this," as the bishop said to the actress.

US, LESLIE CHARTERIS, *Misfortunes of Mr. Teal* (1934). Cited in Whiting 1, p. 73; Mieder, p. 236.

bounce

123   "Bounce," quoth the gun.

GB, NICHOLAS BRETON, *Crossing of Proverbs* (1610). Cited in Lean, p. 742. [*Bounce,* loud burst of noise produced by an explosion.]

bound

124   "I'm bound to be even ere long," was the reflection of a file of newspapers when conveyed to the book bindery establishment.

US (Mass.), *Yankee Blade* (29 Sep. 1849). Cited in Loomis 2, p. 6. Recorded in Bryant (N.Y.).

bounder

125   "What a rotten bounder you turned out to be," murmured the girl disgustedly, looking for a more lively tennis ball.

US (Calif.), *The Pelican,* vol. 30, no. 4 (1924), p. 10. Cited in Loomis 4, p. 241.

bounds

126   "I speak within bounds," as the prisoner said to the jailer.

US (Mass.), *Ballou's Dollar Magazine,* vol. (1856), p. 200. Cited in Loomis 2, p. 6. Recorded in Bryant (N.Y., S.C.).

bower

127   "Will you come into my bower," as the blackleg said when he played his knave of trumps and euchred his antagonist.

US (N.Y.), *Yankee Notions,* vol. 2 (1853), p. 208. Cited in Loomis 2, p. 6. Recorded in Bryant (N.Y.).

boys

128   "Little boys should be seen and not heard," as the boy said when he could not recite his lesson.

US (N.Y.), *Porter's Spirit of the Times,* vol. 1 (1857), p. 338. Cited in Loomis 2, p. 18; Mieder, p. 231. Recorded in Bryant (N.Y.).

breach

129   "Once more into the breach," as the schoolmaster said when he licked the dunce.

US (N.Y.), *Yankee Notions,* vol. 14 (1865), p. 260. Cited in Loomis 2, p. 6. Recorded in Bryant (N.Y.). [*Licked,* whipped, thrashed.]

breast

130   "Make a clean breast of it," as the bishop said to the actress.

US, LESLIE CHARTERIS, *The Saint Goes On* (1935). Cited in Whiting 1, p. 73.

bred

131   "In fancy bred," sang the fly, as he waded through the sponge cake dough.

US (Ohio), *Cincinnati Musical People* (11 Aug. 1881), p. 16. Cited in Whiting 2, p. 10.

brief

132   "Brief let it be," as the barrister said in his conference with the attorney.

GB, *Punch,* vol. 1 (1841), p. 276. Cited in Loomis 3, p. 111.

133 "This is brief and to the point," as the man remarked when he got up off a tack.

US (Iowa), *Keokuk Gate City* (2 Jun. 1881), p. 16. Cited in Whiting 2, p. 10.

bright

134 "Twas bright, 'twas heavenly, but 'tis passed," as the chap said after he spent his last yellow boy.

US (Mass.), *Yankee Blade* (7 Jan. 1846). Cited in Loomis 2, p. 15. [*Yellow boy,* gold coin.]

bring up

135 "Don't bring that up in class," said the professor on the floating university.

US (Calif.), *The Pelican,* vol. 38, no. 6 (1932), p. 38. Cited in Loomis 4, p. 243.

brush

136 "P'raps if vun of us wos to brush, without troubling the man, it 'ud be more agreeable for all parties," as the schoolmaster said wen the young gentleman objected to being flogged by the butler.

GB, CHARLES DICKENS, *Pickwick Papers* (1836). Cited in Maass, p. 213; Baer, p. 179.

137 "We've both had many a brush in our day," as the old sailor said to his cocked hat.

US (N.Y.), *Yankee Notions,* vol. 3 (1854), p. 142. Cited in Whiting 2, p. 4. Recorded in Bryant (Ariz.).

bucking

138 "So much for bucking 'em," as the young man said when he fought the tiger.

US (N.Y.), *New Varieties* (30 Jan. 1871), p. 5. Cited in Whiting 2, p. 9. [The reference is to a line in Colley Cibber's *Richard III* (1700), act 4: "Off with his head--so much for Buckingham."]

bulk

139 "I leave you the bulk of my personal property," as the fat old gentleman said to his lean nephew.

US (N.Y.), *Yankee Notions,* vol. 3 (1854), p. 142. Cited in Whiting 2, p. 5. Recorded in Bryant (Ariz.).

bully

140 "That's bully," as the gentleman said when he got hold of the tough steak.

US (Calif.), *California Golden Era,* vol. 12, no. 37 (1864), p. 7. Cited in Loomis 1, p. 304; Loomis 2, p. 6.

bumper

141   "One bumper at parting," as the man said when he ran against a post.
US (Calif.), *California Golden Era,* vol. 15, no. 17 (1867), p. 3. Cited in Loomis 2, p. 6.

bunch

142   As the Irishman said, "His pigs came in in a bunch, but the last two came in by themselves."
US, c.1945–1980. Recorded in Bryant (N.Y.).

burning

143   "I'm burning to be at the enemy," as the man remarked whose physician had advised him to give up smoking, when he lit a fresh cigar.
US (N.Y.), *Wilkes' Spirit of the Times,* vol. 8 (1863), p. 391. Cited in Loomis 2, p. 6.

burster

144   "Ain't I a burster," as the boiler said to the steamboat captain when it blew him sky high.
US (Pa.), *Alexander's Weekly Messenger* (1839). Cited in Tidwell 2, p. 4.

business

145   "Business first, pleasure arterwards," as King Richard the Third said wen he stabbed the t'other king in the Tower, afore he smothered the babbies.
GB, CHARLES DICKENS, *Pickwick Papers* (1836); US, 1948. Cited in Maass, p. 214; Stevenson, p. 2480; Baer, p. 179.

146   "I'm winding up my business," as the silkworm said to Mr. Cleveland.
US (Pa.), *Alexander's Weekly Messenger* (1839). Cited in Tidwell 2, p. 262.

147   "I've got some urgent business on hand," as the fox said ven the dogs were after him.
US (Pa.), *Alexander's Weekly Messenger* (1839). Cited in Tidwell 2, p. 261.

148   "Rather a soft business," as the mosquito said when he was probing a poet's noddle.
US (Maine), *Yankee Blade* (10 Dec. 1842). Cited in Loomis 2, p. 18. [*Neddle*, head.]

149   "He's too big for his business," as the lady said of the sweep, who stuck fast in the chimney.
US (Maine), *Yankee Blade* (18 Mar. 1846). Cited in Loomis 2, p. 5.

150   "Business before pleasure," as the man said when he kissed his wife before he went out to make love to his neighbor's.
US (N.Y.), *Yankee Notions,* vol. 1 (1852), p. 221. Cited in Whiting 2, p. 8; Loomis 2, p. 6. Recorded in Bryant (Ariz.).

151 "Don't get above your business," as the lady said to the shoemaker who was measuring her ankle in order to ascertain the size of her foot.
US (N.Y.), *Yankee Notions,* vol. 1 (1852), p. 241. Cited in Whiting 2, p. 8; Loomis 2, p. 4; Mieder, p. 231. Recorded in Bryant (Ariz.).

152 "That's my business," as the butcher said when he caught the dog trying to kill his sheep.
US (N.Y.), *Yankee Notions,* vol. 8 (1858), p. 139. Cited in Loomis 2, p. 6.

153 "My business is looking good," said the girl who won first prize at the bathing girl revue.
US (Calif.), *The Pelican,* vol. 34, no. 8 (1929), p. 34. Cited in Loomis 4, p. 243.

154 "And now let's get down to business," as the bishop said to the actress.
US, LESLIE CHARTERIS, *Enter the Saint* (1930). Cited in Whiting 1, p. 73; Mieder, p. 236.

155 "Business before pleasure," as the man said when he kissed his wife before calling on his sweetheart.
GB, JOHN CONNINGTON, *For Murder Will Speak* (1938), p. 224. Cited in Whiting 6, p. 82.

156 "Business before pleasure," as the actress said to the producer when he wanted her to read a script before she relaxed on his couch.
US, CARTER BROWN, *Terror Comes Creeping* (1959), p. 23. Cited in Whiting 6, p. 82.

buss

157 "E pluri-buss-unum," as the saucy fellow said when he put the substance of a dozen common kisses into one emphatic smack.
US (N.Y.), *Yankee Notions,* vol. 14 (1865), p. 196. Cited in Loomis 2, p. 9.

158 "I'll buss the patter," as the young lady said to the man who patted her on the cheek.
US (N.Y.), *Syracuse Sunday Times* (1881). Cited in Whiting 2, p. 5.

but

159 "But me no buts," as the Secesh Transport said to the Federal Ram.
US (N.Y.), *Yankee Notions,* vol. 12 (1863), p. 100. Cited in Loomis 2, p. 6. [A remark from one train to another.]

160 "But soft!" as Hamlet said to the goat.
US (Calif.), *The Wasp,* vol. 3, no. 141 (1879), p. 581. Cited in Loomis 4, p. 231.

butter

161 "I'll pass the butter," as the fellow said to himself as he shied around a ram in the pasture lot.
US (Ind.), *Kokomo Tribune* (1881). Cited in Whiting 2, p. 5.

162 "That butter is too fresh," as the man remarked when the goat lifted him over the garden fence.
US (Mass.), *Lowell Citizen* (4 Aug. 1881), p. 15. Cited in Whiting 2, p. 10.

bygones

163   "We agreed to let bygones be bygones," as the rooster said after he had searched vainly half an hour for an eye pecked out in a fight.

US (Mass.), *Boston Herald* (5 Jan. 1935), p. 14. Cited in Whiting 1, p. 75; Mieder, p. 236.

cake

164   "I suppose that's another case of angel cake," remarked St. Peter as Johnny picked out his little halo and passed down the corridor.

US (Calif.), *The Argonaut,* vol. 32, no. 14 (1893), p. 15. Cited in Loomis 4, p. 234.

165   "You can't eat your cake and have it too," as the man said on shipboard.

US (Calif.), *The Pelican,* vol. 30, no. 4 (1904), p. 85. Cited in Loomis 4, p. 354.

camel

166   "I'd walk a mile for a Camel," murmured the hungry lion, as he watched a caravan crossing the Sahara.

US (Calif.), *The Pelican,* vol. 31, no. 1 (1925), p. 41. Cited in Loomis 4, p. 241; Mieder, p. 235. [The reference is to an advertising slogan for Camel cigarettes.]

capital

167   "Here's a sinking capital," as the earthquake said to the city of Lisbon.

GB, *Punch,* vol. 2 (1842), p. 198. Cited in Loomis 3, p. 112.

care

168   "Let every one take care of themselves," as the jackass said when he was dancing among the chickens.

GB, *The Mirror* (1823). Cited in Williams, p. 93; Kent, p. vii.

carry on

169   "Carry on!" cried the vulture, as he spied the dying horse on the desert.

US (Calif.), *The Pelican,* vol. 45, no. 4 (1938), p. 57. Cited in Loomis 4, p. 244.

case

170   "The case is altered," quoth Plowden.

GB, THOMAS DEKKER, *Batchelars Banquet* (c.1585). Cited in Wilson, p. 105; Whiting 6, p. 94; Taylor 1, p. 202. [The reference is to Edmund Plowden (1581-1585), eminent English jurist; while giving advice on trespassing, he was told that the animals that had trespassed were his.]

171   "It's a trying case," as the culprit said ven the judge passed sentence of death upon him.

US (Pa.), *Alexander's Weekly Messenger* (1839). Cited in Tidwell 2, p. 230.

172   "Your case is a hard one and must be looked into," as the chap said to the oyster.

US (Mass.), *Yankee Blade* (24 Dec. 1845). Cited in Loomis 2, p. 6.

173 "Circumstance h–alters cases," said the Cockney, when he saw two "hard cases" hung.

US (N.Y.), *Yankee Notions,* vol. 5 (1856), p. 181. Cited in Loomis 2, p. 11.

174 "Yours is a very hard case," as the fox said to the oyster.

US (N.Y.), *Yankee Notions,* vol. 8 (1858), p. 172. Cited in Loomis 2, p. 11.

175 "That alters the case," as the watchmaker said when he galvanized a brass watch.

US (Iowa), *Keokuk Constitution* (16 Jun. 1881), p. 16. Cited in Whiting 2, p. 10.

176 "I've got a case on you," remarked the librarian, as he wheeled the bookrack over her foot.

US (Calif.), *The Pelican,* vol. 5, no. 1 (1907), p. 7. Cited in Loomis 4, p. 236.

177 "Well, that's the shortest case on record," sighed the law student, as he finished the last bottle.

US (Calif.), *The Pelican,* vol. 25, no. 1 (1919), p. 1. Cited in Loomis 4, p. 238.

cash

178 "That's equal to cash," as the loafer said ven he found a fip in the streets.

US (Pa.), *Alexander's Weekly Messenger* (1839). Cited in Tidwell 2, p. 230. [*Fip,* short for *fippenny bit,* fivepence.]

catnip

179 "I'm not fond of catnip," as the little girl said ven the pussey bit her nose.

US (Pa.), *Alexander's Weekly Messenger* (1839). Cited in Tidwell 2, p. 261.

caws

180 "Hear me for my caws," as the old crow said when the boy robbed her nest.

US (N.Y.), *Wilkes' Spirit of the Times,* vol. 6 (1862), p. 71. Cited in Loomis 2, p. 6; Browne, p. 201; Mieder, p. 232. [The reference is to a plea by Brutus in Shakespeare's *Julius Caesar* (1599), act 3, scene 2: "Hear me for my cause."]

181 "Hear me for my caws," said the crow to the raven.

US, *Dundreary Joke Book* (1873). Cited in Browne, p. 201; Mieder, p. 232. [See note above.]

cell

182 "This is a cell," remarked a thoroughbred and very bibulous atheist when the policeman shoved him in and returned the key.

US (Calif.), *The Argonaut,* vol. 2, no. 10 (1878), p. 14. Cited in Loomis 4, p. 230.

change

183 "This is a chaynge for the vorse, Mr Trotter," as the gen'l'm'n said ven he got two doubtful shillin's and sixpenn'orth o' pocket pieces for a good half-crown.

GB, CHARLES DICKENS, *Pickwick Papers* (1836). Cited in Maass, p. 211.

184 "We seek no change and least of all such change as they would bring us," as the Mayor of Baltimore said when he vetoed the shinplaster bill.

US (Pa.), *Alexander's Weekly Messenger* (1839). Cited in Tidwell 2, p. 259. ["Shinplasters" were paper tokens issued by rural stores as small change; some storekeepers allegedly baked them to make them so brittle that they would disintegrate in the recipient's pocket.]

185 "I'm 'aving a change a 'air," as the cockney said when he put on a new wig.

US (N.Y.), *Yankee Notions,* vol. 10 (1860), p. 292. Cited in Loomis 2, p. 4. Recorded in Bryant (N.Y., S.C.).

186 "Rum change, this!" as the toper said when the bar-keeper paid him his balance in dirty postage stamps.

US (N.Y.), *Yankee Notions,* vol. 12 (1863), p. 4. Cited in Loomis 2, p. 17. [*Rum,* odd, strange; poor, bad.]

chapmen

187 "I think we will be all chapmen," quoth the good wife when she got a turd on her back.

GB, JAMES KELLY, *Scottish Proverbs* (1712). Cited in Lean, p. 745. [*Chapmen,* peddlers, hawkers, itinerant merchants.]

char

188 "That char is charr'd," as the good wife said when she had hanged her husband.

GB, JOHN RAY, *English Proverbs* (1678); US, 1948. Cited in Lean, p. 749; Stevenson, p. 2481. [*Char is charr'd,* chore is finished.]

189 "That char's charred," as the boy said when he'd killed his father.

GB, J.C. BRIDGE, *Cheshire Proverbs* (1917); US, 1948. Cited in Stevenson, p. 2481. [See note above.]

charge

190 "We make no extra charge for the settin' down," as the king remarked wen he blowed up his ministers.

GB, CHARLES DICKENS, *Pickwick Papers* (1836). Cited in Maass, p. 212; Baer, p. 179.

191 "I'll take charge here," said the murderer, as he seated himself in the electric chair.

US (Calif.), *The Pelican,* vol. 32, no. 4 (1926), p. 88. Cited in Loomis 4, p. 242.

chaw

192 "You don't chaw," as the toad said to the snake when he was about to swallow him whole.

US (Pa.), *Alexander's Weekly Messenger* (1839). Cited in Tidwell 2, p. 261.

check

193 "You can post me a check in the morning," as the actress used to say. She was a perfect lady.

US, LESLIE CHARTERIS, *Wanted for Murder* (1931). Cited in Whiting 1, p. 72.

chicken

194 "You're a queer chicken," as the hen said when she hatched out a duck.

US (Calif.), *Pacific Rural Press,* vol. 1 (1871), p. 108. Cited in Loomis 4, p. 230.

children

195 "What blessings children are!" as the clerk said when he took the fees for christening them.

US (Mass.), *Alexander's Weekly Messenger* (1839). Cited in Whiting 2, p. 4; Loomis 2, p. 5; Tidwell 2, p. 260.

choice

196 "Everyone to his own choice," said the old woman as she kissed the cow.

US, c.1945-1980. Recorded in Bryant (Kans.).

choosey

197 "Can't be choosey," said the old woman as she kissed the cow.

US, c.1945-1980. Recorded in Bryant (Miss.).

Christian

198 "Almost thou persuadest me to be a Christian," as the Jew said to the roasted pork.

GB, 1903. Cited in Lean, p. 741.

civil

199 "It's aye gude to be ceevil," quoth the auld wife when she beckit to the devil.

GB, ALLAN RAMSEY, *Scots Proverbs* (1737). Cited in Lean, p. 746. [*Aye gude,* always good; *beckit,* curtsied.]

civilization

200 "I'm in the land of civilization," as the Irishman said ven he saw the scaffold erected.

US (Pa.), *Alexander's Weekly Messenger* (1839). Cited in Tidwell 2, p. 259.

claims

201   "I have pryer claims to your property," as the burglar said when he entered the house with a jimmy.

US (N.Y.), *Marathon Independent* (17 Feb. 1881), p. 16. Cited in Whiting 2, p. 9.

claws

202   "I'll ratify it, after I put my concluding claws to it," as the cat said when she was watching the mouse.

US (N.Y.), *Yankee Notions,* vol. 3 (1854), p. 142. Cited in Whiting 2, p. 5. Recorded in Bryant (Ohio).

clean

203   "A clean thing's kindly," quo' the good wife when she turned her sark after a month's wear.

GB, ANDREW HENDERSON, *Scottish Proverbs* (1832). Cited in Lean, p. 741. [*Sark,* shirt, chemise.]

clear

204   "Shan't I clear," as the fellow said when he made tracks with a fat rooster.

US (Mass.), *Yankee Blade* (18 Oct. 1843). Cited in Loomis 2, p. 18. [A pun on *Chantecler,* the name of the cock in the medieval fables known as *Le Roman de Renart.*]

205   "I hope I made myself clear," as the water said when it passed through the filter.

US (Calif.), *The Argonaut,* vol. 44, no. 1153 (1899), p. 16. Cited in Loomis 4, p. 235.

206   "It's clear as mud," said the blind man.

US, c.1945-1980. Recorded in Bryant (Oreg., Tex.).

climb

207   "Climb of the unforgotten brave," observed Vice-Admiral Noah, as he reached the summit of Mount Ararat, and stopped to take a mouthful of solace.

US (Calif.), *The Argonaut,* vol. 2, no. 2 (1878), p. 14. Cited in Loomis 4, p. 230.

clothes line

208   "There, that explains where my clothes line went to!" exclaimed an Ohio woman as she found her husband hanging in the stable.

US, 1879. Cited in Browne, p. 202; Mieder, p. 233.

clout

209   "There's more clout than pie," as the schoolboy said when he unwrapped his dinner.

US, 1913. Cited in Wright, p. 163. [*Clout,* cloth.]

clubs

210 "Now is the time to get up clubs," as the boy said when the journalist's dog chased him.

US (N.Y.), *Wilkes' Spirit of the Times,* vol. 7 (1862), p. 215. Cited in Loomis 2, p. 7.

cockfighting

211 "If this don't beat a cock-fightin', nothin' never vill," as the Lord Mayor said ven the chief secretary o'state proposed his missis's health arter dinner.

GB, CHARLES DICKENS, *Pickwick Papers* (1836). Cited in Maass, p. 213.

coincidence

212 That's what Noah Webster said to his wife when she found him in bed with the kitchen wench, "It's just a coincidence."

GB, A. HOBBHOUSE, *Hangover Murders* (1935). Cited in Whiting 1, p. 74. [Noah Webster (1758-1843), American educator, lexicographer, and editor, is famous chiefly for English dictionaries giving spellings and definitions based on American as well as British usage.]

cold

213 "That's a cold one," said the old woman as she stuck her wooden leg out the window.

US, c.1945-1980. Recorded in Bryant (Ill.).

collar

214 "After a collar comes a halter," quoth the tanner of Tamworth when Henry IV called for a collar to make him a squire.

GB, JAMES ORCHARD HALLIWELL, *A Dictionary of Archaic and Provincial Words* (1865). Cited in Lean, p. 741.

collect

215 "Let me collect myself," said the man when he was blown up by a powder-mill.

GB, *Punch,* vol. 2 (1842), p. 96; US (N.Y.), *Yankee Notions,* vol. 11 (1861), p. 25. Cited in Loomis 3, p. 111; Loomis 2, p. 7.

collected

216 "Be collected," as the printer said to a huge batch of old newspaper bills that weren't paid, lying scattered over his desk.

US (Mass.), *Yankee Blade* (26 Nov. 1845). Cited in Loomis 2, p. 7.

colors

217 "At least I can go down with colors flying," said the calciminer when his foot slipped.

US (Calif.), *The Argonaut,* vol. 33, no. 15 (1893), p. 15. Cited in Loomis 4, p. 234.

come

218   "You can't come too often," as the hackney-coachman said to the thunderstorm.

GB, *Punch,* vol. 3 (1842), p. 88. Cited in Loomis 3, p. 112.

219   As the skunk said when the wind changed, "It all comes back to me now."

US, c.1945-1980. Recorded in Bryant (Kans., N.Dak.).

come around

220   "Is this the way you come around a fellow," as the sun said to the earth.

US (Mass.), *Yankee Blade* (30 Dec. 1846). Cited in Loomis 2, p. 7.

221   "Although you consider yourself a brighter fellow than I am, yet I can come round you," as the earth said to the sun.

US (N.Y.), *Yankee Notions,* vol. 10 (1860), p. 4. Cited in Loomis 2, p. 7.

come back

222   "I'll let you know when I come back again," as the rheumatism said to the leg.

GB, *Punch,* vol. 3 (1842), p. 180. Cited in Loomis 3, p. 112.

come clean

223   "I'll have to come clean," as the sheet said to the patent washer.

GB, DOROTHY L. SAYERS, *The Nine Tailors* (1934). Cited in Whiting 1, p. 75.

come down

224   "This is some come-down," said the co-ed, as she lost her petticoat upon the street.

US (Calif.), *The Pelican,* vol. 31, no. 1 (1925), p. 53. Cited in Loomis 4, p. 241.

come in

225   "Come in," as the spider said to the fly.

US (Pa.), *The Casket,* vol. 5 (1830), p. 377. Cited in Loomis 5, p. 51; Tidwell 2, p. 258.

226   "Come in, children—it's going to rain," as the shark said ven he sucked in the little fishes.

US (Pa.), *Alexander's Weekly Messenger* (1839). Cited in Tidwell 2, p. 260.

227   "Come in out of the wet," as the shark said when he swallowed the little Negro.

GB, *Punch,* vol. 2 (1843), p. 31; US (N.Y.), *Yankee Notions,* vol. 8 (1858), p. 138. Cited in Loomis 3, p. 111; Loomis 2, p. 7.

come on

228 "Come on," as the man said to his boot.

US (Pa.), *The Casket,* vol. 5 (1830), p. 377. Cited in Loomis 5, p. 51; Tidwell 2, p. 258.

come out

229 "I shan't come out tonight," as the moon said to the thunderstorm.

GB, *Punch,* vol. 2 (1842), p. 193. Cited in Loomis 3, p. 112.

230 "It will come out all right," as the boy remarked when he was gored by the cow's horn.

US, c.1945-1980. Recorded in Bryant (N.Y., S.C.).

common lot

231 "Ours is a common lot," as the toads said when they got into the clover field.

US (N.Y.), *Yankee Notions,* vol. 1 (1852), p. 76. Cited in Loomis 2, p. 7.

compact

232 "There, now we look compact and comfortable," as the father said ven he cut his little boy's head off to cure him o' squintin'.

GB, CHARLES DICKENS, *Pickwick Papers* (1836). Cited in Maass, p. 210; Williams, p. 94; Baer, p. 179.

company

233 "I'm afraid I'm in low company," as the guy said to the scarecrow.

US (N.Y.), *Wilkes' Spirit of the Times,* vol. 4 (1861), p. 23. Cited in Loomis 2, p. 14. [*Guy,* effigy of Guy Fawkes, English convict; such effigies, stuffed with combustible material, are traditionally displayed and burned on Guy Fawkes Day (5 November) to celebrate the failure of the Gunpowder Plot (1605).]

234 "Bad company," said the thief, as he went to the gallows between the hangman and the monk.

US, 1931. Cited in Taylor 1, p. 217.

complexion

235 "In the bright complexion of my youth I'll have no such word as pale," and she reached for the rouge-box with the clutch of an angel.

US (Calif.), *The Argonaut,* vol. 5, no. 3 (1879), p. 10. Cited in Loomis 4, p. 231.

conclusion

236 "That's a fur-gone conclusion," as the fox said when he lost his tail in a trap.

US (N.Y.), *Marathon Independent* (21 Apr. 1881), p. 15. Cited in Whiting 2, p. 10. Recorded in Bryant (Ohio).

confining

237 "The only trouble with my profession is that it is apt to be a rather confining one," as an ex-convict said.

US (Calif.), *The Argonaut,* vol. 42, no. 1103 (1898), p. 16. Cited in Loomis 4, p. 235.

conquer

238 "I stoop to conquer," said the young lady as she sat on the porch steps and tried to mash the young man in the gloaming.

US (Calif.), *California Golden Era,* vol. 16, no. 20 (1868), p. 1. Cited in Loomis 1, p. 305; Loomis 4, p. 233. [*She Stoops to Conquer* (1773) is a comedy by Oliver Goldsmith; *mash,* flirt with; *gloaming,* twilight.]

239 "She stoops to conquer," as the man said when his wife reached down for the poker.

US (Calif.), *California Golden Era,* vol. 16, no. 20 (1868), p. 1. Cited in Loomis 2, p. 19. [See note above.]

consolation

240 "I'm pretty tough, that's vun consolation," as the wery old turkey remarked wen the farmer said he was afeerd he should be obliged to kill him for the London market.

GB, CHARLES DICKENS, *Pickwick Papers* (1836). Cited in Stevenson, p. 2480.

241 "Well, it's no use talking about it now. It's over and can't be helped, and that's one consolation, as they always say in Turkey, ven they cut the wrong man's head off."

GB, CHARLES DICKENS, *Pickwick Papers* (1836). Cited in Bailey, p. 33; Stevenson, p. 2480; Baer, p. 180.

contain

242 "I just can't contain myself!" said the unfortunate on his ocean voyage.

US (Calif.), *The Pelican,* vol. 31, no. 1 (1925), p. 45. Cited in Loomis 4, p. 241.

content

243 "Keep cool and content and all will go well with you," said the fisherman when he thrust the lobster into a pot of boiling water.

US (Mass.), *Yankee Blade* (28 Jul. 1849). Cited in Loomis 2, p. 7.

244 "Be content with what you have," as the rat said to the trap, when he left part of his tail in it.

US (N.Y.), *Wilkes' Spirit of the Times,* vol. 8 (1863), p. 31. Cited in Loomis 2, p. 7; Browne, p. 202; Mieder, p. 233.

contentibus

245 "Contentibus," quoth Tommy Tomson, "Kiss my wife and welcome."

GB, JAMES KELLY, *Scottish Proverbs* (1721). Cited in Wilson, p. 142.

conversations

246 "No good ever come of exclusive low-toned conversations," as the feller said when he shot the turtle dove.

US, PHOEBE ATWOOD TAYLOR, *Mystery of Cape Cod Tavern* (1933). Cited in Whiting 1, p. 73.

copy

247 "Here's a little copy for you," as the printer's wife said upon an interesting occasion. "It was a fat take."

US (Mass.), *Yankee Blade* (3 Feb. 1849). Cited in Loomis 2, p. 7. [*An interesting occasion,* presumably the birth of a son, the "little copy"; *fat take,* printers' slang for a job that can be quickly done.]

corns

248 "Extracting corns," as the crow said to the farmer.

US (Mass.), *Yankee Blade* (21 Jul. 1847). Cited in Loomis 2, p. 7.

count

249 "On a Count of," said an irate landlord as he knocked down a titled bilk and jumped on top of him.

US (Calif.), *The Wasp,* vol. 3, no. 142 (1879), p. 597. Cited in Loomis 4, p. 231. [*Bilk,* cheater, swindler.]

countenance

250 "I've seen your countenance before," as the rat said to the observant grimalkin.

US (Mass.), *Yankee Blade* (22 Dec. 1849) Cited in Loomis 2, p. 18. [*Grimalkin,* cat.]

251 "I can't countenance such things," as the jolly soldier said, when half of his face was blown away by a shell.

US (N.Y.), *Wilkes' Spirit of the Times,* vol. 6 (1862), p. 151. Cited in Loomis 2, p. 7.

covered

252 "Lie still, I've got you covered," as the rug said to the floor.

US, c.1945-1980. Recorded in Bryant (N.Dak.).

crack

253 "I'll be with you in a crack," as the rifle-ball said to the target.

US (Mass.), *Ballou's Dollar Magazine,* vol. 12 (1860), p. 598. Cited in Loomis 2, p. 7.

254 "Crack it again, my good fellow!" ejaculated a fly that had lit on the folds of a thunder cloud.

US (Wash.), *Walla Walla Union* (30 May 1874), p. 4. Cited in Hines, p. 23.

255 "Another hard crack," remarked the mouse, as he squeezed through the wall.

US (Calif.), *The Pelican,* vol. 31, no. 1 (1925), p. 45. Cited in Loomis 4, p. 241.

crazy

256 "Everybody is crazy over me," said the inmate of the first floor of the insane asylum.

US (Calif.), *The Pelican*, vol. 42, no. 8 (1936), p. 6. Cited in Loomis 4, p. 244.

257 "Young girls are crazy," as the old woman said when she jumped over the straw.

US (N.Y.), 1940. Cited in Thompson, p. 502. [*Straw*, broom; *jumped over the straw*, got married.]

crook

258 "You dirty crook," says the pot to the kettle.

GB, GAVIN HOLT, *Six Minutes Past Twelve* (1933), p. 139. Cited in Whiting 6, p. 506.

crowd

259 "I can't enjoy myself in a crowd," as the herring said when he was packed in a barrel.

US (Mass.), *Yankee Blade* (11 Oct. 1843). Cited in Loomis 2, p. 7.

cry

260 "Much cry and sma' wool," as the barber said when he sheared the sow.

GB, STEPHEN GOSSON, *School of Abuse* (1579). Cited in Lean, p. 744.

261 "A great cry and little wool," quoth the devil when he sheared his hogs.

GB, JAMES HOWELL, *English Proverbs* (1659); US, ALEXANDER HAMILTON, *Itinerarium* (1744). Cited in Wilson, p. 333; Simpson, p. 156; Whiting 5, p. 89; Lean, p. 744; Taylor and Whiting, p. 877; Taylor 2, p. 317; Whiting 3, p. 393. Recorded in Bryant (N.C.). [Cf. no. 880.]

262 "Much cry and sma' wool," as the barber said when he shaved the sow.

US, A. WYNNE, *Toll House Murder* (1935), p. 288. Cited in Whiting 6, p. 142.

cure [See also no. 982.]

263 "Astonishing cure for consumption," as the old lady said when she sprinkled snuff on her boarder's hash.

US (Calif.), *California Spirit of the Times* (27 Jan. 1872). Cited in Loomis 2, p. 7.

cured

264 "I've cured her from lying in the hedge," quoth the good man when he had wed his daughter.

GB, JOHN RAY, *English Proverbs* (1678); US, 1948. Cited in Lean, p. 745; Stevenson, p. 744.

265   "Howsomedever, what can't be cured must be endured," as the feller said when the monkey bit him.

US, WILLIAM THOMPSON, *Major Jones' Courtship* (1848). Cited in Whiting 2, p. 7.

curly

266   "It's curly and crookit," as the devil said o' his horns.

GB, ANDREW HENDERSON, *Scottish Proverbs* (1832). Cited in Lean, p. 746.

current

267   "This is current," as the raft said ven it was going over the shore.

US (Pa.), *Alexander's Weekly Messenger* (1839). Cited in Tidwell 2, p. 261.

cut

268   "That's an unkind cut," as the man said ven his razor slipt.

US (Pa.), *Alexander's Weekly Messenger* (1839). Cited in Tidwell 2, p. 262.

269   "Cut and come again," as the cook said when her mistress discovered them in the larder.

US (Mass.), *Yankee Blade* (17 May 1847). Cited in Loomis 2, p. 7.

270   "Illustrated with cuts," said a young urchin, as he drew his jackknife across the leaves of his grammar.

US (Mass.), *Yankee Blade* (12 Jan. 1850). Cited in Loomis 2, p. 7; Browne, p. 202; Mieder, p. 232.

271   "Cut high, cut low; there's no pleasing you," as the boatswain said to the man he was flogging.

GB, 1903. Cited in Lean, p. 743.

cutting

272   "I'm cutting quite a figure," said the chorus girl, as she sat on the broken bottle.

US (Calif.), *The Pelican,* vol. 27, no. 8 (1922), p. 54. Cited in Loomis 4, p. 240; Halpert 2, p. 117; Mieder, p. 237. Recorded in Bryant (Tenn.).

cut up

273   "I'm dreadfully cut up," as the cod said to the fishmonger.

GB, *Punch,* vol. 2 (1842), p. 31. Cited in Loomis 3, p. 111.

dab

274   "Dab," quoth Dawkins when he hit his wife in the arse with a pound of butter.

GB, JAMES HOWELL, *English Proverbs* (1659). Cited in Wilson, p. 165; Lean, p. 743.

dance

275   "I guess I'll cut in on this dance," said the surgeon as he chloroformed the St. Vitus patient.

US (Calif.), *The Pelican*, vol. 31, no. 1 (1925), p. 11. Cited in Loomis 4, p. 241.

dancing

276   "My dancing days are over," as the duck said vot was trying to take steps on the ice.

US (Pa.), *Alexander's Weekly Messenger* (1839). Cited in Tidwell 2, p. 259; Mieder, p. 230.

dander

277   "You raise my dander," as the goose said ven the boy pulled him through the hole by the tail.

US (Pa.), *Alexander's Weekly Messenger* (1839). Cited in Tidwell 2, p. 259; Mieder, p. 230.

dark

278   "So dark and yet so light," as the man said when he looked at his ton of coal.

US (Calif.), *California Golden Era*, vol. 21, no. 24 (1873), p. 7. Cited in Loomis 1, p. 305; Loomis 2, p. 13.

dark-eyed

279   "Dark-eyed one, come hither to me," as the boxer remarked when he was going the second round with a man with bulging peepers.

US (Maine), *Yankee Blade* (22 Oct. 1842). Cited in Loomis 2, p. 8. [*Bulging peepers,* swollen eyes.]

darkness

280   "Out of darkness cometh forth light," as the printer's devil said when he looked into the ink-keg.

US (Mass.), *Yankee Blade* (22 Apr. 1843). Cited in Loomis 2, p. 8. [*Printer's devil,* printer's apprentice.]

darned

281   "You be darned," as the Yankee said ven he saw a great hole in his stocking.

US (Pa.), *Alexander's Weekly Messenger* (1839). Cited in Tidwell 2, p. 260; Mieder, p. 231.

282   "I'll not cover your heel; I'll be darned if I do," as the ragged stocking said to the novel-reading lady.

US (N.Y.), *Yankee Notions,* vol. 1 (1852), p. 71. Cited in Whiting 2, p. 8; Loomis 2, p. 8.

day

283 "The day we celebrate," as the fat pig said to the cock turkey last Christmas.

US (Pa.), *Alexander's Weekly Messenger* (1839). Cited in Tidwell 2, p. 259.

284 "This is a fine day," as the man who neglected to attend his militia drill said to the collector.

US (Mass.), *Yankee Blade* (28 Jul. 1849). Cited in Loomis 2, p. 10.

285 "Through in one day," as the girl's heel said when she wore thin stockings.

US (Calif.), *Fireman's Journal,* vol. 4 (1857), p. 1. Cited in Loomis 4, p. 230.

286 "Who knows what the day may bring forth," as the man said when he woke up in the morning and found himself in the gutter.

US (N.Y.), *Porter's Spirit of the Times,* vol. 3 (1858), p. 302. Cited in Loomis 2, p. 8.

287 "How dreadful short the days are," as the woman said when she let the breakfast dishes stand until she had read a novel.

US (N.Y.), *Porter's Spirit of the Times,* vol. 4 (1858), p. 94. Cited in Loomis 2, p. 18.

288 So as the mademoiselle said to the doughboy, "Some other day perhaps, but not today."

US, J. Y. DAME, *Murder cum Laude* (1935). Cited in Whiting 1, p. 74. [*Doughboy,* American infantryman in World War I.]

dead

289 "What a dead beat!" cried Carrie, as she opened the door of the crematory.

US (Calif.), *The Pelican,* vol. 24, no. 4 (1918), p. 26. Cited in Loomis 4, p. 238.

dear

290 "I'm on the trail of a dear," as the fellow said when he stepped on one of the female street sweepers.

US (N.Y.), *Yankee Notions,* vol. 13 (1864), p. 120. Cited in Loomis 2, p. 8.

dearer

291 "Each moment makes thee dearer," as the parsimonious tradesman said to his extravagant wife.

US (Calif.), *Fireman's Journal,* vol. 1 (1855), p. 4. Cited in Loomis 4, p. 230.

death

292 "Welcome death," quoth the rat when the trap fell down.

GB, JAMES HOWELL, *English Proverbs* (1659). Cited in Wilson, p. 877; Lean, p. 751.

decimal

293 "Darn that decimal point," said the engineer as the bridge fell down.
US, c.1945-1980. Recorded in Bryant (Kans.).

deer

294 "Vhat a high deer that is!" as the ibex said to the gazelle, ven the gazelle declared she couldn't stoop to converse vith 'em.
US (Pa.), *Alexander's Weekly Messenger* (1839). Cited in Tidwell 2, p. 259. [*High deer,* pun on *idea.*]

degrees

295 "I'm rising by degrees," as the quicksilver said to the thermometer, as it was getting hot.
US (Pa.), *Alexander's Weekly Messenger* (1839). Cited in Tidwell 2, p. 262.

delays

296 "De lays are dangerous," as the unpopular orator remarked when the eggs began to fly.
US (Iowa), *Keokuk Gate City* (2 Jun. 1881), p. 8. Cited in Whiting 2, p. 10.

delighted

297 "Delighted no end," cried the firefly as he backed into the fan.
US (Kans.), 1959. Cited in Koch 1, p. 180.

298 "I'm de-lighted," said the firefly as he accidentally backed into the fan.
US (Kans.), 1959. Cited in Koch 1, p. 180. Recorded in Bryant (Ill., Kans., Nebr., Tenn.).

dependence

299 "I have no dependence on you," as the sailor said when he let go his hold of a rope and tumbled into the sea.
US (Mass.), *Ballou's Dollar Magazine,* vol. 6 (1857), p. 500. Cited in Loomis 2, p. 8.

descended

300 "I am descended from a great house," as the hod-man said when he had come down from the roof of a five-story mansion.
US (Maine), *Yankee Blade* (8 Oct. 1842). Cited in Loomis 2, p. 8. [*Hod-man,* builder's assistant.]

devil

301 "What the devil do you want with me?" as the man said ven he seed the ghost.
GB, CHARLES DICKENS, *Pickwick Papers* (1836). Cited in Maass, p. 213; Bailey, p. 33; Whiting 2, p. 3; Stevenson, p. 2480; Baer, p. 175.

302 "Please give the devil his due," as the printer's apprentice said to his employer on Saturday night.

US (N.Y.), *Yankee Notions*, vol. 1 (1852), p. 9. Cited in Loomis 2, p. 8. [*Devil*, printers' slang for an apprentice.]

dews

303 "Gently the dews are o'er me stealing," as the man said when five due bills were presented to him at once.

US (N.Y.), *Yankee Notions*, vol. 1 (1852), p. 227. Cited in Loomis 2, p. 8.

304 "Where the dews have you been?" as Mrs. Smith remarked when her boy came in with wet feet after a ramble through the fields.

US (Calif.), *Daily Examiner*, vol. 35, no. 157 (1882), p. 4. Cited in Loomis 4, p. 233.

die

305 "I'll die laughing," as the ticklish man said when the sheriff was fixing the rope round his neck to hang him.

US (N.Y.), *Yankee Notions*, vol. 3 (1854), p. 142. Cited in Whiting 2, p. 5; Mieder, p. 232. Recorded in Bryant (N.J.).

306 "I wish I might die," said the sentimental maid, as she stood rubbing the shoulder of her dress with benzine.

US (Calif.), *The Argonaut*, vol. 2, no. 9 (1878), p. 14. Cited in Loomis 4, p. 230.

307 "'Tis sweet to die for those we love," observed the old clothes renovator as he dipped his sweetheart's gown in the dye pot.

US (Calif.), *The Wasp*, vol. 3, no. 148 (1879), p. 693. Cited in Loomis 4, p. 231.

difficulty

308 "This is a difficulty that can't be got over," as the bull said when he tried to leap the five-barred gate.

GB, *Punch*, vol. 3 (1842), p. 178. Cited in Loomis 3, p. 112.

dinner

309 "Dinner--forget," as Sandy said to his dog when he licked the platter.

US (Maine), *Yankee Blade* (29 Oct. 1842). Cited in Loomis 2, p. 8.

disaster

310 "Disaster," cried the pilot as the woman backed into the plane propeller.

US (Kans.), 1960. Cited in Koch 2, p. 196. Recorded in Bryant (Ill., Miss.).

discord

311 "Dis-cord is horrible," as the musical Negro said when he was about to be hung.

US (Mass.), *Yankee Blade* (11 Oct. 1851). Cited in Loomis 2, p. 8.

disgust

312   "I leave you in dis-gust," as the drowning Negro said to his boat which had capsized in a storm.

US (Maine), *Yankee Blade* (24 Dec. 1842). Cited in Loomis 2, p. 8.

313   "I must leave in dis-gust," as the darky said when he bid his friend good night during a thunder storm.

US (N.Y.), *Yankee Notions,* vol. 8 (1858), p. 292. Cited in Loomis 2, p. 8.

dish

314   "She's a sweet dish," he said, as the waiter handed him sago pudding.

US (Calif.), *The Pelican,* vol. 27, no. 2 (1921), p. 13. Cited in Loomis 4, p. 239.

divinity

315   "There is a divinity that shapes our ends," as the pig remarked when he was contemplating the kinks in his tail.

US (N.Y.), *Porter's Spirit of the Times,* vol. 4 (1858), p. 142. Cited in Loomis 2, p. 9. [The reference is to a remark in Shakespeare's *Hamlet* (1601), act 5, scene 2.]

316   "There is a divinity that shapes our ends," as the doughnuts remarked when the girl was making them.

US (Mass.), *Ballou's Dollar Magazine,* vol. 5 (1862), p. 598. Cited in Loomis 2, p. 8. [See note above.]

do

317   "Do as I say and not as I do," as the parson said when they wheeled him home in a wheelbarrow.

GB, A. B. EVANS, *Leichester Phrases* (1848). Cited in Lean, p. 743.

318   "You can't do that again," said the pig to the boy who cut off his tail.

US (Calif.), *California Golden Era,* vol. 12, no. 49 (1864), p. 7. Cited in Loomis 2, p. 6; Mieder, p. 233. Recorded in Bryant (Ariz.).

319   "I'll never do that again," as the monkey said when he fell from the top of the mango tree and broke his back in the fall.

US (Wash.), *Weekly Big Bend Empire* (28 Mar. 1889), p. 3. Cited in Hines, p. 23.

320   As the beetle said when he hit the windshield, "I'll never do that again."

US, c.1945-1980. Recorded in Bryant (Kans.).

dog

321   "Dog cheap," cried Mr. Paradox to his butcher, when he told him his sausages were only eight cents a pound.

US (Mass.), *Boston Herald* (6 Oct. 1853). Cited in Loomis 2, p. 8.

done

322 "There, now it's done and can't be helped," as the cook said when she had roasted and eaten her master's chicken.

GB, *Punch*, vol. 2 (1842), p. 133. Cited in Loomis 3, p. 112.

door

323 "Now where is that revolving door, door, door," said the man as he slipped on the ice while going into the store.

US (Kans.), 1959. Cited in Koch 2, p. 196. Recorded in Bryant (Ky.).

double

324 "V double you X," as the counterfeiter said to his five dollar bill when he was altering it into a ten.

US (N.Y.), *Yankee Notions*, vol. 14 (1865), p. 201. Cited in Loomis 2, p. 21.

down

325 "Now, I'm down upon you," as the extinguisher said to the rush light.

GB, *The Mirror* (1823). Cited in Williams, p. 93. [*Rush light,* candle made with the pith of a rush as a wick.]

326 "I'm down upon you," as the young beard said to the chin.

GB, *Punch*, vol. 3 (1842), p. 238; US (Mass.), *Ballou's Dollar Magazine,* vol. 11 (1860), p. 300. Cited in Loomis 3, p. 113; Loomis 2, p. 8.

327 "I'm down on you," as the man said when coming into collision with the side-walk.

US (Mass.), *Yankee Blade* (24 Feb. 1849). Cited in Loomis 2, p. 8.

328 "Down outside," said the fiddler when he fell out of the window.

US (N.Y.), *Wilkes' Spirit of the Times,* vol. 4 (1861), p. 151. Cited in Loomis 2, p. 8.

329 "I'm down on you," as the feather said to the goose.

US (Pa.), *Philadelphia Sun* (10 Feb. 1881), p. 7. Cited in Whiting 2, p. 8. Recorded in Bryant (Ohio).

330 "I was down once myself," remarked a feather in a lady's hat, when it saw her take a seat on the icy pavement.

US (Ohio), *Steubenville Herald* (3 Mar. 1881), p. 16. Cited in Whiting 2, p. 9.

331 "Down with whiskey!" screamed the temperance orator; and then he downed about three fingers of it.

US (Calif.), *The Wasp*, vol. 9, no. 311 (1882), p. 445. Cited in Loomis 4, p. 232.

332 "I may be down, but I'm not out," exclaimed the second baseman, as he successfully slid into second.

US (Calif.), *The Pelican,* vol. 30, no. 8 (1925), p. 42. Cited in Loomis 4, p. 241.

333 "You can't keep a good man down," as the lion said when he coughed up the Hebrew martyr.

US, WILL IRWIN, *The Julius Caesar Murder Case* (1935); US, 1935. Cited in Whiting 1, p. 74; Mieder, p. 236.

down pat

334 "I've got that down Pat," said Mrs. Flanigan as she gave her son a dose of castor oil.

US (Calif.), *The Pelican,* vol. 27, no. 2 (1921), p. 48. Cited in Loomis 4, p. 239.

draw

335 "Draw it mild," as the boy with the decayed tooth said to the dentist.

GB, *Punch,* vol. 1 (1841), p. 60. Cited in Loomis 3, p. 110.

drawbridge

336 "Raise the drawbridge," cried the flea, as he rode down the river in his matchstick canoe.

US (Kans.), 1959. Cited in Koch 1, p. 180; Mieder, p. 238. Recorded in Bryant (Kans., Ky., Nebr.).

dressed

337 "I am dressed to kill," as the recruit said when he donned his uniform.

US (Mass.), *Cambridge Tribune* (10 Nov. 1881), p. 16. Cited in Whiting 2, p. 11.

dressing

338 "Close the door, I'm dressing," said the salad to the ice box.

US, c.1945-1980. Recorded in Bryant (Kans.).

drift

339 "If I do see your drift, it's my 'pinion that you're a comin' it a great deal too strong," as the mail-coachman said to the snowstorm, ven it overtook him.

GB, CHARLES DICKENS, *Pickwick Papers* (1836). Cited in Maass, p. 209; Baer, p. 175.

340 "I get the drift," sighed the street cleaner the day after the snow storm.

US (Calif.), *The Pelican,* vol. 31, no. 1 (1925), p. 53. Cited in Loomis 4, p. 241; Mieder, p. 235.

drive

341 "The more you drive the firmer I am fixed," as the nail said to the hammer.

US (N.Y.), *Spirit of the Times,* vol. 10 (1840), p. 103. Cited in Whiting 2, p. 7. Recorded in Bryant (Ohio).

drop

342 "We'll take a parting drop together," as the doomed man said to the executioner.

US (Calif.), *California Golden Era,* vol. 8, no. 31 (1860), p. 5. Cited in Loomis 2, p. 8.

343 "I haven't tasted a drop in the last ten years," as the tramp said when the serving-maid tendered him a glass of water.

US (Calif.), *The Wasp,* vol. 6, no. 254 (1881), p. 371. Cited in Loomis 4, p. 232; Whiting 2, p. 10.

344 "I'm only indulging in a drop of the cratur," as the Irishman said when he knocked his wife down for "sassing" him.

US (Mass.), *Somerville Journal* (9 Jun. 1881), p. 16. Cited in Whiting 2, p. 10. [*Cratur,* possibly a pun on *crater* (drinking bowl) and *creature.*

345 "One drop too much," murmured the repentant murderer, as he shot through the deadly trap.

US (Calif.), *The Pelican,* vol. 1, no. 2 (1903), p. 7. Cited in Loomis 4, p. 235.

dust

346 The fly sat upon the axletree of the chariot wheel and said, "What a dust do I raise."

GB, STEPHANO GUAZZO, *Civile Conversation* (1581). Cited in Wilson, p. 271.

347 "What a dust have I raised," quoth the fly upon the coach.

GB, THOMAS FULLER, *Gnomologia* (1732); US, 1931. Cited in Lean, p. 752; Taylor 1, p. 213.

348 "What a dust we raise," said the fly upon the chariot wheel.

US, 1782, Charles Adams, ed. JOHN ADAMS, *Works of John Adams,* vol. 7 (1855). Cited in Whiting 5, p. 123.

349 "What a dust I have made," said the fly behind the flivver.

US, c.1945-1980. Recorded in Bryant (Minn.).

dying

350 "I'm dying for you," as the girl said to the bachelor when she dyed his pantaloons.

US (Mass.), *Yankee Blade* (3 Jun. 1846). Cited in Loomis 2, p. 9.

ear

351 "If we can't hear it, it ain't for the lack of ears," as the ass said to the cornfield.

US (N.Y.), *Yankee Notions,* vol. 8 (1858), p. 274. Cited in Loomis 2, p. 9; Whiting 2, p. 9. Recorded in Bryant (Ariz.).

352 "A splendid ear but a very poor voice," as the organ-grinder said to the donkey.

US (Mass.), *Ballou's Dollar Magazine,* vol. 12 (1860), p. 98. Cited in Loomis 2, p. 9.

353 "This," remarked the rat terrier, when his master had half completed the operation of trimming off his listening things, "this is the off ear."
US (Oreg.), *East Oregonian* (18 Feb. 1878), p. 4. Cited in Hines, p. 23.

easel

354 "Plop goes the easel," cried the artist, as he dropped his paraphernalia to the floor.
US (Calif.), *The Pelican,* vol. 48, no. 4 (1941), p. 8. Cited in Loomis 4, p. 244.

easy

355 "Easy does it," as the girl said to the soldier.
GB, HILARY SAUNDERS, *Sleeping Bacchus* (1951), p. 192. Cited in Whiting 6, p. 195.

356 "This is easy," said the man falling off a log.
US (Kans.), 1959. Cited in Koch 2, p. 196. Recorded in Bryant (Kans.).

357 "Oh well—easy come," as the girl said to the bishop.
GB, NICHOLAS MONSARRAT, *Life Is a Four Letter Word* (1966), p. 346. Cited in Whiting 6, p. 127.

358 Said the monkey to the bear, "'Tis as easy to grin as to growl."
US, c.1945-1980. Recorded in Bryant (N.Y.).

eat

359 "Eat, drink, and be merry, for tomorrow the cook leaves," as the fellow says.
US, EARL BIGGERS, *Seven Keys to Baldpate* (1913). Cited in Whiting 1, p. 73.

eavesdropping

360 "Eaves dropping again," said Adam, as his wife fell out of a tree.
US (Calif.), *The Pelican,* vol. 49, no. 9 (1943), p. 5. Cited in Loomis 4, p. 324; Mieder, p. 234.

element

361 "This is out of my element," as the sturgeon said ven he jum'd in a small boat.
US (Pa.), *Alexander's Weekly Messenger* (1839). Cited in Tidwell 2, p. 259; Mieder, p. 230.

embarrassed

362 "Oh, I'm embarrassed," said the woman as she backed away from the airplane propeller.
US (Idaho), 1966. Cited in Anon, p. 34.

embraces

363 "I want two em-braces," as the printer said to his female compositor.
US (Mass.), *Yankee Blade* (23 Jun. 1849). Cited in Loomis 2, p. 9. [*Em,* a unit of measure in typesetting.]

encore

364 "How nice to get such a hearty encore!" she said, as the half-back was called back after an eighty-yard run.

US (Calif.), *The Argonaut,* vol. 38, no. 4 (1896), p. 16. Cited in Loomis 4, p. 234.

end

365 "What makes you come end foremost," as the man said when the bumble bee stung him.

US (Mass.), *Yankee Blade* (26 Nov. 1845). Cited in Loomis 2, p. 9.

366 "All out; end of the line," the young lady remarked, as she told her last joke.

US (Calif.), *The Pelican,* vol. 28 (1923). Cited in Loomis 4, p. 240.

367 "My end draws near," said the wrestler, as his opponent bent him double.

US (Calif.), *The Pelican,* vol. 46, no. 4 (1939), p. 12. Cited in Loomis 4, p. 244.

368 "This is the end," said the dog's tail to the head.

US (Ky.), c.1949. Cited in Halpert 2, p. 117. Recorded in Bryant (Ky., Tenn.).

369 As the monkey said when he backed into the cactus, "That's the end of my tale."

US (Ky.), c.1950. Cited in Halpert 2, p. 119.

370 "This is the end," said the little boy as his pants fell off.

US (Tenn.), c.1950. Cited in Halpert 2, p. 117.

371 "This is the end of my tale," said the monkey as he backed into the fan.

US (Kans.), 1959. Cited in Koch 1, p. 180. Recorded in Bryant (Kans.).

enemies

372 "We must reconcile ourselves to our enemies when we are dying," remarked an old toper, as he called for a glass of water.

US (Mass.), *Ballou's Dollar Magazine,* vol. 2 (1855), p. 400. Cited in Loomis 2, p. 16.

English

373 "Your English is rotten," said the student, when the Professor missed his shot.

US (Calif.), *The Pelican,* vol. 26, no. 6 (1921), p. 41. Cited in Loomis 4, p. 239.

enough

374 "Oh, quite enough to get, sir," as the soldier said ven they ordered him three hundred lashes.

GB, CHARLES DICKENS, *Pickwick Papers* (1836). Cited in Maass, p. 214; Williams, p. 94; Baer, p. 180.

375 "That will be enough out of you," said the doctor, as he stitched the patient together.

US (Calif.), *The Pelican,* vol. 37, no. 4 (1930), p. 54. Cited in Loomis 4, p. 243.

example

376 "It has always been my aim in life to imitate a good example," as the counterfeiter remarked while working on a new set of dies.

US (Calif.), *The Wasp,* vol. 9, no. 328 (1882), p. 711. Cited in Loomis 4, p. 232.

377 "You are setting us a bad example," as the algebra class said, when the teacher wrote a hard equation on the board.

US (Wash.), *Waitsburg Times* (18 May 1883), p. 1. Cited in Hines, p. 23; Mieder, p. 233.

exchange

378 "An even exchange is no robbery," as the widow said when she swapped herself off for a widower.

US (N.Y.), *Porter's Spirit of the Times,* vol. 3 (1857), p. 270. Cited in Loomis 2, p. 9.

excusez

379 "Excusez," as the duck said to the frog.

GB, *Punch,* vol. 3 (1842), p. 206. Cited in Loomis 3, p. 113. [*Frog,* derisive slang for a French-speaking person.]

exhausting

380 "My, my," said the gas, as it puffed through the muffler, "how exhausting this is!"

US (Calif.), *The Pelican,* vol. 28, no. 3 (1923), p. 32. Cited in Loomis 4, p. 240.

expect

381 "Vell, here I am ven least expected, old gent'lm'n," as the knife said ven he opened the oyster.

US (Pa.), *Alexander's Weekly Messenger* (1837). Cited in Tidwell 2, p. 258.

382 "I've been expecting something. I just didn't know how long it would be," said the June bride.

US (Tex.), 1956. Cited in Hendricks, p. 356. Recorded in Bryant (Ohio).

experience

383 "It's all for the experience," as the feller said when they blew his block off.

US, JOHN DOS PASSOS, *42nd Parallel* (1930). Cited in Whiting 1, p. 73.

extreme

384 "I always heard that extremes were dangerous," said a wight who received a kick in the seat of honor, from a thick boot.

US (Mass.), *Boston Daily Herald* (9 Dec. 1836). Cited in Loomis 2, p. 9. [*Wight,* person.]

385 "One extreme follows the other," as the little dog said when he flew around after his own tail.

US (Pa.), *Alexander's Weekly Messenger* (1839). Cited in Tidwell 2, p. 261; Loomis 2, p. 9; Mieder, p. 230.

eye

386 "Sharp work for the eyes," as the devil said when the broad-wheeled wagon went over his nose.

GB, Samuel Beazley, *Boarding House* (1811). Cited in Kent, p. vii.

387 "It's all in my eye," as the herring said ven he vas strung on a stick.

US (Pa.), *Alexander's Weekly Messenger* (1839). Cited in Tidwell 2, p. 259.

388 "That's all in your eye," as they told the fellow who complained that the streets were dusty.

US (Pa.), *Alexander's Weekly Messenger* (1839). Cited in Tidwell 2, p. 260.

389 "Mind your eye," as the thread said to the needle.

GB, *Punch,* vol. 2 (1842), p. 50; US (Mass.), *Ballou's Dollar Magazine*, vol. 8 (1858), p. 300. Cited in Loomis 3, p. 111; Loomis 2, p. 9.

390 "The eyes have it," as the man said when his better and bigger half dashed the contents of her snuff box in his face.

US (Mass.), *Yankee Blade* (29 Nov. 1843). Cited in Loomis 2, p. 9.

391 "Those dear eyes of thine," as the man said when he bought his wife a pair of five dollar spectacles.

US (N.Y.), *Yankee Notions,* vol. 2 (1853), p. 10. Cited in Whiting 2, p. 8; Loomis 2, p. 8.

392 "I'll give you a poke in the eye," as the thread said to the needle.

US (Mass.), *Ballou's Dollar Magazine,* vol. 3 (1856), p. 600. Cited in Loomis 2, p. 9.

393 "It's all in the eye," as the needle said to the thread on its being run through it.

US (Calif.), *California Spirit of the Times* (23 Apr. 1870). Cited in Loomis 2, p. 9; Whiting 2, p. 9.

394 As the man said when he stuck his foot into the shoe with a nail in it, "There's more in there than meets the eye."

US, c.1945-1980. Recorded in Bryant (Ill.).

face

395 "I'll put a clean face on the matter," as the printer said when he washed the types.

US (Maine), *Yankee Blade* (10 Oct. 1842). Cited in Loomis 2, p. 9. [*Face,* printing surface.]

396 "Onything sets a gude face," quoth the monkey wi' the mutch on.

GB, 1903; US, 1916. Cited in Lean, p. 748; Marvin, p. 359. [*Mutch,* covering for the head.]

fair

397 "Fair enough," murmured the brunette, as she trailed her tresses in the peroxide.

US (Calif.), *The Pelican*, vol. 27, no. 1 (1921), p. 17. Cited in Loomis 4, p. 239.

fall

398 "Now, gen'l'm'n, fall on," as the English said to the French when they fixed bagginets.

GB, CHARLES DICKENS, *Pickwick Papers* (1836). Cited in Maass, p. 210; Baer, p. 180. [*Bagginets*, bayonets.]

false

399 "Tis false!" as the girl said when her beau told her she had beautiful hair.

US (N.Y.), *Yankee Notions*, vol. 1 (1852), p. 9. Cited in Loomis 1, p. 305; Whiting 2, p. 7; Loomis 2, p. 7; Mieder, p. 231. Recorded in Bryant (Ariz.).

fancy

400 "Every Nancy to her fancy," said the old lady as she kissed the cow.

US, c.1945-1980. Recorded in Bryant (N.Y., Ohio, Oreg.).

401 "She has the right to follow her fancy," as the dame said as she kissed the cow.

US, c.1945-1980. Recorded in Bryant (Ohio).

402 "Well, fancy's queer," as the old woman said when she kissed a cow.

US, c.1945-1980. Recorded in Bryant (Wis.).

403 "You to your Nancy and me to my fancy," said the old lady who kissed the cow.

US, c.1945-1980. Recorded in Bryant (N.Y., Ohio, Oreg.).

404 "To each his own fancy," said the old lady as she kissed the cow.

US (Nev.), 1956. Cited in Halpert 2, p. 118.

far

405 "So far, so good," as the boy said when he had finished the first pot of his mother's jam.

US (N.Y.), *Yankee Notions*, vol. 9 (1859), p. 182. Cited in Loomis 2, p. 10.

fare

406 "The fare's reduced," as the chap said when he dined on a single cracker.

US (Mass.), *Yankee Blade* (12 Sep. 1843). Cited in Loomis 2, p. 9.

407 "It's hard, but it's fare," as the coachman said when he charged passengers double price.

US (Mass.), *Yankee Blade* (26 Jun. 1847). Cited in Loomis 2, p. 9.

fat

408 "I'm getting fat," as the loafer said when he was stealing the lard.

US (N.Y.), *Yankee Notions,* vol. 8 (1858), p. 113. Cited in Loomis 2, p. 9.

faun

409 As the buck said to the doe, "Some faun, hey kid?"

US, *Harvard Lampoon,* vol. 109 (1935), p. 50. Cited in Whiting 1, p. 73.

fed

410 "Better fed than taught," said the churl to the parson.

GB, THOMAS FULLER, *Gnomologia* (1732). Cited in Lean, p. 742. [*Churl,* farm laborer, peasant.]

fed up

411 "I'm fed up on that," said the baby, pointing to the high chair.

US (Calif.), *The Pelican,* vol. 40, no. 3 (1933), p. 8. Cited in Loomis 4, p. 244.

feel

412 "I feel for your situation," as the probe said to the bullet.

GB, *Punch,* vol. 33 (1842), p. 238; US (Mass.), *Ballou's Dollar Magazine,* vol. 11 (1860), p. 300. Cited in Loomis 3, p. 113; Loomis 2, p. 10.

413 "I feel for you deeply," said the hungry man, probing about in his soup bowl for a stray oyster.

US (Calif.), *Daily Examiner,* vol. 34, no. 79 (1882), p. 4. Cited in Loomis 4, p. 235.

feeler

414 "I am just throwing out a feeler," remarked the saloon keeper, as he put the blind man into the street.

US (Ind.), *Indianapolis Saturday Review* (3 Mar. 1881), p. 7. Cited in Whiting 2, p. 9.

feeling

415 "There's a mew-tual feeling between us," as the cat said to the kitten.

US (Mass.), *Yankee Blade* (26 Nov. 1845). Cited in Loomis 2, p. 14.

416 "I have a feeling for you," said the lobster to the bait. "I catch on," said the hook. And the lobster, who had a poor appreciation of humor, didn't see the point.

US (Calif.), *The Pelican,* vol. 2, no. 1 (1904), p. 18. Cited in Loomis 4, p. 235.

feelings

417 "You hurt my feelings extremely," as the cat said ven the boy pinched her tail.

US (Pa.), *Alexander's Weekly Messenger* (1839). Cited in Tidwell 2, p. 262.

418 "I hope I haven't hurt your feelings," as the raisin seed said to the tooth.

US (Mass.), *Ballou's Dollar Magazine,* vol. 9 (1859), p. 200. Cited in Loomis 2, p. 11; Browne, p. 202.

419 "I hope I haven't hurt your feelings," as the raisin said to the hollow tooth.

US, PAT ROONEY, *Quaint Conundrums and Funny Gags* (1879). Cited in Browne, p. 202; Mieder, p. 233.

420 "Go on . . . Don't bother about my feelings," as the actress said to the bishop shortly afterwards.

US, LESLIE CHARTERIS, *Wanted for Murder* (1931). Cited in Whiting 1, p. 72.

felt

421 "This certainly is a long felt want," said the editor, as he read the hatter's full column advertisement.

US (Calif.), *The Pelican,* vol. 13, no. 4 (1912). Cited in Loomis 4, p. 237.

fiddle

422 "It sure pays to fiddle your time away," said the violin player, as he drew down his $150 a week.

US (Calif.), *The Pelican,* vol. 28, no. 7 (1923), p. 32. Cited in Loomis 4, p. 240; Mieder, p. 235.

423 "I didn't raise my daughter to be fiddled with," said the pussy cat, as she rescued her offspring from the violin factory.

US (Calif.), *The Pelican,* vol. 38, no. 8 (1932), p. 34. Cited in Loomis 4, p. 243.

figged out

424 "'Tis pleasant to be elegantly figged out," as Eve said when she put on her first apron.

US (N.Y.), *Yankee Notions,* vol. 11 (1862), p. 260. Cited in Loomis 2, p. 10. [*Figged out,* dressed.]

file

425 "Viper, thou gnawest a file," as the editor said to the mouse that was nibbling at his exchanges.

US (Mass.), *Yankee Blade* (29 Sep. 1849). Cited in Loomis 2, p. 10.

filling

426 "This is certainly filling," said the dentist, as he swallowed a part of his tooth.

US (Calif.), *The Pelican,* vol. 31, no. 2 (1925), p. 13. Cited in Loomis 4, p. 241.

filth

427 "Fye on all filthes," quoth the cart to the bullring.

GB, GABRIEL HARVEY, *Letter Book* (1573). Cited in Lean, p. 744.

428 "I hate filth," said the old lady as she washed her dishrag in the duck pond.

US, c.1945-1980. Recorded in Bryant (Ill.).

filthy lucre

429 "Filthy lucre," as the boy said when he picked up a penny from the mud.

US (N.Y.), *Yankee Notions,* vol. 8 (1858), p. 172. Cited in Loomis 2, p. 10.

fini

430 "Fini," as the French girl said when she jumped on her bed after saying her prayers.

GB, JOHN GALSWORTHY, *The Forsyte Saga* (1922); US, 1931. Cited in Stevenson, p. 2480; Taylor 1, p. 210. [*Fini* (French), finished, ended, settled.]

finish

431 "Truly, this is my Finn-ish," groaned the shipwrecked mariner, as his drift-wood raft was shattered on the rocky shores of Finland.

US (Calif.), *The Pelican,* vol. 13, no. 3 (1912). Cited in Loomis 4, p. 236.

432 As the old mule said when the turkey buzzard lit on the fence, "I see my finish."

US, c.1945-1980. Recorded in Bryant (Miss.).

fire

433 "It's hurray, brother John, every fire a turkey," as the boy said.

US, JOHNSON J. HOOPER, *Adventures of Captain Simon Suggs* (1845), p. 168. Cited in Whiting 2, p. 7.

434 "Here will be a good fire anon," quoth the fox when he pissed in the snow.

GB, JAMES ORCHARD HALLIWELL, *A Dictionary of Archaic and Provincial Words* (1865); US (N.C.), 1952. Cited in Lean, p. 744; Whiting 3, p. 408.

435 "It will be a fire when it burns," quoth the toad when he shit on the ice.

GB, 1903; US (N.C.), 1952. Cited in Lean, p. 744; Whiting 3, p. 408.

fireside

436 "I enjoy myself best at my own fireside," as the tongs said ven the andiron invited her to walk.

US (Pa.), *Alexander's Weekly Messenger* (1839). Cited in Tidwell 2, p. 260.

fit

437 "This is a fit time and place," as the mad dog said when he saw the river.

US (Iowa), *Burlington Hawkeye* (11 Aug. 1881), p. 15. Cited in Whiting 2, p. 10.

438 "What a splendid fit," as the tailor said when he threw the epileptic out the door.

US, c.1945-1980. Recorded in Bryant (Minn.).

fizzle

439 "That ended in a fizzle," remarked the diner, as he emptied his bottle of Apollonairis.

US (Calif.), *The Pelican,* vol. 17, no. 4 (1914), p. 26. Cited in Loomis 4, p. 237.

flame

440 "That's a flame of mine," as the bellows said to the fire.

US (N.Y.), *Yankee Notions,* vol. 7 (1858), p. 363. Cited in Loomis 2, p. 10.

441 "I've been to see an old flame," remarked the young man, who had recently journeyed to see Vesuvius.

US (Calif.), *The Argonaut,* vol. 31. no. 20 (1892), p. 15. Cited in Loomis 4, p. 234.

442 "There's my flame," said the fireman.

US (Calif.), *The Pelican,* vol. 31, no. 5 (1926), p. 46. Cited in Loomis 4, p. 242.

flat

443 "You look rather flat," said the tea-kettle to the pancake. "I would take that as an insult," said the cake, "if you had not been steaming it."

US (Mass.), *Yankee Blade* (1 Jan. 1848). Cited in Loomis 2, p. 10; Browne, p. 202; Mieder, p. 233.

444 "You look rather flat," as the tea-kettle said to the pancake.

US, *Ball of Yarn, or, Queer, Quaint, and Quizzical Stories* (1870). Cited in Browne, p. 202; Koch 2, p. 196.

flesh

445 "Flesh of my flesh, and blood of my blood," as the shark said ven he swallowed the man's leg.

US (Pa.), *Alexander's Weekly Messenger* (1839). Cited in Tidwell 2, p. 261.

446   "All flesh is grass," as the horse said when he bit a piece out of a man's arm.

US (Mass.), *Yankee Blade* (7 Aug. 1849). Cited in Loomis 2, p. 10.

447   "I've lost flesh lately," as the butcher said when he sold a quarter of beef to a bad customer.

US (N.Y.), *Yankee Notions,* vol. 1 (1852), p. 209. Cited in Loomis 2, p. 10; Whiting 2, p. 10; Mieder, p. 231.

flock

448   As one shepherd said to another when they saw a storm coming, "Let's get the flock out of here."

US (Calif.), 1959. Cited in Hines, p. 18.

fly

449   Here we may say to papists as the fletcher saith to his bolt, "Fly and be nought."

GB, THOMAS BECON, *Reliques of Rome* (1553). Cited in Lean, p. 744. [*Fletcher,* person who makes arrows.]

450   "I feel as if I should fly," as the dove said ven he saw a boy pick up a stone in the street.

US (Pa.), *Alexander's Weekly Messenger* (1839). Cited in Tidwell 2, p. 261.

451   "Fly not yet," as the waiter said to the ginger-beer on a hot day.

GB, *Punch,* vol. 3 (1842), p. 18. Cited in Loomis 3, p. 112. [Cf. no. 453.]

452   "I feel as though I should fly," as the snipe said on seeing a sportsman approaching.

US (Mass.), *Yankee Blade* (5 Oct. 1850). Cited in Loomis 2, p. 10.

453   "Fly not yet," as the waiter said to the lemon soda on a hot day.

US (N.Y.), *Yankee Notions,* vol. 1 (1852), p. 223. Cited in Loomis 2, p. 10. [Cf. no. 451.]

454   "There are a great many ways of catching flies, but I still adhere to fly paper," said the man when he sat down on a sheet of it.

US (Calif.), *Daily Examiner,* vol. 42, no. 171 (1886), p. 1. Cited in Loomis 4, p. 233.

455   "You think you are getting a little fly, don't you," said the man to the trout, as he leisurely pulled him in.

US (Calif.), *The Argonaut,* vol. 28, no. 8 (1891), p. 15. Cited in Loomis 4, p. 234.

flying colors

456   "We've come off with flying colors," as the ensign said when he ran from the enemy.

US (N.Y.), *Yankee Notions,* vol. 3 (1854), p. 142. Cited in Whiting 2, p. 5.

457 "I came off with flying colors," as the painter said when he fell from the ladder with a palette o'er his thumb.

US (N.Y.), *Wilkes' Spirit of the Times,* vol. 7 (1862), p. 55. Cited in Loomis 2, p. 10. Recorded in Bryant (Ohio).

flying-machines

458 "Flying-machines come a thundering sight higher than they go," said the inventor, picking himself up and surveying the wreck of the flying-apparatus.

US (Calif.), *The Argonaut,* vol. 38, no. 14 (1896), p. 16. Cited in Loomis 4, p. 234.

foe

459 "Bury me with my face to the foe!" cried a cockroach dying in the battle of the Nile.

US (Wash.), *Walla Walla Union* (30 May 1874), p. 4. Cited in Hines, p. 23.

foiled

460 "Foiled!" cried the villain, as he unwrapped a 50 cent cigar.

US (Calif.), *The Pelican,* vol. 26, no. 1 (1920), p. 5. Cited in Loomis 4, p. 238.

followed

461 "Don't look now, but I think we're followed," as one quint said to another.

US (Pa.), c.1935. Cited in Mook, p. 184. Recorded in Bryant (Pa.). [*Quint,* quintuplet. The Dionne quintuplets, born in Ontario on 28 May 1934, were all girls; often photographed for magazines and newspapers, they were famous throughout their infancy and early childhood.]

462 "We are being followed by a pair of heels," said one big toe to the other.

US, c.1945–1980. Recorded in Bryant (Kans.).

food

463 "Sweet food and fruits of early love," as the boy said to the almonds and raisins.

US (N.Y.), *Yankee Notions,* vol. 3 (1854), p. 142. Cited in Whiting 2, p. 4. Recorded in Bryant (Ariz.).

464 "That's food for reflection," as the goat said, when it swallowed the mirror.

US (Calif.), *The Pelican,* vol. 27, no. 8 (1922), p. 26. Cited in Loomis 4, p. 240.

465 "Pardon me for lapping my food," begged the embarrassed guest, as he spilled the gravy into his napkin.

US (Calif.), *The Pelican,* vol. 28, no. 1 (1922), p. 2. Cited in Loomis 4, p. 240.

fool

466   "God help the fool," quoth Pedley (he being one himself).

GB, THOMAS FULLER, *Gnomologia* (1732). Cited in Lean, p. 744.

467   "There's no fool like an old fool," as the old man said when he married his fourth wife.

US, c.1945-1980. Recorded in Bryant (Kans., Nebr., N.Y.).

footnote

468   "Notice the footnote at the bottom of the page," laughed the court fool as the royal attendent's shoes emitted a squeak.

US (Calif.), *The Pelican,* vol. 16, no. 1 (1914). Cited in Loomis 4, p. 237.

footsteps

469   "I'll follow in your footsteps," as one thief said to another when he spelled him on the treadmill.

US (N.Y.), *Yankee Notions,* vol. 3 (1854), p. 154. Cited in Whiting 2, p. 5. Recorded in Bryant (Ohio). [*Spelled,* relieved.]

forth

470   "Let's celebrate the coming forth," as Grant's army said on the third of July, when they heard the Rebs were to march out of Vicksburg and lay down their arms the next day.

US (N.Y.), *Yankee Notions,* vol. 12 (1863), p. 200. Cited in Loomis 2,p. 7.

471   "Come forth!" cried the king, but Daniel stepped on a greasy old piece of lion excrement and only came fifth.

US (Kans.), c.1924-1927. Cited in Porter, p. 159.

fortune

472   "This is a hard fortune," as the counterfeiter said ven he found himself cutting stone in the state prison.

US (Pa.), *Alexander's Weekly Messenger* (1839). Cited in Tidwell 2, p. 259.

473   "Since you will buckle fortune on me back," as Shakespoke says again, "I must hab patience to endure the load."

US, *Minstrel Gags and End Men's Hand-Book* (1875), pp. 50-51. Cited in Browne, p. 201.

foul

474   "Oh, this foul, foul world!" he moaned, as each chicken passed him on the street.

US (Calif.), *The Pelican,* vol. 25, no. 5 (1920), p. 8. Cited in Loomis 4, p. 238.

Frenchmen

475 "Mine Gott! Vat will de Frenchmen make next?" as the Dutchman said the first time he saw a monkey.

US (N.Y.), *Yankee Blade* (8 Feb. 1847). Cited in Loomis 2, p. 14. Recorded in Bryant (Ohio).

friend

476 "No friend like a bosom friend," as the man said when he pulled out a louse.

GB, THOMAS FULLER, *Gnomologia* (1732). Cited in Lean, p. 748.

477 "I've buried my best friend," as the undertaker said when he buried the quack doctor.

US (N.Y.), *Yankee Notions,* vol. 1 (1852), p. 244. Cited in Whiting 2, p. 8; Loomis 2, p. 6.

478 "You stick to me like true friends," as the man said to the tar and feathers after he had been lynched.

US (N.Y.), *Yankee Notions,* vol. 3 (1854), p. 142. Cited in Whiting 2, p. 4. Recorded in Bryant (Ohio).

479 "I'm speaking as to a friend," as Antony said to Caesar, stropping his razor.

US, WILL IRWIN, *The Julius Caesar Murder Case* (1935). Cited in Whiting 1, p. 72.

fun

480 "I take my fun where I find it," said the editor, as he looked over the contributions.

US (Calif.), *The Pelican,* vol. 37, no. 3 (1930), p. 13. Cited in Loomis 4, p. 243.

481 "Isn't it going to be fun?" as the bishop said to the actress.

US, LESLIE CHARTERIS, *The Last Hero* (1930). Cited in Whiting 1, p. 73.

fund

482 "That's part of the sinking fund," as the chap said when a box of specie went to the bottom of the river.

US (N.Y.), *Yankee Notions,* vol. 9 (1858), p. 196. Cited in Loomis 2, p. 12.

gag

483 "That's an old gag," said the cashier, as the bandit stopped up his mouth.

US (Calif.), *The Pelican,* vol. 31, no. 5 (1926), p. 34. Cited in Loomis 4, p. 242.

game

484 "I'm still in the game," said the man, as he tried to pull his hand out of the bear's mouth.

US (Calif.), *The Pelican,* vol. 31, no. 1 (1925), p. 10. Cited in Loomis 4, p. 241.

485   "Every time we get together you think of new games," as the bishop said to the actress.

US, LESLIE CHARTERIS, *Enter the Saint* (1930). Cited in Whiting 1, p. 73.

gammon

486   "I guess there ain't much gammon about this," as the Yankee said when he tried to slice a wooden ham.

US (N.Y.), *Yankee Notions,* vol. 2 (1853), p. 286. Cited in Loomis 2, p. 10.

gaudy

487   "'Tis neat but not gaudy," as they said of the devil when they painted his body pea-green and tied up his tail with red ribbons.

US, 1913. Cited in Wright, p. 161.

488   "Neat but not gaudy," as the devil said when he painted his tail blue.

US (N.Y.), 1940. Cited in Thompson, p. 501; Koch 1, p. 180; Taylor 1, p. 210. Recorded in Bryant (Kans.).

489   "Not gaudy," as the gypsy said, "just plain red and yaller."

Can., c.1945-1980. Recorded in Bryant (Ont.).

490   "That is beautiful but gaudy," said the devil as he painted his tail pea-green.

US (Ky.), c.1950. Cited in Halpert 2, p. 117.

genius

491   "Genius will work its way through," as the poet remarked when he saw a hole in the elbow of his coat.

US (Calif.), *California Spirit of the Times* (27 Jan. 1872). Cited in Loomis 2, p. 21.

get around

492   "I shall soon get round you again," as the earth said to the sun on the 1st of January.

GB, *Punch,* vol. 2 (1842), p. 218. Cited in Loomis 3, p. 112.

get on

493   "You're getting on," as the actress said to the bishop.

US, LESLIE CHARTERIS, *Enter the Saint* (1930). Cited in Whiting 1, p. 72.

get over

494   "I'll never get over this as long as I live," said the hen as she surveyed the ostrich egg.

US (Calif.), *The Pelican,* vol. 29, no. 6 (1924), p. 20. Cited in Loomis 4, p. 240.

get up

495 "You'll never get me up in that thing," said the caterpillar as he gazed up at the butterfly.

US, c.1945-1980. Recorded in Bryant (Kans.).

gip

496 "Gip with an ill rubbing," quoth Badger, when his mare kicked.

GB, JOHN RAY, *English Proverbs* (1678). Cited in Wilson, p. 302. [*Gip,* pettish, perverse; an expression of remonstrance addressed to a horse.]

give

497 "It is more blessed to give than to receive," as the school boy said ven the master flogged him.

US (Pa.), *Alexander's Weekly Messenger* (1839). Cited in Tidwell 2, p. 259; Mieder, p. 230.

gneiss

498 "Is that gneiss?" shouted Herr Doktor to his geology class, holding aloft an armful of rock.

US (Calif.), *The Pelican,* vol. 35, no. 1 (1929), p. 32. Cited in Loomis 4, p. 243.

go

499 "Go here away, go there away," quoth Madge Whitworth when she rode the mare in the tedder.

GB, JAMES SHIRLEY, *Hyde Park* (1637); US, 1931. Cited in Wilson, p. 307; Lean, p. 744; Taylor 1, p. 210. [*Tedder* refers to new-mown grass or hay.]

500 "So here goes," as the boy said when he run by himself.

US, DAVID CROCKETT, *A Narrative of the Life of David Crockett, Written by Himself* (1834). Cited in Whiting 2, p. 6. Recorded in Bryant (Ariz., N.Y.).

501 "Ven are you going to Texas?" as the boy said to the man vot wanted to get trusted at the printing office.

US (Pa.), *Alexander's Weekly Messenger* (1839). Cited in Tidwell 2, p. 261.

502 "We are going very fast," as the man in a consumption said to the locomotive.

US (N.Y.), *Spirit of the Times,* vol. 10 (1840), p. 207. Cited in Whiting 2, p. 7. Recorded in Bryant (Ohio).

503 "That's a pretty go," said the husband when his beautiful wife ran away from him.

US (N.Y.), *Yankee Notions,* vol. 14 (1865), p. 368. Cited in Loomis 2, p. 16; Loomis 1, p. 305.

504 "It was 'all go and no whoa'," as the girl said when she was a slidin' the greased balluster.

US, PALMER COX, *Squibbs of California* (1874). Cited in Loomis 2, p. 10.

505 "Go, father, and fare worse," as the son said to the old man sent to jail for wife beating.

US (Va.), *Richmond Baton* (10 Feb. 1881), p. 15. Cited in Whiting 2, p. 9. Recorded in Bryant (N.J.).

506 "I shall go tomorrow," said the king. "You shall wait for me," said the wind.

US (Wash.), *Waitsburg Times* (26 Jan. 1883), p. 4. Cited in Hines, p. 23.

go down

507 "I must go down to the sea again," said the fried halibut, as the passenger leaned over the rail.

US (Calif.), *The Pelican,* vol. 39, no. 1 (1932), p. 6. Cited in Loomis 4, p. 243.

good

508 "It's gude to be merry and wise," quoth the miller when he moutered twice.

GB, JAMES KELLY, *Scottish Proverbs* (1721). Cited in Lean, p. 746. [*Moutered,* collected a toll due to the owner of a mill for the privilege of having grain ground.]

509 "It's for my own good," vich is the reflection with vich the penitent schoolboy comforted his feelings ven they flogged him.

GB, CHARLES DICKENS, *Pickwick Papers* (1836); US, 1989. Cited in Maass, p. 214; Mieder, p. 234.

510 "Every evil is followed by some good," as the man said when his wife died the day after he became bankrupt.

US (Pa.), *Alexander's Weekly Messenger* (1838). Cited in Tidwell 2, p. 258; Mieder, p. 230.

511 "Overcome evil with good," as the preacher said when he knocked a rascal down with the Bible.

US (Mass.), *Yankee Blade* (22 Jan. 1848). Cited in Loomis 2, p. 15.

512 "Return good for evil," as the match said when lighting the pipe of the man who had struck it.

US (Wash.), *Walla Walla Union* (22 Jul. 1871), p. 1. Cited in Hines, p. 23; Mieder, p. 234.

513 "I promised mother I'd be good," cried the egg as it ran from the shell.

US (Calif.), *The Pelican,* vol. 31, no. 1 (1925), p. 45. Cited in Loomis 4, p. 241.

514 "I punish my wife with good words," said the old man as he threw the Bible at his wife.

US, 1931; US (Ky.), c.1950. Cited in Taylor 1, p. 215; Halpert 2, p. 119; Mieder, p. 237. Recorded in Bryant (Ill., Wis.).

goodness

515 "Your goodness overpowers me," as the gentleman murmured to the champagne when he couldn't rise from his chair.

GB, *Punch,* vol. 3 (1842), p. 240. Cited in Loomis 3, p. 113.

516 "For goodness sake," sighed the young modern, as he wearily trudged home from an auto ride.

US (Calif.), *The Pelican*, vol. 35, no. 3 (1929), p. 46. Cited in Loomis 4, p. 243.

goodwill

517 "I do what I can or I will do my goodwill," quoth the fellow when he threshed in his cloak.

GB, JOHN MANNINGHAM, *Diary* (1602). Cited in Wilson, p. 395; Lean, p. 745.

518 "I kill'd her for goodwill," said Scot when he killed his neighbor's mare.

GB, JOHN RAY, *English Proverbs* (1678). Cited in Lean, p. 745.

go off

519 "I'm ready to go off by the train," as the barrel of gunpowder said to Guy Faux.

GB, *Punch*, vol. 1 (1842), p. 50; US (N.Y.), *New Varieties* (22 May 1871), p. 11. Cited in Whiting 2, p. 9; Loomis 3, p. 111. [The reference is to Guy Fawkes, English conspirator convicted in the Gunpowder Plot (1605).]

go out

520 "Go out for a while; you're getting me too hot," as the lamp shade said to the lamp.

US (Calif.), *The Pelican*, vol. 39, no. 9 (1933), p. 2. Cited in Loomis 4, p. 244.

go through

521 "I go through my work," as the needle said to the idle boy. "But not until you're hard pushed," as the idle boy said to the needle.

US (N.Y.), *Yankee Notions*, vol. 9 (1859), p. 17. Cited in Loomis 2, p. 10; Thompson, p. 502; Hines, p. 23.

gouging

522 "No gouging," as the chap said when he felt the critters in his head.

US (Mass.), *Yankee Blade* (26 Nov. 1845). Cited in Loomis 2, p. 10. [*Critters,* creatures (e.g., fleas or lice).]

grace

523 "Grace before meats," as the belle said when she took in the last reef in her corset just before dinner.

US (N.Y.), *Yankee Notions*, vol. 13 (1864), p. 132. Cited in Loomis 2, p. 10.

grate

524 "This is a grate country," as Pat said when he got in the lock-up.

US (Mass.), *Yankee Blade* (31 Jul. 1847). Cited in Loomis 2, p. 11.

525 "I'm in a grate scrape," as the nutmeg agonizingly said to the grater.
US (N.Y.), *Yankee Notions*, vol. 1 (1852), p. 88. Cited in Whiting 2, p. 8; Loomis 2, p. 10. Recorded in Bryant (N.J.).

526 "This is a grate prospect," as the prisoner said in peeping out of his cell window.
US (N.Y.), *Porter's Spirit of the Times*, vol. 4 (1858), p. 14; *Yankee Notions*, vol. 7 (1858), p. 119. Cited in Loomis 2, p. 10.

grave

527 "This is making light of a grave proposition," gleefully laughed the incendiary, as he touched a match to the crematory.
US (Calif.), *The Pelican*, vol. 2, no. 2 (1904), p. 7. Cited in Loomis 4, p. 235.

528 "These are grave charges," murmured the hopeless one, as he perused the bill for the burial of his mother-in-law.
US (Calif.), *The Pelican*, vol. 12, no. 3 (1912). Cited in Loomis 4, p. 236.

grease

529 "To grease we give our shining blades," as the father of the family said when he rose to perform the solemn duty of carving a fat goose on Christmas Day.
US (N.Y.), *Yankee Notions*, vol. 15 (1866), p. 67. Cited in Loomis 2, p. 11. Recorded in Bryant (N.Y.).

green

530 "Green, but dangerous," as the asparagus said to the copper kettle in which it was boiled.
US (Mass.), *Ballou's Dollar Magazine*, vol. 10 (1859), p. 600. Cited in Loomis 2, p. 11.

grilling

531 "Suffering Sappho, but this is grilling work," said the cook, as he poured more grease on the waffle iron.
US (Calif.), *The Pelican*, vol. 13, no. 3 (1912). Cited in Loomis 4, p. 236.

grind

532 "One enjoys a good grind now and then," said the humorous cannibal, as he devoured the valedictorian.
US (Calif.), *The Pelican*, vol. 26, no. 4 (1920), p. 44. Cited in Loomis 4, p. 238. [*Grind,* slang for an industrious student.]

grip

533 "Now I've got you in my grip," hissed the villain, shoving his toothpaste into his valise.
US (Calif.), *The Pelican*, vol. 29, no. 5 (1923), p. 37. Cited in Loomis 4, p. 240.

grit

534 "I am clear grit," as the grindstone said to the razor.
US (Pa.), *Alexander's Weekly Messenger* (1839). Cited in Tidwell 2, p. 259.

ground

535 "I'm gaining ground," as the sand bar said to the river.
US (Mass.), *Yankee Blade* (8 Jan. 1845). Cited in Loomis 2, p. 11.

536 "I'll hit the ground soon," said the man when he fell off the top of the barn.
US (Tenn.), 1950. Cited in Halpert 2, p. 118.

gulp

537 "Gulp!" quoth the wife when she swallowed her tongue.
GB, 1903. Cited in Lean, p. 744.

guts

538 "It takes guts to do this," said the moth, as he popped on the windshield.
US (Calif.), *The Pelican,* vol. 47, no. 6 (1941), p. 9. Cited in Loomis 4, p. 244; Koch 1, p. 180. Recorded in Bryant (Ill., Kans., Wis.).

habit

539 "The fours of habit," said the gambler softly, as he dealt himself all the aces in the pack.
US (Calif.), *Daily Examiner,* vol. 34, no. 65 (1882), p. 4. Cited in Loomis 4, p. 232.

half-cracked

540 "You're half-cracked," said the squirrel to the pecans. And they replied, "That's because we're nuts about you."
US (Calif.), *The Pelican,* vol. 34, no. 1 (1928), p. 3. Cited in Loomis 4, p. 243.

hand

541 "I do not ask thee for thy hand," as the child said when gazing earthward o'er its parent's knee.
US (Calif.), *The Argonaut,* vol. 2, no. 9 (1878), p. 14. Cited in Loomis 4, p. 230.

542 "It's easy enough after you get your hand in," was the reply of the criminal with the fetters on his wrist.
US (Calif.), *The Wasp,* vol. 6, no. 250 (1881), p. 318. Cited in Loomis 4, p. 232.

543 "Best hand I ever held," said a fellow as he impudently squeezed a lady's fingers.
US (Calif.), *The Wasp,* vol. 11, no. 379 (1883), p. 10. Cited in Loomis 4, p. 233.

544 "You'll have to hand it to him!" remarked the football fan, as the left end dropped a forward pass.

US (Calif.), *The Pelican,* vol. 26, no. 6 (1921), p. 41. Cited in Loomis 4, p. 239.

545 "Give this little girl a great big hand," said the cannibal's small daughter, as he was serving dinner.

US (Calif.), *The Pelican,* vol. 40, no. 4 (1933), p. 42. Cited in Loomis 4, p. 244.

546 "Let's walk hand in hand in hand," said the boy octopus to his girl friend.

US (Kans.), 1959. Cited in Koch 1, p. 180.

hang

547 "Thereby hangs a tail," as the monkey said ven he placed his hand on his rump.

US (Pa.), *Alexander's Weekly Messenger* (1839). Cited in Tidwell 2, p. 259.

548 "Well, now I've got the hang of this business," as the culprit said when he found himself at last on the gallows.

US, *Ball of Yarn, or, Queer, Quaint, and Quizzical Stories* (1870). Cited in Browne, p. 202; Mieder, p. 232.

549 "Yes, I guess I'll have to hang around here," murmured the convicted murderer, as he entered the prison.

US (Calif.), *The Pelican,* vol. 25, no. 3 (1918), p. 45. Cited in Loomis 4, p. 238. Recorded in Bryant (Kans.).

550 Said the corset to the plump lady, "I'll hang around you all day."

US, c.1945-1980. Recorded in Bryant (Kans.).

551 "Guess I'll hang around a little while," said the prisoner from the gallows.

US (Kans.), 1960. Cited in Koch 2, p. 196; Mieder, p. 238.

hanged

552 "You be hanged," said the artist to his painting when he sent it in to the exhibition.

US (Calif.), *The Wasp,* vol. 3, no. 141 (1879), p. 581. Cited in Loomis 4, p. 231.

hanging

553 As the Irishman said, "Hangin's too good for her, they ought to kick her tail."

US (N.Y.), HELEN REILLY, *The Dead Can Tell* (1940), p. 85. Cited in Whiting 6, p. 287.

hard

554 "Too hard on me," said the corn to the tight boot.

GB, *Punch,* vol. 2 (1842), p. 31; US (Mass.), *Yankee Blade* (10 Apr. 1844). Cited in Loomis 3, p. 111; Loomis 2, p. 11.

555 "You're a hard customer," as the fellow said when he ran against the post.

US (Mass.), *Yankee Blade* (26 Nov. 1845). Cited in Loomis 2, p. 11.

556 "I didn't think you'd be so hard on me," as the shark said when he bit the anchor.

US (Mass.), *Ballou's Dollar Magazine,* vol. 5 (1857), p. 200. Cited in Loomis 2, p. 11.

hardship

557 "I have passed through great hardships," as the schooner said after sailing through a fleet of iron ships.

US (Mass.), *Ballou's Dollar Magazine,* vol. 5 (1857), p. 200. Cited in Loomis 2, p. 11; Mieder, p. 231.

hard times

558 "Hard times! And we must make the most of what little we have," as the grocer said when he watered the vinegar.

US (N.Y., Calif.), *Yankee Notions,* vol. 1 (1852), p. 9. Cited in Loomis 1, p. 305; Whiting 2, p. 7. Recorded in Bryant (Ohio).

559 "Hard times, and we must make the most of what little we have," as the grocer said when he sanded his sugar and watered his wine.

US (N.Y.), *Yankee Notions,* vol. 1 (1852), p. 75. Cited in Loomis 2, p. 14.

harping

560 "Still harping on, my daughter," as the father said to the young lady who was continually twanging on the wires of her instrument.

US (N.Y.), *Yankee Notions,* vol. 15 (1866), p. 4. Cited in Loomis 2, p. 11.

haste

561 "Make no more haste when you come down than when you went up," as the man said to him on the tree top.

GB, ANON., *Merry Tales, Wittie Questions and Quick Answers* (1567). Cited in Lean, p. 747.

562 "The more haste the worse speed," quoth the tailor to his long thread.

GB, JAMES KELLY, *Scottish Proverbs* (1721); US, 1916. Cited in Lean, p. 749; Wilson, p. 356; Marvin, p. 357.

563 "Excuse my haste," as the locomotive said to the cow on the railroad.

US (Pa.), *Alexander's Weekly Messenger* (1839). Cited in Tidwell 2, p. 262.

564 "Yours in haste," as the thief said ven the constable cotched him.

US (Pa.), *Alexander's Weekly Messenger* (1839). Cited in Tidwell 2, p. 261. [*Cotched,* caught.]

hat

565 "It's all around my hat," as the hypocrite said when he put on mourning for his departed wife.

US (Mass.), *Ballou's Dollar Magazine,* vol. 10 (1860), p. 200. Cited in Loomis 2, p. 4.

head

566 "Two heads are better than one," quoth the woman when she had her dog with her to the market.

GB, THOMAS FULLER, *Gnomologia* (1732); US, 1916. Cited in Lean, p. 751; Wilson, p. 851; Marvin, p. 363.

567 "Two heads are better than one," as the cabbage-head said to the lawyer.

US (Maine), *Yankee Blade* (22 Oct. 1842). Cited in Loomis 2, p. 11.

568 "Shouldn't wonder if that made my head ache!" as the sailor said when the cannon ball smashed his skull.

US (N.Y.), *Yankee Notions,* vol. 3 (1854), p. 142. Cited in Whiting 2, p. 9. Recorded in Bryant (Ariz.).

569 "Who says two heads are better than one?" exclaimed Jaggs as he woke up the next morning and took a dose of bromo-soda.

US (Calif.), *The Wasp,* vol. 3, no. 142 (1879), p. 597. Cited in Loomis 4, p. 234.

570 "Heads, I win," said the executioner, as he let the guillotine fall.

US (Calif.), *The Pelican,* vol. 30, no. 1 (1924), p. 23. Cited in Loomis 4, p. 240.

571 It's what the monkey said to Mary Queen of Scots just before her execution, "Keep your head screwed on."

GB, G. BEATON, *Jack Robinson* (1933). Cited in Whiting 1, p. 74.

headwork

572 "Some headwork," said the barber, as he clicked the shears on the next frosh.

US (Calif.), *The Pelican,* vol. 11, no. 1 (1911). Cited in Loomis 4, p. 236. [*Frosh,* high-school or college freshman.]

health

573 As the old beggarman said to his dame, "God send you your health as long as I live."

GB, BRIAN MELBLANCKE, *Philotimus* (1583). Cited in Lean, p. 742.

574 "Here's a health to all good lasses," as the boy said when he licked a stick which he had plunged by mistake into a barrel of sperm oil.

US (Mass.), *Yankee Blade* (28 Jul. 1847). Cited in Loomis 2, p. 12.

hear

575 "I shall be glad to hear from you at all times," as the deaf man said to the ear-trumpet.

GB, *Punch,* vol. 2 (1842), p. 96. Cited in Loomis 3, p. 111.

heart

576   ''My heart is thine,'' as the cabbage said to the cook maid.
GB, *Punch*, vol. 2 (1842), p. 82. Cited in Loomis 3, p. 111.

577   ''You'll break my heart,'' as the oak said to the hatchet.
GB, *Punch*, vol. 2 (1842), p. 43. Cited in Loomis 3, p. 111.

578   ''Ah me, my heart is full!'' sighed the girl who had been taking advantage of her leap-year privilege until she found herself engaged to five men.
US (Calif.), *The Argonaut*, vol. 38, no. 14 (1896), p. 16. Cited in Loomis 4, p. 234.

heat

579   '''Tis a blessed heat tho','' as the old woman said when her house was on fire.
GB, G. F. NORTHALL, *Folk Phrases of Four Counties* (1894). Cited in Lean, p. 750.

heaven

580   ''This smacks of heaven!'' as the youth said as he kissed the maiden's cheek.
US (N.Y.), *Yankee Notions*, vol. 12 (1863), p. 4. Cited in Loomis 2, p. 18.

heck

581   ''Heck,'' quoth Howie when he swallowed his wife's clue.
GB, 1903. Cited in Lean, p. 745. [*Clue*, ball of thread.]

hee haw

582   ''Hee Haw!'' said the mule as the straw tickled his upper lip.
US (Ky.), c.1950. Cited in Halpert 2, p. 120.

heir

583   ''Another heir cut,'' cried the barber, as he bound up his young offspring's finger.
US (Calif.), *The Pelican*, vol. 31, no. 1 (1925), p. 45. Cited in Loomis 4, p. 241.

hell

584   ''Well, then, you go to hell!'' as the Frenchman said.
US (N.Y.), JOHN NEAL, *Down-Easters*, vol. 1 (1833), p. 97. Cited in Whiting 2, p. 6. Recorded in Bryant (Ohio).

585   ''Hell, yes!'' murmured the devil picking up the phone receiver.
US (Calif.), *The Pelican*, vol. 27, no. 3 (1921), p. 11. Cited in Loomis4, p. 239.

586   ''Hell,'' said the Duchess.
GB, AGATHA CHRISTIE, *Murder on the Links* (1923). Cited in Taylor 6, p. 32.

587   "Where in the Hell are you going?" said the devil to his wife in the subway.

US (Calif.), *The Pelican,* vol. 31, no. 7 (1926), p. 87. Cited in Loomis 4, p. 242; Mieder, p. 234.

hell fire

588   "Hell fire!" shouted the Duchess as she jumped out the window with a cigar in her mouth.

US (Ala.), 1939. Cited in Halpert 2, p. 117.

help

589   "It is in vain to help those who don't help themselves," as the chap said in the apple tree.

US (Pa.), *Alexander's Weekly Messenger* (1839). Cited in Tidwell 2, p. 259; Mieder, p. 230.

590   "Shall I help you down?" as the shark said to the man who was floating upon the water.

US (Mass.), *Yankee Blade* (29 Oct. 1845). Cited in Loomis 2, p. 8.

591   "Well, it can't be helped now," as the monkey said when he fell out of the cocoa-nut tree.

US, THOMAS B. ALDRICH, *Story of a Bad Boy* (1869). Cited in Whiting 2, p. 9. Recorded in Bryant (N.J.).

heps

592   "Fie upon heps," quoth the fox because he could not reach them.

GB, JOHN RAY, *English Proverbs* (1678). Cited in Lean, p. 744. [*Heps,* fruit of the dog rose.]

here

593   "That's neither here nor there," as the crow said when an egg fell out of her nest.

US (Wash.), *Weekly Big Bend Empire* (28 Mar. 1889), p. 3. Cited in Hines, p. 23; Mieder, p. 233.

594   "'Ere we are, sir," as Bertie said to Gertie.

US, QUENTIN PATRICK, *Murder at Cambridge* (1933). Cited in Whiting 1, p. 72.

595   "That's neither here nor there," as the steeplejack said when his foot slipped.

US (N.Y.), 1940. Cited in Thompson, p. 502.

herring

596   "Deal gently with the 'erring," as the Cockney fish dealer said to a customer.

US (Calif.), *California Spirit of the Times* (1 Jan. 1870). Cited in Loomis 2, p. 11.

hide

597 "I'll hide you where nobody can find you," as the schoolmaster said when he took the truant into the cellar to larrup him.

US (N.Y.), *Yankee Notions*, vol. 3 (1854), p. 142. Cited in Whiting 2, p. 5. [*Larrup*, whip, flog, give a hiding.]

hit

598 "Well hit," quoth Hickman when he smote his wife on the buttock with a beer pot.

GB, WILLIAM HAZLITT, *Four Elements*, in *Old Plays* (1570). Cited in Lean, p. 751.

599 "Why don't you hit one of your own size?" as the tenpenny nail said to the sledge hammer.

GB, *Punch*, vol. 2 (1842), p. 31. Cited in Loomis 3, p. 111.

hoe

600 "Ah-ha!" said the farmer to his corn. "Oh! hoe!" said the corn to the farmer.

US (Mass.), *Yankee Blade* (22 Jul. 1848). Cited in Loomis 2, p. 11.

601 "Hoe for the sea-shore," as the youth said who did garden work for his vacation money.

US (Calif.), *Daily Examiner*, vol. 34, no. 45 (1882), p. 4. Cited in Loomis 4, p. 232.

602 "Sale hoe!" shouted the hardware clerk, as he sold another planting instrument.

US (Calif.), *Daily Examiner*, vol. 34, no. 86 (1882), p. 4. Cited in Loomis 4, p. 232.

hog

603 "Go it, porkey—root, hog, or d-i-e!" as Shakapeel said when Caesar stabbed him in the House of Representatives.

US (N.Y.), *Yankee Notions*, vol. 1 (1852), p. 272. Cited in Whiting 2, p. 8. [The proverb "Root, hog, or die" is the refrain of an American folk song of 1856.]

hold

604 "Hold your jaw," as the man said when his head was in the lion's mouth.

GB, *Punch*, vol. 2 (1842), p. 43. Cited in Loomis 3, p. 111.

hold up

605 "You had to hold me up to do it," said the sweet young thing, after the big, tall man had stolen a kiss.

US (Calif.), *The Pelican*, vol. 26, no. 3 (1920), p. 42. Cited in Loomis 4, p. 238.

hole

606 Said the sieve to the needle, "You've a hole in your head."

Can., c.1945-1980. Recorded in Bryant (Ont.).

home

607 "Home is home," as the Devil said when he found himself in the Court of Sessions.

GB, ANDREW HENDERSON, *Scottish Proverbs* (1832). Cited in Simpson, p. 112.

608 "Home sweet home," as the loafer said ven the constable was taken him to prison.

US (Pa.), *Alexander's Weekly Messenger* (1839). Cited in Tidwell 2, p. 261; Mieder, p. 230. Recorded in Bryant (Ohio).

609 "There's no place like home," as the loafer said ven he crept under a market stall for a night's repose.

US (Pa.), *Alexander's Weekly Messenger* (1839). Cited in Tidwell 2, p. 259; Mieder, p. 230.

610 "Home, Sweet Home," as the loafer said to the sugar hogshead.

US (Mass.), *Yankee Blade* (31 Jul. 1847). Cited in Loomis 2, p. 20.

611 "Home sweet home!" as the vagrant said when he was sent to prison for the third time.

US (N.Y.), *Yankee Notions,* vol. 3 (1854), p. 142. Cited in Tidwell 2, p. 261; Whiting 2, p. 4. Recorded in Bryant (Ohio).

612 "What is home without a mother?" as the young lady said when she sent her old lady to chop wood.

US (Calif.), *California Spirit of the Times,* vol. 33 (18 May 1871), p. 1. Cited in Loomis 2, p. 14; Loomis 4, p. 230.

613 "Harrogate Wells," said the Devil when flying o'er, "I think I am getting near home by the smells."

GB, VINCENT LEAN, *Collectanea,* vol. 1 (1902). Cited in Wilson, p. 355. [Harrogate, in Yorkshire, is noted for its sulfurous springs.]

614 "Home was never like this," said Mr. Henpeck as he was shown about the deaf and dumb asylum.

US (Calif.), *The Argonaut,* vol. 61, no. 1586 (1907), p. 80. Cited in Loomis 4, p. 236.

honors

615 "Honors foller one another pooty fast," as the feller said, when his wife had triplets.

US, PALMER COX, *Squibbs of California* (1874). Cited in Loomis 2, p. 11.

hookey

616 "Hookey," as the carp said when he saw a worm at the end of the line.

GB, *Punch,* vol. 1 (1841), p. 276. Cited in Loomis 3, p. 111.

hope

617   "I hope better," quoth Benson, when his wife bid him "Come in cuckold."

GB, JOHN RAY, *English Proverbs* (1678). Cited in Lean, p. 745; Wilson, p. 384.

618   "If it wasn't for hope the heart would break," as Mrs. Perkins said, when she buried her seventh husband and looked anxiously among the funeral crowd for another.

US (Mass.), *Boston Herald* (23 Jul. 1853). Cited in Loomis 2, p. 11.

619   "This is running all my hopes into the ground," said the old girl, as she stood weeping beside the grave of the man to whom she was engaged to be married.

US (Calif.), *The Wasp,* vol. 10, no. 353 (1883), p. 2. Cited in Loomis 4, p. 233.

horn

620   "Won't you take a horn," as the mad bull said to the loafer.

US (N.Y.), *Yankee Notions,* vol. 12 (1863), p. 363. Cited in Loomis 2, p. 11.

hot

621   "How very hot you are," as the roast beef said to the horse radish.

GB, *Punch,* vol. 2 (1842), p. 50; US (N.Y.), *New Varieties* (22 May 1871), p. 11. Cited in Whiting 2, p. 9; Loomis 3, p. 111.

622   "I'll make it hot for you," said the waiter, as he took the soup back into the kitchen.

US (Calif.), *The Pelican,* vol. 33, no. 7 (1928), p. 46. Cited in Loomis 4, p. 243.

623   "That's a hot number," said the steer, as a branding iron was pressed against his leg.

US (Calif.), *The Pelican,* vol. 51, no. 8 (1945), p. 39. Cited in Loomis 4, p. 245; Mieder, p. 230.

hounds

624   "We hounds slew the hare," quoth the small dog.

GB, JAMES CARMICHAEL, *Proverbs on Scots* (c.1628); US, 1916. Cited in Wilson, p. 872; Lean, p. 751; Marvin, p. 364.

hours

625   "There's cheat in all trades but hours," observed the clock-dial. "You are a handsome punster," rejoined the bell. "Another word and I'll strike!" said the hammer.

US (Mass.), *Yankee Blade* (18 Nov. 1846). Cited in Loomis 2, p. 11.

house

626 "I fear my house will be shaken down," mutters a mouse, as the walls of the cathedral rock with the throes of the earthquake.

US (Wash.), *Walla Walla Union* (30 May 1874), p. 4. Cited in Hines, p. 24.

627 "This'll be on the house," said the sea gull, as he headed toward shore.

US (Calif.), *The Pelican,* vol. 36, no. 1 (1930), p. 35. Cited in Loomis 4, p. 243.

hunch

628 "I've got a hunch," said the dwarf, when the doctors asked him what his ailment was.

US (Calif.), *The Pelican,* vol. 13, no. 4 (1912). Cited in Loomis 4, p. 237; Mieder, p. 234.

hurrah

629 "Hurrah!" as the old maid shouted waving her wooden leg.

US (Ky.), c.1950. Cited in Halpert 2, p. 118.

630 "Hurrah!" shouted the old maid as she jumped out the window.

US (Tenn.), c.1950. Cited in Halpert 2, p. 118.

hurray

631 "There now!—see there!—didn't I tell ye so," as the old woman said when the hog eet the grinstone, "Hurray!"

US, JOHN NEAL, *Down-Easters,* vol. 1 (1833), p. 118. Cited in Whiting 2, p. 6; Taylor and Whiting, p. 409.

hurry

632 "Don't be in a hurry. It's one at a time here," as the old woman said at the wirligog.

US, 1913. Cited in Wright, p. 161. [*Wirligog,* whirligig.]

hurt

633 "It won't hurt me and it may amuse you," as the big man said when his little wife beat him.

US, LOUISA MAY ALCOTT, *Little Women* (1869). Cited in Taylor and Whiting, p. 236.

husband

634 "I'm beginning to miss my husband," said Mrs. Murphy, as the rolling pin grazed her husband's head and hit the wall.

US (Calif.), *The Pelican,* vol. 28, no. 8 (1923). Cited in Loomis 4, p. 240.

icy

635 "Icy," said the blind man as he opened the icebox door.

US, 1959. Cited in Taylor 4, p. 290.

idle

636   "You're my idle," as the quizzical husband said to his lazy wife.

US (N.Y.), *Yankee Notions,* vol. 12 (1863), p. 196. Cited in Loomis 2, p. 12.

ill

637   "There's nae ill in a merry wind," quo' the wife when she whistled through the kirk.

GB, 1903, US, 1916. Cited in Lean, p. 750; Marvin, p. 363; Whiting 1, p. 75; Mieder, p. 236. [*Kirk,* church.]

impossible

638   "Nought's impossible," as the old woman said when they told her the calf had swallowed the grindlestone.

US, 1913. Cited in Wright, p. 162.

impression

639   "That's my impression," as the die said to the dollar.

US (N.Y.), *Yankee Notions,* vol. 1 (1852), p. 76. Cited in Loomis 2, p. 12.

640   "That is my impression," as the typo said when he kissed the young lady.

US (Mass.), *Ballou's Dollar Magazine,* vol. 14 (1861), p. 398. Cited in Loomis 2, p. 12. [*Typo,* typographer.]

641   "I'm laboring under a false impression," as the die said to the counterfeiter.

US (N.Y.), *Wit and Wisdom* (14 Jul. 1881), p. 16. Cited in Whiting 2, p. 10.

improvement

642   "Here's to internal improvement," as Dobbs said when he swallowed a dose of salts.

US (N.Y.), *Yankee Notions,* vol. 6 (1857), p. 303. Cited in Loomis 2, p. 12.

impudence

643   "I like your impudence," as a pretty girl said when her beau kissed her.

US (N.Y.), *Yankee Notions,* vol. 11 (1862), p. 237; *Wilkes' Spirit of the Times,* vol. 7 (1862), p. 94. Cited in Loomis 2, p. 12.

inconvenience

644   "Wery sorry to 'casion any personal inconwenience, ma'am," as the housebreaker said to the old lady when he put her on the fire.

GB, CHARLES DICKENS, *Pickwick Papers* (1836). Cited in Maass, p. 211; Baer, p. 178.

indebted

645   "I shall be indebted to you for life," as the man said to his creditors when he ran away to Australia.

US (Calif.), *Carrie and Damon's California Almanac* (1856), p. 12. Cited in Loomis 2, p. 12.

inducement

646   "That's vat I calls a strong inducement to go round," as the man said yesterday ven he came to a mud puddle so deep he couldn't get over without swimming.

US (Pa.), *Alexander's Weekly Messenger* (1839). Cited in Tidwell 2, p. 259.

industry

647   "Industry must prosper," as the pickpocket said when he stole three handkerchiefs before breakfast.

US (N.Y.), *Yankee Notions,* vol. 3 (1854), p. 142. Cited in Whiting 2, p. 5; Mieder, p. 232. Recorded in Bryant (Ariz.).

648   "Industry must prosper," as the man said when holding the baby for his wife to chop wood.

US (N.Y.), *Porter's Spirit of the Times,* vol. 3 (1857), p. 174. Cited in Loomis 2, p. 12.

inkstand

649   "My inkstand is stationary," as the schoolmaster said when he found it nailed to his desk.

US (N.Y.), *Porter's Spirit of the Times,* vol. 7 (1859), p. 151. Cited in Loomis 2, p. 19.

insecure

650   "To be insecure is to be unsafe," said the ocean wave when it beat against the cable.

US, 1916. Cited in Marvin, p. 364.

insult

651   "This I call adding insult to injury," as the parrot said ven they not only took him from his native land, but made him talk the English langvidg arterwards.

GB, CHARLES DICKENS, *Pickwick Papers* (1836); US (Pa.), *Alexander's Weekly Messenger* (1837). Cited in Maass, p. 213; Tidwell 2, p. 258.

652   "That's vat I call addin' insult to injury," as the rabbit said, ven they sewed his mouth up, and then told him to vistle.

US (Pa.), *Alexander's Weekly Messenger* (1839). Cited in Tidwell 2, p. 259; Mieder, p. 230.

intentions

653   "All good feelin', sir, the wery best intentions," as the gen'l'm'n said ven he run way from his wife 'cos she seemed unhappy with him.
GB, CHARLES DICKENS, *Pickwick Papers* (1836). Cited in Maass, p. 210; Stevenson, p. 2480; Bailey, p. 33; Baer, p. 178.

interruption

654   "Sorry to do anythin' as may cause interruption to such wery pleasant proceedings," as the king said wen he dissolved the parliament.
GB, CHARLES DICKENS, *Pickwick Papers* (1836). Cited in Maass, p. 212; Baer, p. 179; Mieder, p. 224.

introduce

655   "Permit me to introduce myself," as the oyster knife said to the native.
GB, *Punch*, vol. 2 (1824), p. 50; US, *Ball of Yarn, or, Queer, Quaint, and Quizzical Stories* (1870). Cited in Loomis 3, p. 111; Browne, p. 202; Mieder, p. 233.

intrude

656   "I hope I don't intrude," as the knife said to the oyster.
US (Pa.), *The Casket*, vol. 5 (1830), p. 377. Cited in Loomis 5, p. 51; Tidwell 2, p. 258. Recorded in Bryant (Pa.).

657   "Sorry to intrude," as the bull said when he rushed into the china shop.
US, FRANCIS DURIVAGE, *Three Brides* (1856). Cited in Taylor and Whiting, p. 46. Recorded in Bryant (N.Y.).

ironed

658   "After you've been ironed, you'll be hung up to dry," as the sheriff pleasantly remarked to the criminal.
US (Maine), *Yankee Blade* (28 Aug. 1842). Cited in Loomis 2, p. 12.

is

659   As the old hermit of Prague, that never saw pen and ink, very wittily said to a niece of King Gorboduc: "That that is, is."
GB, WILLIAM SHAKESPEARE, *Twelfth Night* (1601), act 5, scene 2. Cited in Lean, p. 742.

660   "Wotever is, is right," as the young nobleman's uncle remarked wen they put him down in the pension list 'cos his mother's uncle's wife's grandfather vunce lit the king's pipe with a portable tinderbox.
GB, CHARLES DICKENS, *Pickwick Papers* (1836). Cited in Baer, p. 179; Mieder, p. 224.

661   "Ah, this is as it should be," as the gentleman said ven he bought a handsome print of the new houses of parliament.
US (Pa.), *Alexander's Weekly Messenger* (1837). Cited in Tidwell 2, p. 258.

jam

662   "Black bury jam," said he, as he gazed at the overcrowded cemetery for colored people.
US (Calif.), *The Argonaut,* vol. 3, no. 12 (1878), p. 14. Cited in Loomis 4, p. 230.

663   "Don't get in a jam," said one strawberry to the other.
US, c.1945-1980. Recorded in Bryant (Kans.).

join

664   "We'd be awfully glad to have you join us," remarked the prospective bridegroom to the justice.
US (Calif.), *The Pelican,* vol. 27, no. 1 (1921), p. 15. Cited in Loomis 4, p. 239.

joke

665   "This is carrying a joke too far," remarked the perspiring humorist as he set out for the next newspaper office.
US (Calif.), *The Pelican,* vol. 2, no. 4 (1904), p. 10. Cited in Loomis 4, p. 235.

joys

666   "My joys are buried deep," as the loafer said when his whiskey bottle tumbled into the river.
US (Pa.), *Alexander's Weekly Messenger* (1839). Cited in Tidwell 2, p. 261.

jump

667   "O Lord, how you made me jump!" as the grasshopper said when he was created.
US (N.Y.), 1940. Cited in Thompson, p. 501. Recorded in Bryant (N.Y.).

kick

668   "That's the kick," said Paddy when he kicked his wife into the fire.
GB, 1903. Cited in Lean, p. 749.

kidding

669   "I believe you are kidding me," said the surprised father, as the stork arrived with triplets.
US (Calif.), *The Pelican,* vol. 28, no. 7 (1923), p. 47. Cited in Loomis 4, p. 240.

killing

670   The dead man rose up and said, "It's killing me!"
US (Ky., Tenn.), c.1950. Cited in Halpert 2, p. 119.

kindness

671   "Kill him with kindness," said the mother as the father cuddled his little son.
US, c.1945-1980. Recorded in Bryant (Ill.).

kneaded

672 "Oh, I see I'm very much kneaded here," as the batch of bread said, "and I must rise in consequence."

US (Mass.), *Yankee Blade* (29 Sep. 1849). Cited in Loomis 2, p. 12.

knell

673 "You ain't done right by my knell," said the departed spirit to the village sexton.

US (Calif.), *The Pelican,* vol. 35, no. 1 (1929), p. 36. Cited in Loomis 4, p. 243.

knifing

674 "I guess this is knifing through scenter," said the ex-football man, as he stabbed the skunk.

US (Calif.), *The Pelican,* vol. 31, no. 5 (1926), p. 34. Cited in Loomis 4, p. 242.

knock

675 "I don't come without knocking," as the bullet said when it asked the fox if he couldn't give it lodging in his upper story.

US (Mass.), *Yankee Blade* (26 Nov. 1845). Cited in Loomis 2, p. 12.

676 "Ah," exclaimed the conceited rifle. "I always knock 'em cold."

US (Calif.), *The Pelican,* vol. 27, no. 8 (1922), p. 11. Cited in Loomis 4, p. 240.

knot

677 "I see thee, knot," as the culprit on the scaffold said to the rope.

US (N.Y.), *Spirit of the Times,* vol. 10 (1840), p. 262. Cited in Whiting 2, p. 7.

678 "I would rather knot," as Jack Ketch said when asked if he wished to retire from business.

US (N.Y.), *Yankee Notions,* vol. 12 (1863), p. 196. Cited in Loomis 2, p. 12.

knotty

679 "That's a very knotty affair," said the culprit looking at the rope. "It is because you have been naughty yourself," was the answer.

US (N.Y.), *Wilkes' Spirit of the Times,* vol. 4 (1861), p. 87. Cited in Loomis 2, p. 12. Recorded in Bryant (N.Y.).

know

680 As the old lady said, "What you don't know can't hurt you."

US (N.Y.), HUGH PENTECOST, *The Shape of Fear* (1964), p. 46. Cited in Whiting 6, p. 356.

labor

681 "Labor is going up," sighed the employer, as he watched the aeroplane soar away with three ship-builders on board.

US (Calif.), *The Pelican,* vol. 25, no. 3 (1919), p. 25. Cited in Loomis 4, p. 238.

lane

682 "It is a long lane that has no turning," as the eel said to the aqueduct.
US (Mass.), *Yankee Blade* (14 Jun. 1851). Cited in Loomis 2, p. 13.

lass

683 "A lass! I am no more," as the girl said when she got married.
US (N.Y.), *Yankee Notions,* vol. 2 (1849), p. 53. Cited in Loomis 2, p. 4.

684 "A lass, a lass!" exclaimed an old bachelor, who wanted to marry. "Alas! Alas!" he cried after he had been married awhile.
US (Wash.), *Walla Walla Union* (23 May 1874), p. 4. Cited in Hines, p. 22.

last

685 "Last but not least," as the old lady said when she kissed the cow.
US, c.1945-1980. Recorded in Bryant (Ohio).

late

686 "To late y-war," qouth Beautee, whan it paste.
GB, GEOFFREY CHAUCER, *Troilus and Criseyde* (c.1385), book 2, line 398. Cited in Taylor 1, p. 203. [In modern English, this line may be rendered as "'Too late aware,' quoth Beauty, when it passed."]

687 "You're late," as Paddy Loughran said to the ghost.
US, 1913. Cited in Wright, p. 163.

laugh

688 "Laugh that off," said the fat man's wife, as she sewed his vest button on with wire.
US (Calif.), *The Pelican,* vol. 42, no. 6 (1936), p. 52. Cited in Loomis 4, p. 244.

lay

689 "'Tis my last lay," as the hen cackled when she deposited her eggs in the nest.
US (Mass.), *Yankee Blade* (3 Jul. 1847). Cited in Loomis 2, p. 12; Whiting 2, p. 9.

laying

690 "I'm laying down the law," said the client ven he floored his counsellor.
US (Pa.), *Alexander's Weekly Messenger* (1839). Cited in Tidwell 2, p. 259; Loomis 2, p. 12; Mieder, p. 230.

691 "I am laying for you," as the old hen said to the chap who was hunting for her nest.
US (Calif.), *California Golden Era,* vol. 6, no. 17 (1868), p. 3. Cited in Loomis 1, p. 305; Loomis 2, p. 12. Recorded in Bryant (Ariz., Ohio).

leaf

692 "By your leaf," as the caterpillar said when he dined off the cauliflower.
US (Mass.), *Ballou's Dollar Magazine,* vol. 5 (1857), p. 500. Cited in Loomis 2, p. 12.

693 "Oh! Leaf me not," as the book said to the student.
US (Pa.), *Philadelphia Herald* (15 Sep. 1881), p. 7. Cited in Whiting 2, p. 11.

leak

694 "Everything must leak," quoth the wren when she pissed into the sea.
GB, JAMES ORCHARD HALLIWELL, *A Dictionary of Archaic and Provincial Words* (1865). Cited in Lean, p. 743.

learn

695 "Vether it's worth goin' through so much to learn so little," as the charity boy said ven he got to the end of the alphabet, "is a matter o' taste."
GB, CHARLES DICKENS, *Pickwick Papers* (1836). Cited in Maass, p. 209; Stevenson, p. 2480.

leave

696 "I'll take no leave of you," quoth the baker to the pillory.
GB, ROBERT CODRINGTON, *Select Proverbs* (1672). Cited in Lean, p. 746.

697 "It is well to leave something for those who come after us," said the gentleman when he threw a barrel in the way of a constable who was chasing him.
US (Calif.), *California Golden Era,* vol. 15, no. 4 (1866), p. 7. Cited in Loomis 1, p. 304; Loomis 2, p. 7.

lent

698 "I keep lent," as the borrowed dollar said to the slow paymaster.
US (N.Y.), *Yankee Notions,* vol. 14 (1865), p. 260. Cited in Loomis 2, p. 13.

lesson

699 "Boy, I've sure learned my lesson," said the convicted criminal as he stood at the gallows.
US (Idaho), 1966. Cited in Anon, p. 34. Recorded in Bryant (Idaho).

let off

700 "I'll let you off this time," as the horse said when he capsized his rider in the mud.
US (Mass.), *Yankee Blade* (11 Oct. 1843). Cited in Loomis 2, p. 13.

let out

701 "That lets me out," said the burglar, when he found a file in his mince pie.
US (Calif.), *The Pelican,* vol. 16, no. 2 (1914). Cited in Loomis 4, p. 237.

702 "This lets me out," said the pickpocket as he lifted the jailer's pass key.
US (Calif.), *The Pelican,* vol. 26, no. 5 (1921), p. 45. Cited in Loomis 4, p. 238.

liar

703 "He is the greatest liar on 'earth," as the cockney said of the lap–dog he often saw lying before the fire.
GB, *Punch,* vol. 1 (1841), p. 276. Cited in Loomis 3, p. 111.

liberty

704 "The price of liberty is eternal vigilance," said the debtor when the constable was following in his footsteps.
US (Pa.), *Alexander's Weekly Messenger* (1839). Cited in Tidwell 2, p. 261; Mieder, p. 230. [The reference is to a speech delivered in 1790 by John Philpot Curran, Irish judge: "The condition upon which God hath given liberty to man is eternal vigilance."]

lick

705 "Come out here and I'll lick the whole on ye," as the boy said to the molasses candy.
US (Mass.), *Yankee Blade* (1 Dec. 1849). Cited in Loomis 2, p. 13.

706 "It takes me to lick lasses," as the Yankee school–master said when he whipped the girls.
US (Mass.), *Yankee Blade* (2 Feb. 1850). Cited in Loomis 2, p. 13.

lie

707 "You lie," as the physician said to his prostrate patient, when the latter said he could get up.
US (Pa.), *Alexander's Weekly Messenger* (1839). Cited in Tidwell 2, p. 262.

708 "How we printers lie," as our devil said when he got up too late for breakfast.
US (Maine), *Yankee Blade* (3 Sep. 1842). Cited in Loomis 2, p. 13. [*Devil,* printer's apprentice.]

life

709 "Anything for a quiet life," as the man said ven he took the sitivation at the lighthouse.
GB, CHARLES DICKENS, *Pickwick Papers* (1836). Cited in Maass, p. 212.

710 "If you walley my precious life don't upset me," as the gen'l'm'n said to the driver wen they was a carryin' him to Tyburn.
GB, CHARLES DICKENS, *Pickwick Papers* (1836). Cited in Maass, p. 210; Stevenson, p. 2480; Baer, p. 176. [Tyburn was a place of execution in London, near the present location of the Marble Arch.]

711 "Life let us cherish," as the butcher whistled to himself as he fed the fat pig for Christmas.
GB, *Punch,* vol. 2 (1842), p. 133. Cited in Loomis 3, p. 112.

712   "My life has been a blank," groaned the cartridge as he lay on the field after the sham battle.

US (Calif.), *The Pelican*, vol. 2, no. 4 (1904), p. 20. Cited in Loomis 4, p. 235.

light

713   "Light's heartening," quoth the thief to the Lammas mune.

GB, ALLAN CUNNINGHAM, *Glossary to Burns* (1834). Cited in Lean,p. 747. [*Lammas*, harvest festival traditionally celebrated in England on 1 August, when bread baked from the first crop of wheat was blessed in church; *mune*, moon.]

714   "Let the light beam on me," as the fellow said when a scantling struck him.

US (N.Y.), *Wilkes' Spirit of the Times*, vol. 1 (1859), p. 199. Cited in Loomis 2, p. 4. Recorded in Bryant (N.Y.). [*Scantling*, piece of wood.]

715   "Let there be light," murmured the raven-haired beauty, as she drew forth the peroxide bottle.

US (Calif.), *The Pelican*, vol. 11, no. 1 (1911). Cited in Loomis 4, p. 236; Mieder, p. 234.

like

716   "Every man where he likes," quoth the goodman when he kissed his cow.

GB, JOHN HEYWOOD, *English Proverbs* (1546); US 1948. Cited in Wilson, p. 228; Lean, p. 743; Taylor 2, p. 317. Recorded in Bryant (Ill., N.Y.).

717   "Like will to like," as the devil said to the collier.

GB, THOMAS BECON, *Lord's Supper and Pope's Mass* (1599); US, 1948. Cited in Wilson, p. 465; Lean, p. 747; Taylor 2, p. 317. [*Collier*, coal miner.]

718   "Like will to like," as the scabbed squire said to the mangy knight when they both met in a dish of buttered fish.

GB, BEN JONSON, *A Tale of a Tub* (1633). Cited in Lean, p. 747.

liking

719   "Everyone to his liking," as the old woman said when she kissed her cow.

US, c.1945-1980. Recorded in Bryant (Ill., R.I.).

line

720   "Anything in my line," as the hangman said to the judge.

US (Mass.), *Yankee Blade* (26 Nov. 1845). Cited in Loomis 2, p. 13.

721   "I don't like to patronize that line," as the culprit said to the hangman.

US (N.Y.), *Yankee Notions*, vol. 10 (1860), p. 196. Cited in Loomis 2, p. 13.

722   "Drop me a line," as the drowning man said to the fellow on deck.

US (N.Y.), *Wilkes' Spirit of the Times*, vol. 6 (1862), p. 183. Cited in Loomis 2, p. 13.

723 "I'm afraid I have left out some of my best lines," remarked the actress petulantly, as she finished dressing in haste.

US (Calif.), *The Pelican,* vol. 15, no. 1 (1913). Cited in Loomis 4, p. 237.

724 "Drop me a line," remarked the second mate, as he fell overboard.

US (Calif.), *The Pelican,* vol. 31, no. 2 (1925), p. 59. Cited in Loomis 4, p. 242.

725 "Well, that's the end of the line," said the pencil as the lead broke.

US, c.1945–1980. Recorded in Bryant (Kans.).

link

726 "The last link is broken that bound me to thee," as the convict said ven he escaped from his chains.

US (Pa.), *Alexander's Weekly Messenger* (1839). Cited in Tidwell 2, p. 261.

727 "The last link is broken that bound me to thee," as the horse said when he kicked off his traces and ran away from the plow.

US (Mass.), *Yankee Blade* (6 Jan. 1847). Cited in Loomis 2, p. 13.

lip

728 "Take, oh, take those lips away," as the gudgeon said to the shark.

US (Pa.), *Alexander's Weekly Messenger* (1839). Cited in Tidwell 2, p. 259. [The reference is to a line in Shakespeare's *Measure for Measure* (1604), act 4, scene 1: "Take, O take those lips away"; *gudgeon,* a fish.]

729 "None of your lip," as the teetotaler said to the cider pitcher.

US (Wash.), *Walla Walla Union* (30 May 1874), p. 4. Cited in Hines, p. 24; Mieder, p. 234.

little

730 "Every little helps," quoth the wren when she pissed in the sea.

GB, WILLIAM CAMDEN, *Remains Concerning Britaine* (1605); US (N.C.), 1952. Cited in Simpson, p. 67; Lean, p. 743; Whiting 3, p. 371.

731 "There's little to reck," quoth the knave to his neck.

GB, ALLAN CUNNINGHAM, *Glossary to Burns* (1834); US, 1916. Cited in Lean, p. 758; Marvin, p. 363. [*To reck,* to be concerned for, to take heed of.]

732 "A dreadful little for a shilling," said a penurious fellow to a physician who dealt him out an emetic.

US (Mass.), *Ballou's Dollar Magazine,* vol. 3 (1856), p. 200. Cited in Loomis 2, p. 13.

733 "I know by a little what a great deal means," as the gander said when he saw the tip of a fox's tail sticking out of a hollow tree.

US (N.Y.), *Yankee Notions,* vol. 10 (1860), p. 264. Cited in Loomis 1, p. 305; Loomis 2, p. 13; Hines, p. 24; Mieder, p. 234.

734 "Every little helps," as the captain said when he threw his wife overboard to lighten the ship.

GB, F. COWAN, *Sea Proverbs* (1894); US, 1948. Cited in Lean, p. 744; Taylor 2, p. 317; Stevenson, p. 2481.

735 "A little will go a long way," said the man, as he spit off the Woolworth building.
US (Calif.), *The Pelican*, vol. 17, no. 1 (1914), p. 27. Cited in Loomis 4, p. 237; Mieder, p. 235.

736 "Every little helps," as the old woman said when she beat up a dead fly in her currant cake.
GB, HULBERT FOOTNER, *Easy to Kill* (1931), p. 80. Cited in Whiting 6, p. 379.

737 "Every little helps," said Mr. Little and took the six little Littles out to help him saw a pile of wood.
US, 1931. Cited in Taylor 1, p. 220. Recorded in Bryant (Ark.).

little bit

738 "Every little bit helps," said the lady, as she spit in the ocean.
US, JOHN DUTTON, *Letters from New England* (1867). Cited in Koch 1, p. 180; Mieder, p. 238. Recorded in Bryant (Idaho, Kans., Ky., Ohio, Tenn.).

739 "Well, a little bit goes a long way," as the monkey said when he shit over the cliff.
US (Kans.), c.1924–1927. Cited in Porter, p. 159.

740 "Every little bit helps," said the old fisherman to his wife, as he threw the fish net on the bed on a cold winter night.
US, c.1945–1980. Recorded in Bryant (Fla.).

741 "Every little bit helps," said the old lady as she threw the dish water in the ocean.
US, c.1945–1980. Recorded in Bryant (Ill., Miss.).

742 "Every little bit helps," said the old woman as she threw the water on the ceiling to drown her husband with.
US, c.1945–1980. Recorded in Bryant (Miss.).

743 "Every little bit helps," said the seagull as he spat in the ocean.
US, c.1945–1980. Recorded in Bryant (Ind., Ohio).

744 "Every little bit helps," as the old lady said when she pissed in the ocean to help drown her husband.
US (Ky.), 1950. Cited in Anon, p. 34; Mieder, p. 237. Recorded in Bryant (Idaho, Ky., N.Y., Tenn.).

745 "Every little bit helps," as the old woman said when she spit in the cistern.
US (Ky.), 1950. Cited in Mieder, p. 237. Recorded in Bryant (Ky., Tenn.).

746 "Every little bit helps," said the old lady as she pissed in the sea.
US (Ky.), 1956. Cited in Halpert 2, p. 117; Whiting 6, p. 379. Recorded in Bryant (Ariz., Idaho, Ky., Minn., Ohio, Tenn.).

747 "Every little bit helps," said the ant as he peed in the ocean.

US (Idaho), 1966. Cited in Anon, p. 34. Recorded in Bryant (Idaho, N.Y., S.C.).

little things

748 "These are the little things that count," cried the salesman, as he demonstrated the adding machine.

US (Calif.), *The Pelican,* vol. 29, no. 4 (1923), p. 51. Cited in Loomis 4, p. 240.

749 "It is the little things that tell," said sister to her new beau, as they left Johnny stranded under the chesterfield.

US (Calif.), *The Pelican,* vol. 32, no. 5 (1927), p. 23. Cited in Loomis 4, p. 242. Recorded in Bryant (Idaho). [*Chesterfield,* sofa.]

live

750 "I would now live always," as the pirate said when he was going to the gallows.

US (Pa.), *Alexander's Weekly Messenger* (1839). Cited in Tidwell 2, p. 262.

loanly

751 "It is loanly here," as the sentimental pawnbroker's daughter said of her father's shop.

US (Calif.), *California Spirit of the Times* (26 May 1870). Cited in Loomis 2, p. 13; Mieder, p. 231.

local color

752 "I've just been gathering a bit of local color," remarked the sheik, as he brushed the lapels of his coat.

US (Calif.), *The Pelican,* vol. 31, no. 4 (1925), p. 42. Cited in Loomis 4, p. 242. [*Sheik,* a masterful man irresistible to women; *The Sheik* (1921), a novel by E. M. Hull, was made into a film starring Rudolph Valentino.]

locks

753 "I have a great aversion to Auburn locks," as the criminal said when he took lodging in the Auburn prison.

US (Mass.), *Yankee Blade* (10 Mar. 1849). Cited in Loomis 2, p. 4. Recorded in Bryant (N.Y.). [Auburn, New York, is the site of a state prison built in 1816.]

lode

754 "You took a lode off my mind," as the seller of a worthless mine said to the speculative purchaser.

US (Calif.), *Daily Examiner,* vol. 43, no. 44 (1882), p. 4. Cited in Tidwell 1, p. 216; Loomis 4, p. 232.

lodging

755 "Wake up here and pay for your lodging," said the Deacon as he nudged the sleepy stranger with the contribution box.

US (Mass.), *Yankee Blade* (29 Jan. 1848). Cited in Loomis 2, p. 13.

long

756 "'Twa'n't long," as the old lady said when they saved her from drowning.

US, MICHAEL GRAVES, *Bubblin's an' B'ilin's at the Center* (1934). Cited in Whiting 2, p. 11.

757 "'Twa'n't long, though," as the feller said arter the weddin' ceremony.

US, MICHAEL GRAVES, *Bubblin's an' B'ilin's at the Center* (1934). Cited in Whiting 2, p. 11.

758 "It won't be long now," as the monkey said, when he caught his tail in the lawnmower.

US, 1945. Cited in Jones, p. 236; Halpert 2, p. 119; Taylor 2, p. 317. Recorded in Bryant (Ind., Iowa, Ky., Minn., N.Dak., N.J., Ohio, Tenn., Tex., Wis.).

759 As the old dog said as he lost his tail in the meat grinder, "Won't be long now."

US, c.1945-1980. Recorded in Bryant (N.Y.).

760 "It won't be long now," as the monkey said when they cut off his tail.

US, c.1945-1980. Recorded in Bryant (Minn.).

761 "It won't be long now," said grandma as she climbed into our barber's chair.

US, c.1945-1980. Recorded in Bryant (Oreg.).

762 "It won't be long now," said the man as the train cut off his dog's tail.

US, c.1945-1980. Recorded in Bryant (Ohio).

763 "So long," said the chimp, sliding off the giraffe's neck.

US (Kans.), 1959. Cited in Koch 1, p. 180; Mieder, p. 237. Recorded in Bryant (Kans.).

long run

764 "I think I shall do well in the long run," as the fellow said when he cleared for Texas.

US (Mass.), *Yankee Blade* (10 Sep. 1845). Cited in Loomis 2, p. 13.

longshoreman

765 "That's a longshoreman," he observed as six-feet two inches of a stevedoer passed by.

US (Calif.), *The Wasp*, vol. 3, no. 146 (1879), p. 661. Cited in Loomis 4, p. 231. [*Stevedoer*, stevedore.]

look

766 "That's one way to look at it," said the mouse as she ran across the mirror.

US (Idaho), 1966. Cited in Anon, p. 34.

looked

767 "I've just looked in to see if you are doing well," as the cook said to the lobster when she lifted the lid up.

GB, *Punch,* vol. 3 (1842), p. 188. Cited in Loomis 3, p. 113. [Cf. no. 769.].

768 "This must be looked into," as the young lady said to the mirror.

US (Mass.), *Yankee Blade* (7 Aug. 1844). Cited in Loomis 2, p. 13.

769 "I've just looked in to see if you are doing well," as the cook said to the lobster when she lifted up the sauce-pan lid.

US (Mass.), *Yankee Blade* (20 May 1846). Cited in Loomis 2, p. 13. [Cf. no. 767.]

770 "This must be looked into," as the spoiled child said to his father's watch when he heard it tick.

US (Mass.), *Ballou's Dollar Magazine,* vol. 6 (1857), p. 400. Cited in Loomis 2, p. 13.

looking

771 "Are you looking for anyone in particular?" as the rat said to the cat ven she was a peeping down his hole.

US (Pa.), *Alexander's Weekly Messenger* (1839). Cited in Tidwell 2, p. 261; Loomis 2, p. 13.

772 "Are you looking for anyone in particular?" as the mite said to the microscope.

GB, *Punch,* vol. 3 (1842), p. 146. Cited in Loomis 3, p. 112.

773 "Are you looking for anyone in particular?" as the rat said when he saw the cat watching him.

US (Mass.), *Yankee Blade* (26 Nov. 1845). Cited in Loomis 2, p. 13.

774 "That's one way of looking at it," said the ant as it sat down on the mirror.

US (Tenn.), c.1950. Cited in Halpert 2, p. 117; Mieder, p. 236. Recorded in Bryant (Ky., Tenn.).

looks

775 "All the world looks up to me," as the thief said when he stood in the pillory.

US (N.Y.), *Yankee Notions,* vol. 3 (1854), p. 142. Cited in Whiting 2, p. 5. Recorded in Bryant (N.J.).

loss

776 "It's a to-e-tal loss," as the sailor said when the shark bit his leg off.

US (N.Y.), *Yankee Notions,* vol. 3 (1854), p. 142. Cited in Whiting 2, p. 4.

lost

777 "Though lost to sight, to memory dear," as the maiden said to her lover when his face was buried in beard and whiskers.

US (Mass.), *Ballou's Dollar Magazine,* vol. 11 (1860), p. 498. Cited in Loomis 2, p. 13.

lot

778 "They're a rum lot," as the devil said of the Ten Commandments.

GB, 1903. Cited in Lean, p. 750. [*Rum,* strange, bad, poor.]

Lot's wife

779 "Lot's wife had nothing on me," said the convict, as he turned to a pile of stone.

US (Calif.), *The Pelican,* vol. 35, no. 1 (1929), p. 44. Cited in Loomis 4, p. 243. [Lot's wife was turned into a pillar of salt (*Genesis* 19.26).]

love

780 "Every man as he loveth," as the good woman said when she kissed her cow.

GB, GEORGE HERBERT, *Outlandish Proverbs* (1640). Cited in Lean, p. 743.

781 "Thou know'st that I love thee!" as the cat said to the mouse.

US (Pa.), *Alexander's Weekly Messenger* (1839). Cited in Tidwell 2, p. 261.

782 "Thou, thou know'st I love thee," as the loafer said to the liquor.

US (Pa.), *Alexander's Weekly Messenger* (1839). Cited in Tidwell 2, p. 262.

783 "How I love thee, none can tell," as the toper said to the gin bottle.

US (Mass.), *Yankee Blade* (23 Aug. 1843). Cited in Loomis 2, p. 13.

784 "I have not loved lightly," as the man thought who married a wealthy widow weighing two hundred.

US (Mass.), *Yankee Blade* (24 Nov. 1849). Cited in Loomis 2, p. 13.

785 "Love thy neighbor," as the parson said to the man who lived next door to the pigsty.

US (N.Y.), *Yankee Notions,* vol. 1 (1852), p. 9. Cited in Whiting 2, p. 7; Loomis 2, p. 13; Mieder, p. 232. Recorded in Bryant (Ohio).

786 "I'll banquet on the smiles of love," as the hungry poet said when he thought about his mistress about dinner time.

US (N.Y.), *Yankee Notions,* vol. 3 (1854), p. 142. Cited in Whiting 2, p. 5. Recorded in Bryant (Ohio).

787 "Write me as one who loves his fellow men," as the cannibal said to his missionary.

US (Calif.), *California Golden Era,* vol. 18, no. 19 (1870), p. 7. Cited in Loomis 1, p. 305; Loomis 2, p. 14.

788   "Write me as one who loves his fellow men," said a cannibal to a reporter.

US (Calif.), *The Argonaut,* vol. 1, no. 38 (1877), p. 7. Cited in Loomis 4, p. 230.

789   "Love lightens labor," as the man said when he saw his wife doing his work for him.

US (Mo.), *Saint Louis Spirit* (12 May 1881), p. 8. Cited in Whiting 2, p. 10. Recorded in Bryant (N.J.).

790   "I love you for yourself alone," as the blackbird said when he swallowed the gooseberry.

US (Wash.), *Weekly Big Bend Empire* (28 Mar. 1889), p. 24. Cited in Hines, p. 24; Mieder, p. 233.

791   "I love you, my black darling," breathed the furnace warmly. "Hot air," retorted the coal. Her thoughts were with a former flame.

US (Calif.), *The Pelican,* vol. 3, no. 1 (1905), p. 16. Cited in Loomis 4, p. 235.

792   "Love me, love my doggerel," said the poet to his lady.

US (Calif.), *The Pelican,* vol. 26, no. 2 (1920), p. 10. Cited in Loomis 4, p. 238; Mieder, p. 235.

793   "I'm entangled in your love," said the octopus to his girl friend as she hugged him.

US (Kans.), 1959. Cited in Koch 1, p. 180; Mieder, p. 238.

low cusses

794   "You are one of the low cusses," as the chap said when he saw the locust digging out of the ground.

US (Mass.), *Yankee Blade* (12 Aug. 1846). Cited in Loomis 2, p. 14.

lump

795   "Here I am, sir, all of a lump," as the old man said what found the sixpence.

GB, CHARLES DICKENS, *Pickwick Papers* (1836). Cited in Baer, p. 87.

Luther Burbank

796   "Here is one Luther Burbank didn't try," said the coed, as she crossed her legs.

US (Calif.), *The Pelican,* vol. 50, no. 8 (1944), p. 8. Cited in Loomis 4, p. 245. [Luther Burbank (1849-1926), American horticulturist, developed many new and improved varieties of fruits, vegetables, and flowers.]

mainstay

797   "That was my mainstay," said the lady, as her corset ripped.

US (Calif.), *The Pelican,* vol. 32, no. 6 (1927), p. 63. Cited in Loomis 4, p. 242.

make

798 "I'll make one," quoth Kirkham, when he danced in his clogs.

GB, JOHN RAY, *English Proverbs* (1678); US, 1931. Cited in Lean, p. 746; Taylor 1, p. 210; Wilson, p. 395. [*Clogs,* shoes with thick wooden soles, commonly worn by factory workers in the north of England.]

799 "I'll neither make nor mar," as the young cock said when he saw the auld cock's neck thrawn.

GB, 1903. Cited in Lean, p. 746. [*Thrawn,* twisted, misshapen.]

man

800 "Every man for himself," as the jackass said when he stamped among the young turkies.

US (N.Y.), *Spirit of the Times,* vol. 10 (1840), p. 230. Cited in Whiting 2, p. 7.

manners

801 "After me is manners," as the turtle soup said to the cold punch.

GB, *Punch,* vol. 2 (1842), p. 167. Cited in Loomis 3, p. 112.

many

802 "What are we among so many?" as the two-pronged fork said to the dish of green peas.

GB, 1903. Cited in Lean, p. 752.

march

803 "I stole a march on them all right," said the kleptomaniac, as she walked out of the Ten-Cent Store with a sheet of music in her muff.

US (Calif.), *The Pelican,* vol. 24, no. 5 (1919), p. 1. Cited in Loomis 4, p. 238.

mark

804 "Mark and learn," as the schoolboy said when his back had been marked for not learning his lesson.

US (N.Y.), *Yankee Notions,* vol. 15 (1866), p. 4. Cited in Loomis 2, p. 14.

805 "Well, I've made my mark in the world," said the prisoner as the officer took his fingerprints.

US (Calif.), *The Wasp,* vol. 3, no. 146 (1879), p. 677. Cited in Loomis 4, p. 240.

806 "I leave my mark in life," boasted the pencil. "But not until you are lead," retorted the ruler, "and even then it takes me to keep you straight."

US (Calif.), *The Pelican,* vol. 3, no. 1 (1905), p. 7. Cited in Loomis 4, p. 236.

master

807 "A new master, a new, and hang up the old," as the porters cry in Stirbridge Fair.

GB, THOMAS BECON, *Worckes* (1563). Cited in Lean, p. 741.

808 "Many masters," quoth the toad to the harrow, when every tine turned her over.

GB, DAVID FERGUSON, *Scottish Proverbs* (1641); US, 1931. Cited in Lean, p. 748; Taylor 1, p. 209; Taylor 2, p. 317; Koch 1, p. 180; Williams, p. 93.

match

809 "A match," quoth Hatch when he got his wife by the breech.

GB, JOHN RAY, *English Proverbs* (1678). Cited in Lean, p. 741.

810 "A match," quoth Jack when he kissed his dame.

GB, JOHN RAY, *English Proverbs* (1678). Cited in Lean, p. 741.

measure

811 "I'll take your measure," as the tailor said when he cabbaged his neighbor's half-bushel.

US (N.Y.), *Yankee Notions,* vol. 11 (1862), p. 376. Cited in Loomis 2, p. 14. [*Cabbaged,* stole.]

812 "I am forced into the measure," as Tom Thumb said when he was crammed into a quart cup.

US, PAT ROONEY, *Quaint Conundrums and Funny Gags* (1879). Cited in Browne, p. 202.

813 "Measure in all things," said the tailor and beat his wife with a yardstick.

US, 1948. Cited in Taylor 2, p. 317.

meat

814 "It is dry meat," said the country fellow when he lost the hare.

GB, PETER HEYLIN, *Animadvina* (1659). Cited in Wilson, p. 207.

815 "There's baith meat and music here," quoth the dog when he ate the piper's bag.

GB, ANDREW HENDERSON, *Scottish Proverbs* (1832); US, 1916. Cited in Lean, p. 750; Marvin, p. 363. [*Baith,* both.]

816 "We two shall meat again," barked one pup to another, as they started for the butcher's.

US (Calif.), *The Pelican,* vol. 31, no. 1 (1925), p. 45. Cited in Loomis 4, p. 241.

meet

817 "I'll meet you at the corner," said one wall to another.

US, c.1945-1980. Recorded in Bryant (Kans., N.Dak.).

melancholy

818   "Away with melancholy," as the little boy said ven his schoolmissis died.

GB, CHARLES DICKENS, *Pickwick Papers* (1836). Cited in Maass, p. 209.

melon

819   "It's no use," said the boy as he saw the old man coming over the fence with the ox whip. "I can'telope with that melon."

US (Calif.), *The Argonaut,* vol. 5, no. 7 (1879), p. 7. Cited in Loomis 4, p. 231.

mention

820   "Pray, don't mention it," as the man said when he was told by the tax-collector that his rates were due.

US (Mass.), *Ballou's Dollar Magazine,* vol. 2 (1855), p. 500. Cited in Loomis 2, p. 14.

mercy

821   "God have mercy on our people," said Oswald, falling to the ground.

GB, BEDE, *Historia Ecclesiastica* (c.731), trans. T. Miller, EETS (1890), pp. 95-96. Cited in Whiting 4, p. 32. [The reference is to King Oswald of Northumbria (c.605-641), a Christian convert killed in battle against pagan forces.]

822   "Lord, have mercy upon the soul," as St. Oswald said when he fell to the earth.

GB, JOHN BRAND, *Popular Antiquities* (1795). Cited in Lean, p. 747. [See note above.]

messages

823   "Messages carefully delivered," as the ear trumpet said to the old maid.

GB, *Punch,* vol. 3 (1842), p. 239; US (N.Y.), *Yankee Notions,* vol. 1 (1852), p. 224. Cited in Loomis 3, p. 113; Loomis 2, p. 14.

milk

824   "You seem to be full of the milk of human kindness," as the monkey said when he sucked the cocoa nut.

US (Maine), *Yankee Blade* (22 Oct. 1842). Cited in Loomis 2, p. 14.

millions

825   "Millions for de fence," as the darky said when a bull was chasing him through a field.

US (N.Y.), *Porter's Spirit of the Times,* vol. 2 (1857), p. 90. Cited in Loomis 2, p. 8. [The reference is to an epigram coined in 1797 by Charles Cotesworth Pinckney: "Millions for defense, but not one cent for tribute."]

826   "Astor and I," said the New York bootblack, "are worth millions."

US (Wash.), *Walla Walla Union* (20 Jan. 1872), p. 4. Cited in Hines, p. 22. [John Jacob Astor (1763-1848), American financier, was famous for his wealth, as were many of his descendants.]

827   "There's millions in it," said the inventor, as he scratched his dome.
US (Calif.), *The Pelican,* vol. 27, no. 2 (1921), p. 18. Cited in Loomis 4, p. 239.

mince

828   "I am not going to mince the matter," as the cook said when asked to make a batch of pies. She was "some pumpkins."
US (Mass.), *Yankee Blade* (29 Dec. 1849). Cited in Loomis 2, p. 14.

mind

829   "He won't do it if he hasn't a mind to," as the man said by his jackass.
US, 1913. Cited in Wright, p. 163.

mine

830   "What's hers is mine; what's mine is my own," quoth the husband.
GB, ROBERT FORBY, *Vocabulary of East Anglia* (1830). Cited in Lean, p. 752.

mismanage

831   "I miss-man-age," exclaimed a fifteen-year-old hopelessly sighing for a mustache.
US (Calif.), *The Wasp,* vol. 4, no. 196 (1880), p. 645. Cited in Loomis 4, p. 231.

missal

832   "Here's an illuminated missal for you," remarked the wife of the book-collector, as she threw a lighted lamp at her husband's head.
US (Calif.), *The Argonaut,* vol. 31, no. 13 (1892), p. 15. Cited in Loomis 4, p. 234.

mission

833   "That's my mission in life," said the monk, as he pointed to his monastery.
US (Calif.), *The Pelican,* vol. 19, no. 3 (1915), p. 36. Cited in Loomis 4, p. 237.

mock

834   "Mock not," quoth Mumford, when his wife called him cuckold.
GB, JAMES HOWELL, *English Proverbs* (1659). Cited in Wilson, p. 537.

moderate

835   "Be moderate in all things," as the boy said to his schoolmaster when the latter was whipping him.
US (Mass.), *Ballou's Dollar Magazine,* vol. 5 (1857), p. 200. Cited in Loomis 2, p. 14.

mole

836   "There's a mole in't," quo' the man when he swallowed the dishclout.
GB, 1903. Cited in Lean, p. 750. [Cf. no. 845.]

money

837 "God send us some money, for they are little thought of that want it," quoth the Earl of Eglinton at his prayers.

GB, JOHN RAY, *English Proverbs* (1678). Cited in Lean, p. 744.

838 "Money is very tight," as the thief said who was trying to break open a bank vault.

US (Pa.), *Alexander's Weekly Messenger* (1839). Cited in Loomis 1, p. 305; Tidwell 2, p. 259; Loomis 2, p. 20; Mieder, p. 231.

839 "Put money in thy purse," as the pickpocket said when he robbed a man of an empty one.

US (Calif.), *California Golden Era,* vol. 17, no. 32 (1869), p. 7. Cited in Loomis 1, p. 305; Loomis 2, p. 16.

840 "This is going to run into money," said the monkey as he peed in the cash register.

US (Kans.), c.1924–1927. Cited in Porter, p. 158; Anon, p. 34. Recorded in Bryant (Idaho).

monkey

841 "That's my glandfather," said the spry old man, as he pointed to the monkey.

US (Calif.), *The Pelican,* vol. 31, no. 2 (1925), p. 8. Cited in Loomis 4, p. 241.

842 "I'll be a monkey's uncle," said the monkey as his sister had a baby.

US (Kans.), 1959. Cited in Koch 1, p. 180; Mieder, p. 238. Recorded in Bryant (Kans.).

morning

843 "A good morning to you; I hope you are well!" as the boa-constrictor said to the emigrant when he was going to make a meal of him.

US (N.Y.), *Yankee Notions,* vol. 15 (1866), p. 164. Cited in Loomis 2, p. 11.

morsel

844 "I was taken by a morsel," says the fish.

GB, JAMES KELLY, *Scottish Proverbs* (1721). Cited in Lean, p. 745.

mote

845 "There's a mote in it," said the man, when he swallered the dish rag.

US, KAY STRAHAN, *Merriwether Mystery* (1933). Cited in Whiting 1, p. 74. [Cf. no. 836.]

motion

846 "That motion is out of order," as the chairman of a political meeting said when he saw a ruffian raising his arm to throw a rotten egg.

US (Mass.), *Ballou's Dollar Magazine,* vol. 9 (1859), p. 200. Cited in Loomis 2, p. 14.

847   "Well, I think I'll put the motion before the house," said the chorus girl, as she danced out on the stage.

US (Calif.), *The Pelican,* vol. 35, no. 3 (1929), p. 46. Cited in Loomis 4, p. 243.

mouth

848   "Keep your mouth shut," said Daniel, as he entered the lion's den.

US (Calif.), *The Pelican,* vol. 30, no. 3 (1924), p. 67. Cited in Loomis 4, p. 241.

moving

849   "I'm moving in very high circles," as the sweep said when he turned himself round in a chimney-pot.

GB, *Punch,* vol. 2 (1842), p. 161. Cited in Loomis 3, p. 112.

muckhill

850   "You make a muckhill on my trencher," quoth the bride.

GB, JOHN RAY, *English Proverbs* (1687). Cited in Lean, p. 752. [*Trencher,* wooden platter.]

mud

851   "This settles you. Your name is mud," said the raindrop to the particle of dust.

US (Calif.), *The Pelican,* vol. 27, no. 8 (1922), p. 47. Cited in Loomis 4, p. 240; Mieder, p. 235.

mum

852   "Just keep Mum," as the fellow said to the keeper of the poorhouse, when he left his maternal parent at that institution.

US (N.Y.), *Wit and Wisdom* (31 Mar. 1881), p. 15. Cited in Whiting 2, p. 10.

music

853   "Sweet music," as the little boy said when he played on his sugar whistle.

US (Pa.), *Alexander's Weekly Messenger* (1839). Cited in Tidwell 2, p. 260.

854   "I give lessons in music and drawing," as the donkey said when he began to bray and drag a cart after him.

US (Mass.), *Yankee Blade* (18 Sep. 1847). Cited in Loomis 2, p. 14.

855   "There's music in the heir," was a father's remark as he paced the midnight floor with his crying son in his arms.

US (Oreg.), *East Oregonian* (29 Jul. 1881), p. 4. Cited in Hines, p. 24; Mieder, p. 234.

856   "There is music in that sole," said the cook as she threw a fish upon the frying pan and it commenced fizzling.

US (Calif.), *The Wasp,* vol. 3, no. 146 (1897), p. 661. Cited in Loomis 4, p. 231.

857 "I'm simply carried away with the music," remarked the monkey from the top of the organ, as the grinder started away.

US (Calif.), *The Pelican,* vol. 2, no. 4 (1904), p. 15. Cited in Loomis 4, p. 235.

858 "Music by Handel," said the Frosh, as he wound up the Victrola.

US (Calif.), *The Pelican,* vol. 36, no. 2 (1930), p. 39. Cited in Loomis 4, p. 243. [*Frosh,* high-school or college freshman.]

must

859 "Well, if I must, I must," as the brewer said when his customers requested him to brew nothing but musty ale.

US (N.Y.), *Yankee Notions,* vol. 11 (1862), p. 351. Cited in Loomis 2, p. 14.

name

860 "What's in a name?" as the actress said to the bishop when he told her she reminded him of Aspasia.

US, LESLIE CHARTERIS, *The Saint in New York* (1935). Cited in Whiting 1, p. 72.

nature

861 "I only assisted natur', ma'm," as the doctor said to the boy's mother, arter he'd bled him to death.

GB, CHARLES DICKENS, *Pickwick Papers* (1836). Cited in Baer, p. 180.

naughty

862 "Naughty, naughty," said the sweet young thing, as the score keeper put up a double zero.

US (Calif.), *The Pelican,* vol. 26, no. 8 (1921), p. 34. Cited in Loomis 4, p. 239.

neck

863 "A rough neck," the sweet young thing exclaimed, as our hero strutted his stuff.

US (Calif.), *The Pelican,* vol. 33, no. 5 (1928), p. 49. Cited in Loomis 4, p. 242.

neckties

864 "Talking about neckties, here's something that is perfectly killing," gayly remarked the Western sheriff, as he deftly arranged the noose.

US (Calif.), *The Argonaut,* vol. 43, no. 1116 (1898), p. 16. Cited in Loomis 4, p. 234.

nerve

865 "I like your nerve!" said the young lady, as she examined her partner's zoological drawing.

US (Calif.), *The Pelican,* vol. 26, no. 2 (1920), p. 43. Cited in Loomis 4, p. 238.

866 "Well, of all the nerve!" murmured the lady dentist, as she investigated the molar.

US (Calif.), *The Pelican,* vol. 27, no. 2 (1921), p. 13. Cited in Loomis 4, p. 239.

net

867 "This is net gain," as the spider said to the fly.
US (N.Y.), *Yankee Notions,* vol. 1 (1852), p. 67. Cited in Loomis 2, p. 14.

868 "Our nets are floating wide," as the girls said of their ribbons.
US (N.Y.), *Yankee Notions,* vol. 1 (1852), p. 76. Cited in Loomis 2, p. 14.

869 "Caught in her own net," as the man said when he saw the fair sex
kitched in her crinoline.
US (Mass.), *Ballou's Dollar Magazine,* vol. 11 (1860), p. 100. Cited in Loomis 2, p. 14; Loomis
1, p. 304.

news

870 "Here is news," quoth the fox when he let a fart in the morning.
GB, ANON., *Marriage of Wit and Wisdom* (c.1590). Cited in Lean, p. 745.

871 "No noose is good news," as the man said when reprieved.
US (Calif.), *California Golden Era,* vol. 14, no. 43 (1866), p. 5. Cited in Loomis 1, p. 304; Loomis
2, p. 14; Hines, p. 24; Mieder, p. 234. Recorded in Bryant (Ohio).

next

872 "What next?" as the frog said when his tail fell off.
GB, THOMAS HOOD, *Hood's Owen* (1839); US (N.Y.), 1940. Cited in Lean, p. 752; Thompson,
p. 501. Recorded in Bryant (N.Y.).

873 "What next?" as the woman said to the man who kissed her in the
tunnel.
GB, THOMAS HALIBURTON, *Nature and Human Nature,* vol. 2 (1855). Cited in Taylor and
Whiting, p. 409.

874 "Who next?" as the whale said after Jonah.
US, LANGDON MITCHELL, *New York Idea* (1906). Cited in Stevenson, p. 2481. Recorded in
Bryant (N.Y.).

875 "What next?" as the toad said when his tail dropped off.
US, 1940. Cited in Thompson, p. 501. Recorded in Bryant (N.Y.).

night

876 "This is my idea of a night out," as the bishop said to the actress.
US, LESLIE CHARTERIS, *Enter the Saint* (1930). Cited in Whiting 1, p. 73.

nine lives

877 "I have nine lives," said the kitten.
US (N.Y.), L. FRANK BAUM, *Dorothy and the Wizard of Oz* (1908), p. 33. Cited in Whiting 6,
p. 96.

noise

878 "You can't make noise here," as the wooden pavement said to the omnibus.

GB, *Punch,* vol. 3 (1842), p. 146. Cited in Loomis 3, p. 112.

879 "I am going—and you need not make so much noise about it," as the cannon ball said to the cannon.

US (Mass.), *Ballou's Dollar Magazine,* vol. 13 (1861), p. 598. Cited in Loomis 2, p. 14.

880 "Much noise and little wool," said the devil when he sheared a pig.

US, 1931. Cited in Taylor 1, p. 219; Mieder, p. 225. Recorded in Bryant (Minn., Oreg.). [Cf. no. 261.]

nonsense

881 "That is shear nonsense," as the convict remarked when he saw his wavy locks fall off under the influence of the penitentiary barber.

US (N.Y.), *Yankee Notions,* vol. 12 (1863), p. 109. Cited in Loomis 2, p. 18.

nose

882 "You sing through your nose," as the man said to his tea-kettle.

US (N.Y.), *Spirit of the Times,* vol. 10 (1840), p. 207. Cited in Whiting 2, p. 7.

883 "There's nose sorrow there," as the fellow said, who had a severe cold.

US (N.Y.), *Marathon Independent* (19 May 1881), p. 16. Cited in Whiting 2, p. 10.

884 As the little pig says, "Mama, how happens it that you have so long a nose?"

US, c.1945-1980. Recorded in Bryant (N.Y.).

note

885 "If you know'd who was near, Sir, I rayther think you'd change your note," as the hawk remarked to himself vith a cheerful laugh, ven he heerd the robin redbreast a singin' round the corner.

GB, CHARLES DICKENS, *Pickwick Papers* (1836). Cited in Maass, p. 211.

886 "That's a hell of a note," remarked the impresario, as the diva took a mighty gulp and pounced savagely on a high E.

US (Calif.), *The Pelican,* vol. 26, no. 8 (1921), p. 2. Cited in Loomis 4, p. 239.

nothing

887 "It's nothing when you're used to it," as the eels said while they were being skinned alive.

GB, JONATHAN SWIFT, *Polite Conversation* (1738). Cited in Lean, p. 747; Wilson, p. 582.

888 "Nothing is certain," as the fisherman said when he always found it in his nets.

GB, *Punch,* vol. 1 (1841), p. 276. Cited in Loomis 3, p. 111.

889 "Out of place and nothing to take to," as the man said when he fell out of the balloon.

GB, *Punch*, vol. 2 (1842), p. 126. Cited in Loomis 3, p. 112.

890 "You've got nothing on me," said Aphrodite to Venus.

US (Calif.), *The Pelican*, vol. 27, no. 5 (1921), p. 40. Cited in Loomis 4, p. 239.

891 "There's nothing I particularly want to do tonight," as the bishop said to the actress.

US, LESLIE CHARTERIS, *Enter the Saint* (1930). Cited in Whiting 1, p. 73.

notice

892 "You are beneath my notice," as the balloonist said to the receding crowd of gaping citizens.

US (Calif.), *The Wasp*, vol. 3, no. 148 (1879), p. 698. Cited in Loomis 4, p. 231.

notion

893 "Everybody to his own notion," as the girl said when she kissed the calf.

US, c.1945-1980. Recorded in Bryant (Miss., Wis.).

894 "Every feller to his own notion," said the old lady as she kissed her cow.

US (Ky.), 1956. Cited in Halpert 2, p. 118.

895 "Everyone to their own notion," as the old woman said when she kissed the cow.

US (Ky., Tenn.), 1956. Cited in Halpert 2, p. 118. Recorded in Bryant (Ala., Ark., Kans., Miss., Ohio, Tex., W.Va.).

oblige

896 "I should be charmed to oblige you," as the actress said to the bishop.

US, LESLIE CHARTERIS, *Enter the Saint* (1930). Cited in Whiting 1, p. 72.

observations

897 "What a deal of observations we excite!" said the bumble bee buzzing along in the trail of a comet.

US (Wash.), *Walla Walla Union* (30 May 1874), p. 4. Cited in Hines, p. 25.

ocean

898 "A life on the ocean wave!" as the ship said ven he fell into the Atlantic.

US (Pa.), *Alexander's Weekly Messenger* (1839). Cited in Tidwell 2, p. 262.

899 "We leave the very ocean split asunder!" exclaims a perch darting along in the wake of a whale.

US (Wash.), *Walla Walla Union* (30 May 1874), p. 4. Cited in Hines, p. 25.

off

900 "I'm off," as the fly said when he crept out of the mustard pot.

US, ROBERT BAILEY THOMAS, *Old Farmer's Almanack, 1793 to the Present* (1822). Cited in Loomis 5, p. 51.

901 "I'm off!" as the fly said that lit on the mustard pot.

US (Pa.), *The Casket,* vol. 8 (1832), p. 286. Cited in Loomis 2, p. 15.

902 "I'm off when you talk of working," as the cork said to the ginger pop.

US (N.Y.), *Porter's Spirit of the Times,* vol. 6 (1859), p. 126. Cited in Loomis 2, p. 21.

903 "They're off," cried the monkey as he backed into the lawn mower.

US (Kans.), 1924. Cited in Porter, p. 158; Brewster, p. 268; Halpert 2, p. 120. Recorded in Bryant (Ind., Tenn.).

904 "It's all off," as the monkey said, when he caught his tail in the lawn mower.

US, 1945. Cited in Jones, p. 236. Recorded in Bryant (Ind., Tex., Wis.).

oil

905 "Oil on the brain," exclaimed Jones as he broke a bottle of oil over the head of his friend Brown.

US (Calif.), *California Golden Era,* vol. 15, no. 3 (1886), p. 3. Cited in Loomis 1, p. 304; Loomis 2, p. 15. Recorded in Bryant (N.Y.).

one

906 "One for us tew an' one for you tew," as the Irishman said when he was dividin' the four dollars 'twixt him self an' his tew frinds.

US (N.Y.), ROWLAND ROBINSON, *Uncle Lisha's Shop* (1887). Cited in Whiting 2, p. 11.

907 "That's one on me," said the whale, as the U.S.S. *New Yorker* dropped her anchor on his head.

US (Calif.), *The Pelican,* vol. 33, no. 1 (1927), p. 6. Cited in Loomis 4, p. 242.

onward

908 "Onward and occupation!" as the girl said when her beau was afraid to pop the question.

US (Mass.), *Yankee Blade* (1 Jan. 1848). Cited in Loomis 2, p. 15.

opinion

909 "Everyone to his own opinion," said the old lady as she kissed the cow.

US, c.1945–1980. Recorded in Bryant (Miss., Oreg.).

opportune

910 "That's hoppertune," said the Englishman as the band struck up a waltz; and then, sure enough, the people began to hop round the room.

US (Calif.), *The Wasp,* vol. 3, no. 146 (1879), p. 661. Cited in Loomis 4, p. 231.

opposition

911 "Opposition is the life of trade," as the sky rocket said to the firefly.

US (Pa.), *Alexander's Weekly Messenger* (1839). Cited in Tidwell 2, p. 260; Mieder, p. 230.

912 "Confound all opposition," as the owner of a watering machine said when a heavy shower of rain came on.

US (N.Y.), *Wilkes' Spirit of the Times,* vol. 3 (1861), p. 279. Cited in Loomis 2, p. 15.

orders

913 "Ye're early with your orders," as the bride said at the church door.

GB, ALEXANDER HISLOP, *Proverbs of Scotland* (1870). Cited in Lean, p. 752.

out

914 "Out vith it," as the father said to the child, ven he swallowed a farden.

GB, CHARLES DICKENS, *Pickwick Papers* (1836). Cited in Stevenson, p. 2480; Baer, p. 175. [*Farden,* farthing.]

overhead

915 "I'm overhead and ears in debt," as the fellow said when he had on a hat that wasn't paid for.

US (Maine), *Yankee Blade* (8 Oct. 1842). Cited in Loomis 2, p. 15.

owe

916 "We all owe something to our country," said the Briton who went abroad without having paid his income-tax.

GB, *Punch,* vol. 58 (1879), p. 257. Cited in Loomis 3, p. 113.

pain

917 "I'll spare no pains," as the quack said when he sawed off his patient's leg for the rheumatism.

US (N.Y.), *Yankee Notions,* vol. 2 (1853), p. 16. Cited in Loomis 2, p. 15.

918 "You give me a pain in the neck," said the doomed man at the guillotine to the executioner.

US (Kans.), 1959. Cited in Koch 2, p. 160; Mieder, p. 9. Recorded in Bryant (Kans.).

paint

919 "Look out for paint," as the girl said when the fellow went to kiss her.

US (N.Y.), *Yankee Notions,* vol. 8 (1858), p. 367. Cited in Tidwell 2, p. 261; Loomis 2, p. 15.

paintings

920   "I am passionately fond of paintings," as the young beau said when he kissed the rouged cheeks of his sweetheart.

US (Mass.), *Ballou's Dollar Magazine,* vol. 6 (1857), p. 400. Cited in Loomis 2, p. 15.

pair

921   "They're a bonny pair," as the craw said o' his feet.

GB, 1903. Cited in Lean, p. 750. [*Craw,* crow.]

922   "They're a bonny pair," as the de'il said o' his cloots.

GB, 1903. Cited in Lean, p. 750. [*Cloots,* hoofs.]

pants

923   "This is a pair of pants," ejaculated the young man, as he cantered along the road with a bulldog sampling his coat tails.

US (Calif.), *Daily Examiner,* vol. 35, no. 157 (1882), p. 4. Cited in Loomis 4, p. 233.

paper

924   "Stop my paper," as the fellow said ven he was running away.

US (Pa.), *Alexander's Weekly Messenger* (1839). Cited in Tidwell 2, p. 259.

pardon

925   "I beg your pardon!" sang out the convict, as the governor passed down the corridor.

US (Calif.), *The Argonaut,* vol. 32, no. 7 (1893), p. 12. Cited in Loomis 4, p. 234.

parents

926   "Contrary to what you are thinking, students, my parents were married when I was born," said the instructor while putting his fifth consecutive pop quiz on the board.

US (Idaho), 1966. Cited in Anon, p. 34. Recorded in Bryant (Idaho).

Paris

927   "So this is Paris," said the leg to the garter.

US (Calif.), *The Pelican,* vol. 25, no. 5 (1920), p. 21. Cited in Loomis 4, p. 238.

part

928   Quoth the baker to the pillory, "I fear we part not yet."

GB, JOHN HEYWOOD, *English Proverbs* (1546). Cited in Wilson, p. 27.

929   "We part to meet no more," as the turtle soup said to the platter when an alderman entered the room.

US (Mass.), *Yankee Blade* (8 Jan. 1845). Cited in Loomis 2, p. 15.

930 "I'll take your part," as the dog said when he robbed the cat of her portion of the dinner.

US (Mass.), *Ballou's Dollar Magazine,* vol. 3 (1856), p. 400. Cited in Loomis 2, p. 20; Mieder, p. 237. Recorded in Bryant (Ky., N.Y.).

931 "I must have some part of you to take with me," he cried, as he pinched her cheek.

US (Calif.), *The Pelican,* vol. 26, no. 8 (1921), p. 39. Cited in Loomis 4, p. 239.

pass

932 "I pass," as the brag player said ven he slipped out of one door as he saw the constable entering another.

US (Pa.), *Alexander's Weekly Messenger* (1839). Cited in Tidwell 2, p. 260.

933 "You don't pass here," as the counter said to the bad shilling.

GB, *Punch,* vol. 2 (1842), p. 82; US (Pa.), *Alexander's Weekly Messenger* (1839). Cited in Loomis 3, p. 111; Loomis 2, p. 15; Mieder, p. 230.

pastors

934 "A change of pastors makes fat calves," as the minister reasoned when he accepted a higher call.

US (Maine), *Yankee Blade* (18 Oct. 1842). Cited in Loomis 2, p. 15.

pat

935 "I'll pat the busser," as the young lady said when she boxed the young man's jaw.

US (Ohio), *Steubenville News* (1881). Cited in Whiting 2, p. 5.

patronize

936 "I'll not pat-ronize this house," as the Irishman said when the landlord told him he kept no liquor.

US (Mass.), *Yankee Blade* (15 Jan. 1845). Cited in Loomis 2, p. 15.

paws

937 "I paws for reply," as the cat said to the owl.

US (Pa.), *Alexander's Weekly Messenger* (1839). Cited in Tidwell 2, p. 259; Loomis 2, p. 15.

paying

938 "Paying dear for good company," as the rook said when he was put in the pigeon pie.

US (Mass.), *Ballou's Dollar Magazine,* vol. 9 (1859), p. 300. Cited in Loomis 2, p. 15.

peace

939 "Peace be with you," as the fox said to the trap that caught his tail.

US (N.Y.), *Yankee Notions,* vol. 1 (1852), p. 90. Cited in Loomis 2, p. 15.

peel

940 "Peel forever!" as the church bells said to the Conservative hearts.

GB, *Punch,* vol. 1 (1841), p. 101. Cited in Loomis 3, p. 111. [Sir Robert Peel (1788-1850), British statesman, was the founder of the Conservative party.]

pen

941 "Your pen wants mending," as the shepherd said to the stray sheep.

GB, *Punch,* vol. 2 (1842), p. 82. Cited in Loomis 3, p. 111.

942 "Excuse haste and bad pen," said the pig as he broke out of his enclosure and ran off.

US (Calif.), *The Wasp,* vol. 9, no. 319 (1882), p. 566. Cited in Loomis 4, p. 232.

penny

943 "A penny for your thoughts," as the cheap newspaper reader said to the editor of a daily.

US (Mass.), *Ballou's Dollar Magazine,* vol. 8 (1858), p. 300. Cited in Loomis 2, p. 15.

944 "Mony a thing's made for the penny," as the auld wife said when she saw the plack man.

US, 1916. Cited in Marvin, p. 358; Taylor 1, p. 209. [*Plack,* small copper coin issued by James III of Scotland, worth four pennies Scots.]

permitted

945 "This is the thing that ought not to be permitted," as the fox said when he found the henroost empty.

US (Wash.), *Weekly Big Bend Empire* (28 May 1889), p. 3. Cited in Hines, p. 25; Mieder, p. 234.

personalities

946 "Personalities are disagreeable," as the loafer said ven the butcher's dog snapped his teeth through his leg.

US (Pa.), *Alexander's Weekly Messenger* (1839). Cited in Taylor 3, p. 260.

perspire

947 "How we perspire!" said the beefsteak to the gridiron.

US, ROBERT BAILEY THOMAS, *Old Farmer's Almanąck, 1793 to the Present* (1821). Cited in Loomis 5, p. 51. [*Gridiron,* broiling grate.]

picking

948 "This is easy picking," remarked the banjo player, as he started in with a new tune.

US (Calif.), *The Pelican,* vol. 7, no. 4 (1909). Cited in Loomis 4, p. 236.

pickle

949 "Will any other lady have a pickle!" as the girl said when she tumbled into a hogshead of brine.

US (Mass.), *Yankee Blade* (17 Jan. 1847). Cited in Loomis 2, p. 15. [*Hogshead,* large cask or barrel.]

pinch

950 "I could stay here in a pinch," he said, as they took him to a cell.

US (Calif.), *The Pelican,* vol. 16, no. 2 (1914). Cited in Loomis 4, p. 237.

pitch

951 "Pitch," shouted the baseball player, as he stepped on the newly poured black-top highway.

US (Kans.), 1959. Cited in Koch 2, p. 196. Recorded in Bryant (Kans.).

pity

952 "How I pity the poor fellows whose business requires them to be out on a night like this," said the policeman, looking out from the side door.

US (Calif.), *The Argonaut,* vol. 34, no. 11 (1894), p. 16. Cited in Loomis 4, p. 234.

place

953 "A place for everything and everything in its place," as an old lady said when she stowed the broom, bellows, balls of yarn, cards, caps, curry-comb, three cats and a gridiron into an old oven.

US (Mass.), *Yankee Blade* (18 May 1848). Cited in Loomis 2, p. 15.

plant

954 As the farmer said to the potato, "I'll plant you now and dig you later."

US, c.1945-1980. Recorded in Bryant (Ill.).

please

955 "Anything to please the child," as the nurse said when she let the baby crawl out the third story window.

US (Pa.), *Alexander's Weekly Messenger* (1839). Cited in Tidwell 2, p. 261; Loomis 2, p. 4; Mieder, p. 230. Recorded in Bryant (N.Y.).

pleasure

956 "I can take no pleasure in you when you get in your snappish ways," as the rat said to the trap.

US (Mass.), *Yankee Blade* (15 Sep. 1849). Cited in Loomis 2, p. 18.

957 "I'll do it for you with pleasure," as the carpenter said when the hang-man asked him to make a gallows.

US (N.Y.), *Yankee Notions,* vol. 3 (1854), p. 142. Cited in Whiting 2, p. 5.

958 "It was a pleasure, but kind of unexpected," as the starvin' man said when someone threw the soup at him.

US, PETER A. TAYLOR, *Mystery of the Cape Cod Players* (1933). Cited in Whiting 1, p. 75; Browne, p. 202; Mieder, p. 236.

959 As the bear said while he buggered the porcupine, "A little pleasure, a lot of pain."

US, c.1945-1980. Recorded in Bryant (Wash.).

960 As the monkey said when diddling the porcupine, "There is always some pain with pleasure."

US, c.1945-1980. Recorded in Bryant (Wash.).

pledge

961 "Why don't you take the pledge?" as the woman said to her good man when she handed him the little 'un.

US (Mass.), *Yankee Blade* (7 Oct. 1846). Cited in Loomis 2, p. 16.

poetry

962 "I occasionally drop into poetry," as the man said when he fell into the waste basket.

US (Calif.), *Daily Examiner,* vol. 34, no. 121 (1882), p. 4. Cited in Loomis 4, p. 232.

point

963 "I'm particularly uneasy on this point," as the fly said when the young gentleman stuck him on the end of a needle.

GB, *Punch,* vol. 3 (1842), p. 122; US (N.Y.), *Yankee Notions,* vol. 1 (1852), p. 223. Cited in Loomis 3, p. 112; Whiting 2, p. 8; Loomis 2, p. 16; Mieder, p. 231. Recorded in Bryant (Ohio).

964 "I may feel the point, but I don't see the joke," as the sheep said to the butcher's knife.

US (Calif.), *Fireman's Journal,* vol. 2 (1855), p. 1. Cited in Loomis 4, p. 230.

965 "Do you see the point?" asked the needle of the cloth as it passed through it. "No, but I feel it," replied the cloth with a groan.

US (Calif.), *The Wasp,* vol. 8, no. 296 (1882), p. 202. Cited in Loomis 4, p. 232.

966 "That isn't the point," as the man said to the assassin who tried to stab him with the hilt of a dagger.

US (N.Y.), ISAAC BANGS, *A House-Boat on the Styx* (1896). Cited in Whiting 2, p. 11.

967 "I have a few more points to touch upon," said the after-dinner tramp, as he scaled the barbed wire fence.

US (Calif.), *The Pelican,* vol. 17, no. 2 (1914), p. 12. Cited in Loomis 4, p. 237.

968 "I got the point," said the man as he pulled the hornet off his neck.

US (Tenn.), c.1950. Cited in Halpert 2, p. 118; Mieder, p. 237. Recorded in Bryant (Tenn.).

pointed

969 "Very good, but rather pointed," as the fish said when it swallowed the bait.

US (Pa.), *Alexander's Weekly Messenger* (1839). Cited in Tidwell 2, p. 260; Loomis 1, p. 305; Loomis 2, p. 16. Recorded in Bryant (Ohio).

port

970 "I guess we'll make port," said the sailor, as he threw in another handful of raisins.

US (Calif.), *The Pelican,* vol. 29, no. 4 (1923), p. 55. Cited in Loomis 4, p. 240.

potato

971 "There is more parade than potatoes," as the Irishman said of the dinner table at a fashionable hotel.

US (Mass.), *Ballou's Dollar Magazine,* vol. 3 (1856), p. 600. Cited in Loomis 2, p. 15.

972 Said Aristotle unto Plato, "Have another sweet potato?" Said Plato unto Aristotle, "Thank you, I prefer the bottle."

US, c.1945–1980. Recorded in Bryant (N.Y., S.C.).

pot luck

973 "Come and take pot luck," as the cook said to the live lobster.

GB, *Punch,* vol. 2 (1842), p. 112. Cited in Loomis 3, p. 112.

pray

974 "Let us pray," as the hawk said to its nestling.

US, 1873. Cited in Browne, p. 202; Mieder, p. 233.

present

975 "It isn't the size of the present that gives it its value," as the gentleman said when his wife gave him four boys at a birth.

US (N.Y.), *Yankee Notions,* vol. 2 (1853), p. 262. Cited in Whiting 2, p. 8. Recorded in Bryant (Ariz.).

press

976 "Let us try to elevate the press," as the boy said when he sent up a kite made of Copperhead newspapers.

US (N.Y.), *Yankee Notions,* vol. 12 (1863), p. 228. Cited in Loomis 2, p. 9. [*Copperhead newspapers,* Northern newspapers sympathetic to the South during the American Civil War, so called by Northerners (Yankees). A copperhead is a poisonous North American snake.]

977 "Excuse the freedom of the press," as the editor said when he hugged his neighbor's wife.

US (N.Y.), *Yankee Notions,* vol. 14 (1865), p. 196. Cited in Loomis 2, p. 16.

978   "As we go to press," facetiously said the young journalist, as he put his arm around her waist.

US (Calif.), *The Wasp,* vol. 10, no. 355 (1883), p. 2. Cited in Loomis 4, p. 233.

pressed

979   "I'm very much pressed for time," as the man said when his wife hugged and kissed him to coax a gold watch out of him.

US (Mass.), *Yankee Blade* (10 Sep. 1845). Cited in Loomis 2, p. 16.

pressing

980   "I have a pressing engagement," said the man as he took his pants to the cleaners.

US (Ky.), c.1950. Cited in Halpert 2, p. 118; Mieder, p. 237. Recorded in Bryant (Ky., Tenn.).

pressure

981   "There is a great pressure in the money market," as the mouse remarked when a keg of silver rolled over his nose.

US (Maine), *Yankee Blade* (20 Aug. 1842). Cited in Loomis 2, p. 16; Whiting 2, p. 8.

prevention

982   "Prevention is better than cure," as the pig said when it ran away with all its might to escape the killing attentions of the pork butcher.

GB, *Punch,* vol. 43 (1862), p. 90; US (N.Y.), *Yankee Notions,* vol. 12 (1863), p. 101. Cited in Loomis 3, p. 113; Loomis 2, p. 7.

pride

983   "Fly pride," says the peacock.

GB, WILLIAM SHAKESPEARE, *The Comedy of Errors* (1594), act 4, scene 3. Cited in Lean, p. 744; Taylor 3, p. 170.

984   "Pride must have a fall," exclaimed a mechanic, as he knocked down a dandy who had abused him.

US (Pa.), *The Casket,* vol. 8 (1833), p. 480. Cited in Loomis 5, p. 51.

principle

985   "Hooroar for the principle," as the money lender said ven he wouldn't renew the bill.

GB, CHARLES DICKENS, *Pickwick Papers* (1836). Cited in Stevenson, p. 2480; Baer, p. 177.

986   "I'm a northern man with southern principles," as the Yankee said when he was eating rice and molasses.

US (Maine), *Yankee Blade* (8 Oct. 1842). Cited in Loomis 2, p. 16.

987   "I'm always in favor of carrying out a principle," as one of the b'hoys said when he kicked his master into the street.

US (Mass.), *Yankee Blade* (6 Jan. 1847). Cited in Loomis 2, p. 16.

988 "The principle of the thing is what I care for," as a creditor said to a debtor whose note he held.
US (Mass.), *Webster Times* (12 May 1881), p. 16. Cited in Whiting 2, p. 10. Recorded in Bryant (Oreg.).

promises

989 As the pansy said to the angry sailor, "Now you're making promises."
US, J. Y. DANE, *Murder cum Laude* (1935). Cited in Whiting 1, p. 74.

proposition

990 "That's a self-evident proposition," as the cat's-meat-man said to the servant maid when she called him no gentleman.
GB, CHARLES DICKENS, *Pickwick Papers* (1836). Cited in Bailey, p. 32; Baer, p. 178.

puffs

991 "You couldn't get along without my puffs," as the engine said to the steamboat.
US (Mass.), *Yankee Blade* (30 Sep. 1848). Cited in Loomis 2, p. 16.

puke

992 "You're a puke," as the whale disrespectfully said to Jonah when he disgorged that emigrant prophet.
US (N.Y.), *Yankee Notions,* vol. 13 (1863), p. 228. Cited in Loomis 2, p. 16.

punch

993 "I'm losing my punch," she said, as she left the cocktail party in a hurry.
US (Calif.), *The Pelican,* vol. 42, no. 1 (1935), p. 32. Cited in Loomis 4, p. 244.

punishment

994 "Capital punishment," as the boy said when the mistress seated him with the girls.
US (Calif.), *Carrie and Damon's California Almanac* (1856). Cited in Loomis 2, p. 6.

995 "That's what I call capital punishment," as the boy said when his mother shut him up in the closet among the preserves.
US (Mass.), *Ballou's Dollar Magazine,* vol. 10 (1859), p. 600. Cited in Loomis 2, p. 6.

996 "This is a true corporal punishment," said the sophomore, as he drilled his awkward squad.
US (Calif.), *The Pelican,* vol. 22, no. 3 (1915), p. 13. Cited in Loomis 4, p. 238.

pupil

997 "You have a pupil under the lash," as the man said when he looked into a pedagogue's eye.
US (Mass.), *Yankee Blade* (19 Jan. 1850). Cited in Loomis 2, p. 16.

998 "I guess I've lost another pupil," said the professor, as his glass eye rolled down the kitchen sink.

US (Calif.), *The Pelican,* vol. 47, no. 8 (1941), p. 33. Cited in Loomis 4, p. 244.

puss

999 "I'll bat the puss, sir," the cook said when striking with the poker.

US (Mo.), *Modern Argo* (21 Apr. 1881), p. 9. Cited in Whiting 2, p. 6.

1000 "I'll puss the batter," as the kitten said when it flung itself into the buckwheat conglomeration prepared for the morning meal.

US (Mo.), *Modern Argo* (21 Apr. 1881), p. 8. Cited in Whiting 2, p. 6.

put out

1001 "I was terribly put out about it," as the fellow said who was kicked down stairs for making a row.

US (Mass.), *Yankee Blade* (3 Apr. 1844). Cited in Loomis 2, p. 16.

1002 "Be quiet, can't you—you put me out!" as the fire said to the hose pipe.

US (N.Y.), *Yankee Notions,* vol. 8 (1858), p. 100. Cited in Loomis 2, p. 16.

quarter

1003 "I'll give no quarter to his changing his halves," as the bummer said, who had button-holed a Bodiean.

US (Calif.), *The Wasp,* vol. 4, no. 196 (1880), p. 80. Cited in Loomis 4, p. 232.

quest

1004 "Thee beest a queer quest," as the boy said to the owl.

US, 1913. Cited in Wright, p. 163. [*Quest,* possibly a variant of *queest,* ring-dove, wood-pidgeon.]

quietness

1005 "Quietness is best," as the fox said when he bit the cock's head off.

GB, ROBERT HOLLAND, *Cheshire Glossary* (1886); US, 1913. Cited in Wilson, p. 660; Wright, p. 161.

rabbit

1006 "No one knows where the rabbit has his runways nor how high he jumps," the old lady said when she put the rabbit snare on the roof.

US (Idaho), 1966. Cited in Anon, p. 34. Recorded in Bryant (Idaho).

racer

1007 "Yes, you're a racer, to be sure," cried the devil to the crab.

GB, JOHN WOLCOTT, *Middlesex Election* (1794). Cited in Lean, p. 752; Wilson, p. 689.

races

1008 "This is certainly doping the races," chuckled the villain, as he placed knock-out drops in the glasses of the Chinaman and the Negro.

US (Calif.), *The Pelican,* vol. 2, no. 5 (1904), p. 17. Cited in Loomis 4, p. 235.

rag-tag

1009 "It's sort of rag-tag an' bobtail," as ole man Blair used to say when the fellers at the wharf used to ask him about his corn beef.

US, PETER A. TAYLOR, *Deathblow Hill* (1935). Cited in Whiting 1, p. 74; Mieder, p. 236.

railery

1010 "Come, none of your railery," as the stage-coach said indignantly to the steam-engine.

GB, *Punch,* vol. 1 (1841), p. 101. Cited in Loomis 3, p. 111.

railing

1011 "What's the use of railing?" as the stage driver said when he saw the locomotive leave the track and run across lots.

US (Mass.), *Yankee Blade* (8 Apr. 1848). Cited in Loomis 2, p. 16.

rainest

1012 "Thou rainest in this bosom," as the chap said when a basin of water was thrown over him by the lady he was serenading.

US (N.Y.), *Porter's Spirit of the Times,* vol. 3 (1857), p. 7. Cited in Loomis 2, p. 8. Recorded in Bryant (N.Y.).

raise

1013 "I'll raise you two," said the wealthy lady to the orphans.

US (Calif.), *The Pelican,* vol. 26, no. 9 (1921), p. 32. Cited in Loomis 4, p. 239.

random

1014 "How are you?" "Pretty much at random, sir," as Frank Duffy said when he slept in the big tavern.

US (N.Y.), *Spirit of the Times,* vol. 10 (1840), p. 207. Cited in Whiting 2, p. 7.

rank

1015 "My offence is rank," as the French nobleman said when he was about to be guillotined at the Revolution.

US (Mass.), *Yankee Blade* (20 May 1846). Cited in Loomis 2, p. 16.

1016 "I can boast of rank," as the butter said to the cheese. "And I am strong and mighty," as the cheese replied to the butter.

US (Mass.), *Yankee Blade* (10 Mar. 1849). Cited in Loomis 2, p. 16.

rate

1017   "We sure do rate," said Mr. Dun to Mr. Bradstreet.

US (Calif.), *The Pelican,* vol. 28, no. 5 (1923), p. 43. Cited in Loomis 4, p. 240. [R. G. Dun & Co. and the Bradstreet Co. were famous publishers of current business news; the firms merged in 1933 to form Dun & Bradstreet, Inc.]

raw

1018   "Raw stuff," said the bride, as she watched the butcher weigh the chops.

US (Calif.), *The Pelican,* vol. 28, no. 2 (1922), p. 12. Cited in Loomis 4, p. 240.

raze

1019   "I am going to raze a pig sty," said Jenkins, and he straightway knocked one down.

US (Mass.), *Boston Daily Evening Transcript* (15 Mar. 1834). Cited in Loomis 2, p. 16; Loomis 5, p. 51.

rear

1020   "To the rear," said Johnnie's ma, reaching for the strap.

US (Calif.), *The Wasp,* vol. 17, no. 541 (1886), p. 6. Cited in Loomis 4, p. 233.

1021   "You go on ahead, I'll bring up the rear," said the girdle to the hat.

US, c.1945-1980. Recorded in Bryant (Kans.).

reckoning

1022   "The hour of reckoning has come," said the cashier, as he opened his books and prepared to run up a column of figures.

US (Idaho), *Colfax Commoner* (27 Apr. 1888), p. 3. Cited in Hines, p. 24; Mieder, p. 233.

recommended

1023   "Strongly recommended for family use," as the Yorkshire schoolmaster said of the pickled birch.

GB, *Punch,* vol. 3 (1842), p. 182. Cited in Loomis 3, p. 112.

reflection

1024   "None of your unkind reflections," as the old maid said to the looking glass.

US, PAT ROONEY, *Quaint Conundrums and Funny Gags* (1879). Cited in Browne, p. 202; Mieder, p. 233.

reformed

1025   "He has reformed and behaves much better," as the rich family said of the poor relation when a legacy was left him.

US (Mass.), *Yankee Blade* (18 Mar. 1847). Cited in Loomis 2, p. 17. Recorded in Bryant (N.Y.).

rehearse

1026   "We'll have to rehearse that," said the undertaker, as the coffin fell out of the car.

US (Calif.), *The Pelican,* vol. 42, no. 7 (1936), p. 47. Cited in Loomis 4, p. 244.

rejoice

1027   "Rejoice, bucks," quo' Brodie, when he shot at the buryin' and thought it was a weddin'.

US, 1916. Cited in Marvin, p. 359.

relief

1028   "You give me great relief," as the marble said to the sculptor.

US (Pa.), *Alexander's Weekly Messenger* (1839). Cited in Tidwell 2, p. 262.

1029   "What a relief," murmured the celebrated sculptor, Phidias, as he put the finishing touches on the Parthenon frieze.

US (Calif.), *The Pelican,* vol. 6, no. 5 (1909). Cited in Loomis 4, p. 236.

remains

1030   "That remains to be seen," said the elephant, as he walked in the fresh cement.

US (Calif.), *The Pelican,* vol. 48, no. 8 (1942), p. 5. Cited in Loomis 4, p. 245; Mieder, p. 234.

remark

1031   "This is a personal remark," as the prisoner said when the judge told him to hold out his right hand.

US (N.Y), *Yankee Notions,* vol. 3 (1854), p. 142. Cited in Whiting 2, p. 5. Recorded in Bryant (Ohio).

remembering

1032   "I presume you won't charge me anything for just re-membering me," said a one-legged sailor to a wooden leg manufacturer.

US (N.Y.), *Wilkes' Spirit of the Times,* vol. 3 (1860), p. 39. Cited in Loomis 2, p. 17.

remittent

1033   "Oh, that my father was seized with remittent fever," sighed a young spendthrift at college.

US (N.Y.), *Wilkes' Spirit of the Times,* vol. 3 (1860), p. 39. Cited in Loomis 2, p. 17.

rents

1034   "Rents collected," as the darning-needle said to the pantaloons.

GB, *Punch,* vol. 3 (1842), p. 178. Cited in Loomis 3, p. 112.

1035 "Rents are enormous," as the loafer said on looking at his pants.

US (Mass.), *Yankee Blade* (31 Jul. 1847). Cited in Loomis 2, p. 17.

1036 "Rents have risen," was the jocose remark of the astute small boy when a nail caught in a previously small tear in his coat tail, and ripped the garment up to his neck.

US (Wash.), *Walla Walla Union* (4 Dec. 1875), p. 4. Cited in Hines, p. 25.

reservations

1037 "I b'lieve it, but with res'vations," like the feller said when they told him for the third time it was corn beef hash he was eatin'.

US, PHOEBE ATWOOD TAYLOR, *Sandbar Sinister* (1934). Cited in Whiting 1, p. 73.

responsibility

1038 "I'll take responsibility," as the woman said when the baby began to cry.

US (Maine), *Yankee Blade* (3 Dec. 1842). Cited in Loomis 2, p. 17.

retainer

1039 "A retainer at the bar," as the boy said when caught by a dog, just as he was about to climb on the orchard fence.

US (Mass.), *Ballou's Dollar Magazine,* vol. 12 (1860), p. 198. Cited in Loomis 2, p. 17. Recorded in Bryant (N.Y., S.C.).

return

1040 "What an ungrateful return!" said a defeated candidate when a count of his votes proved him to be in the minority.

US (Mass.), *Ballou's Dollar Magazine,* vol. 10 (1859), p. 100. Cited in Loomis 2, p. 17.

reverberation

1041 "What a prodigious reverberation!" says a woodpecker, tapping a hollow tree on the roaring verge of Niagara.

US (Wash.), *Walla Walla Union* (30 May 1874), p. 4. Cited in Hines, p. 25.

re-wive

1042 "I guess he'll re-wive," as the gentleman said when his friend fainted away at his wife's funeral.

US (N.Y.), *Spirit of the Times,* vol. 10 (1840), p. 231. Cited in Whiting 2, p. 7. Recorded in Bryant (Ohio).

Rhine

1043 "I'm going up the Rhine," as the bluebottle fly said when he was shinning up a newly smoked ham.

US (Mass.), *Yankee Blade* (11 Sep. 1852). Cited in Loomis 2, p. 17.

rich

1044 "Come Sir, this is rayther too rich," as the young lady said ven she remonstrated with the pastry cook, arter he'd sold her a pork pie as had got nothin' but fat inside.

GB, CHARLES DICKENS, *Pickwick Papers* (1836). Cited in Maass, p. 212.

ring

1045 "Now your talk has the true ring," said the girl to her lover, when he began to talk of a diamond circlet.

US (Calif.), *The Wasp,* vol. 14, no. 443 (1885), p. 14. Cited in Loomis 4, p. 233.

rise

1046 "Don't rise for me," as the customer said when the man charged two cents more a pound for beef.

US (Pa.), *Alexander's Weekly Messenger* (1839). Cited in Tidwell 2, p. 260.

1047 "Come, get up, it's time to rise," as Baron Rothschild said to the Spanish Funds.

GB, *Punch,* vol. 3 (1842), p. 88. Cited in Loomis 3, p. 112. [Nathan Mayer Rothschild (1777-1836), member of an international banking family, founded a London firm in 1805; made an Austrian baron in 1822, he never formally assumed the title.]

1048 "Come, get up, it's time to rise," as Mr. Squizzle said to his railroad shares.

US (Mass.), *Ballou's Dollar Magazine,* vol. 4 (1856), p. 400. Cited in Loomis 2, p. 17.

1049 "I aspire to rise high in the church," remarked the man who was making alterations in the steeple.

US (Calif.), *The Pelican,* vol. 2, no. 5 (1904), p. 22. Cited in Loomis 4, p. 235.

rising

1050 "Provisions is rising," as the fellow said when he threw up his dinner.

US (Maine), *Yankee Blade* (14 Jan. 1843). Cited in Loomis 2, p. 17.

road

1051 "A hobby road," as the man said when he fell over the cow.

GB, JOHN BROCKETT, *Glossary of Northcountry Words* (1825). Cited in Lean, p. 741. [*Hobby,* rough, uneven.]

1052 "That's a rale road," observed an Irishman referring in an approving manner to a good turnpike.

US (Calif.), *The Wasp,* vol. 3, no. 147 (1879), p. 677. Cited in Loomis 4, p. 231.

1053 "Knobby road," as the man said when he stumbled over a cow.

US, 1913. Cited in Wright, p. 163.

roam

1054   "Some love to roam," as the fellow said ven he legged it away from the constable.

US (Pa.), *Alexander's Weekly Messenger* (1839). Cited in Tidwell 2, p. 261.

rob

1055   "Don't rob yourself," as the farmer said to the lawyer who called him hard names.

US (Pa.), *Alexander's Weekly Messenger* (1839). Cited in Tidwell 2, p. 259; Loomis 2, p. 17.

rock

1056   "This is the rock of ages," said a tired father who had kept the cradle going for two hours, and the baby still awake.

US (Calif.), *Daily Examiner,* vol. 35, no. 59 (1882), p. 4. Cited in Loomis 4, p. 232.

room

1057   "There's plenty of room inside," as the pauper said to the penny loaf.

GB, *Punch,* vol. 2 (1842), p. 193; US (Mass.), *Yankee Blade* (4 May 1848). Cited in Loomis 3, p. 112; Loomis 2, p. 12.

rope

1058   "I thought I had given her rope enough," said Pedley when he hanged his mare.

GB, JOHN RAY, *English Proverbs* (1678). Cited in Lean, p. 745; Wilson, p. 683.

rotation

1059   "Reg'lar rotation," as Jack Ketch said, ven he tied the men up.

GB, CHARLES DICKENS, *Pickwick Papers* (1836). Cited in Maass, p. 211; Whiting 2, p. 3; Baer, p. 180.

rotten

1060   "Something rotten in Denmark," as the fellow said when he swallowed the egg.

US (Pa.), *Alexander's Weekly Messenger* (1839). Cited in Tidwell 2, p. 259. [The reference is to a remark in Shakespeare's *Hamlet* (1601), act 1, scene 4: "Something is rotten in the state of Denmark."]

rough   [See also nos. 1068 and 1069.]

1061   "Rough as it runs," as the boy said when his ass kicked him.

GB, JOHN RAY, *English Proverbs* (1678). Cited in Lean, p. 748.

1062   "Here's where I get away with some rough stuff," said the burglar, as he swiped a roll of sandpaper.

US (Calif.), *The Pelican,* vol. 18, no. 1 (1915), p. 22. Cited in Loomis 4, p. 237.

1063 "Rough, rough," said the dog as he sat on sandpaper.

US (Ky.), c.1950. Cited in Halpert 2, p. 117; Koch 1, p. 180. Recorded in Bryant (Kans., Ky., Nebr.).

roughly

1064 "This is, roughly, what I intend to do," she explained, hitting her husband in the eye.

US (Calif.), *The Pelican,* vol. 30, no. 3 (1924), p. 5. Cited in Loomis 4, p. 241.

roundhouse

1065 As the one-armed lady laid down her ax, she said, "You'll never corner me in the roundhouse."

US (N.J.), c.1950. Cited in Halpert 2, p. 117.

rouser

1066 "Ain't I a rouser?" as the stage driver said ven he vaked the wrong passenger.

US (Pa.), *Alexander's Weekly Messenger* (1839). Cited in Tidwell 2, p. 260.

rub

1067 "Here's where the rub comes," said the washerwoman, as she leaned over her scrub-board.

US (Calif.), *The Pelican,* vol. 29, no. 3 (1923), p. 2. Cited in Loomis 4, p. 240; Mieder, p. 235.

ruff   [See also no. 1063.]

1068 "Ruff! Ruff!" said the dog when he sat on the gravel.

US (Ky.), c.1950. Cited in Halpert 2, p. 117. Recorded in Bryant (Ky.).

1069 "Ruff," cried the dog as he sat on the cactus.

US (Kans.), 1959. Cited in Koch 1, p. 180; Mieder, p. 237. Recorded in Bryant (Kans., Nebr.).

ruined

1070 "I'm ruined," as the old woman said when her house was on fire, "but it's a cold night and I may as well warm myself."

US (Calif.), *California Golden Era,* vol. 18. no. 18 (1870), p. 7. Cited in Loomis 1, p. 305; Loomis 2, p. 17; Browne, p. 202.

rule

1071 "If I can't rule my daughter, I'll rule my goods," quoth Wood.

GB, JOHN RAY, *English Proverbs* (1670); US, 1931. Cited in Lean, p. 746; Taylor 1, p. 210; Wilson, p. 808.

1072 "Poor rule that won't work both ways," as the boy said when he threw the rule back at his master.

US (Mass.), *Ballou's Dollar Magazine,* vol. 3 (1856), p. 99. Cited in Loomis 2, p. 17.

ruler

1073 "Ruler ruin," as the boy said when he threw the teacher's ferule into the stove.

US (Wash.), *Weekly Big Bend Empire* (28 May 1874), p. 3. Cited in Whiting 2, p. 10; Hines, p. 25. [The reference is to a line in John Dryden's *Absalom and Achitophel* (1681): "Resolved to ruin or to rule the state."]

run

1074 "Don't run," as the fellow said ven he gave the constable leg bail.

US (Pa.), *Alexander's Weekly Messenger* (1839). Cited in Tidwell 2, p. 261. [*To give leg bail,* to run away, to take unauthorized leave.]

run down

1075 "I'm getting that run down feeling," said the cow as the freight train bore down on her.

US (Kans.), 1959. Cited in Koch 1, p. 180; Mieder, p. 237. Recorded in Bryant (Kans.).

1076 "Oh, I feel run down," said the man who got hit by a truck.

US (Kans.), 1959. Cited in Koch 2, p. 196; Mieder, p. 238. Recorded in Bryant (Kans.).

runner

1077 "Ye look like a rinner," quo' the de'il to the lobster.

GB, JAMES KELLY, *Scottish Proverbs* (1721). Cited in Lean, p. 752; Wilson, p. 689.

running

1078 "I have been running ever since I was born and I am not tired now," as the brook said to Captain Barclay.

GB, *Punch,* vol. 1 (1841), p. 276. Cited in Loomis 3, p. 111.

1079 "I'm running this!" asserted Mr. Henpeck, starting the water for his morning bath.

US (Calif.), *The Pelican,* vol. 21. no. 8 (1917), p. 4. Cited in Loomis 4, p. 237.

rye

1080 "I'm going through the rye," sang the man, as he gazed at his fast diminishing stock.

US (Calif.), *The Pelican,* vol. 31, no. 7 (1926), p. 26. Cited in Loomis 4, p. 242.

safety

1081 "Upon you depends my safety," confided the ballet dancer to her skirt. "You mean I depend on your safety," corrected the skirt, as the pin tore through the cloth.

US (Calif.), *The Pelican,* vol. 3, no. 1 (1905), p. 14. Cited in Loomis 4, p. 236.

sassafras

1082 "I'd like it better if they'd only scent it with sassyfrass," remarked a Sutter Street boy as he chewed away at the last remnant of a half a pound of carpenter's glue.

US (Calif.), *The Argonaut,* vol. 2, no. 3 (1878), p. 14. Cited in Loomis 4, p. 230.

satin

1083 "Get thee behind me, satin," as the actress said when she kicked the train of her dress out of the way.

US (Calif.), *The Wasp,* vol. 3, no. 131 (1879), p. 426. Cited in Loomis 4, p. 231.

satisfied

1084 "But I'm not nearly satisfied yet," as the actress said to the bishop.

US, LESLIE CHARTERIS, *Enter the Saint* (1930). Cited in Whiting 1, p. 72.

sauce

1085 "None of your sauce," as the boy said to the crab apple.

US (Mass.), *Yankee Blade* (26 Nov. 1845). Cited in Loomis 2, p. 17.

saving

1086 "It's a saving of one half," as the toper said when his wife died.

GB, *Punch,* vol. 2 (1842), p. 218. Cited in Loomis 3, p. 112.

saw

1087 "I saw you," as the wood sawyer said to the log of wood.

US (Pa.), *Alexander's Weekly Messenger* (1839). Cited in Tidwell 2, p. 262.

scent

1088 "You have scent for me and here I am," as the mustard remarked to the Limburger cheese. "Spread yourself if you're strong enough," growled the cheese.

US (Iowa), *Keokuk Gate City* (6 Oct. 1881), p. 16. Cited in Whiting 2, p. 11.

1089 "He'll be scent up for ten days," remarked the skunk pensively, as the police led his victim off.

US (Calif.), *The Pelican,* vol. 12, no. 1 (1912). Cited in Loomis 4, p. 236.

1090 "I certainly make a scent go a long way," remarked the garbage man. "Giddap!"

US (Calif.), *The Pelican,* vol. 32, no. 4 (1926), p. 49. Cited in Loomis 4, p. 242.

1091 "There's a lot of common scents there," said the spitz, as it passed the dog pound.

US (Calif.), *The Pelican,* vol. 37, no. 3 (1930), p. 30. Cited in Loomis 4, p. 243.

1092   As the mama skunk said to her little ones, "Do as I tell you or I'll cut you off without a scent."

US (Mass.), *Harvard Lampoon,* vol. 109 (1935), p. 60. Cited in Whiting 1, p. 75.

scholar

1093   "I'm not much of a scholar, but I can sling ink," as the schoolboy said when he shied the inkstand at his teacher's head.

US (Calif.), *California Golden Era,* vol. 18, no. 16 (1870), p. 7. Cited in Loomis 1, p. 305; Loomis 2, p. 18. [*Shied*, threw.]

scrape

1094   "Vot a scrape I'm in now," as the fish said to the voman who vas rubbing down his back with a knife.

US (Pa.), *Alexander's Weekly Messenger* (1839). Cited in Tidwell 2, p. 260; Mieder, p. 230.

1095   "I've got into an awful scrape," as the chin said to the blunt razor.

US (N.Y.), *Yankee Notions,* vol. 8 (1858), p. 127. Cited in Loomis 2, p. 17.

1096   "I shall never get out of this scrape alive," as the hog said when they were rubbing the bristles of his back with clam shells and scalding water.

US (Calif.), *California Golden Era,* vol. 8, no. 50 (1860), p. 6. Cited in Loomis 2, p. 17.

scream

1097   "Don't touch me, or I'll scream!" as the engine whistle said to the stoker.

GB, *Punch* (Almanack for 1854); US (N.Y.), *Wilkes' Spirit of the Times,* vol. 5 (1861), p. 135. Cited in Loomis 3, p. 113; Loomis 2, p. 17.

1098   "I scream by steam," said the whistle to the locomotive.

US, *Ball of Yarn, or, Queer, Quaint, and Quizzical Stories* (1870). Cited in Browne, p. 202.

sea

1099   Like the old blind man said, "There's no sea to it. It's all dry land."

US (Ky.), c.1950. Cited in Halpert 2, p. 119; Taylor 4, p. 290. Recorded in Bryant (Ky., Tenn.).

seam

1100   "We are not what we seam," as the sewing machine said to the needle.

US (Wis.), *Peck's Sun* (24 Mar. 1881), p. 15. Cited in Whiting 2, p. 9. Recorded in Bryant (N.J.).

seat

1101   "Pray keep your seat," as the cockney sportsman said to the wild rabbit.

GB, *Punch,* vol. 2 (1842), p. 167. Cited in Loomis 3, p. 112.

sediment

1102 "What I sediment," as the river murmured during high water.

US (Iowa), *Keokuk Gate City* (19 May 1881), p. 16. Cited in Whiting 2, p. 10.

see

1103 "Marry, that I would see!" quoth blind Hew.

GB, JOHN HEYWOOD, *The Pardoner and the Frere* (1533). Cited in Lean, p. 747.

1104 "That would I fain see," quoth the blind George of Holloway.

GB, JOHN HEYWOOD, *The Pardoner and the Frere* (1533). Cited in Wilson, p. 238; Lean, p. 747; Stevenson, p. 2481; Taylor 4, p. 287.

1105 "I wish I could see," quoth blind Hugh.

US, WILLIAM WINTHROP (1678), cited in John Winthrop, ed., *Winthrop Papers*, vol. 5, ser. 8 (1863-1892); GB, JONATHAN SWIFT, *Polite Conversation* (1738). Cited in Whiting 5, p. 228; Lean, p. 747; Stevenson, p. 198; Wilson, p. 238; Taylor 4, p. 287.

1106 "We'll say nothing, but we'll see," as blind Pete said to his dog.

GB, *Fraser's Magazine,* vol. 6 (1832), p. 506. Cited in Lean, p. 752; Taylor 4, p. 287.

1107 "Wery glad to see you, indeed, and hope our acquaintance may be long 'un," as the gen'l'm'n said to the fi'pun' note.

GB, CHARLES DICKENS, *Pickwick Papers* (1836); US, 1916. Cited in Maass, p. 210; Marvin, p. 363. [*Fi'pun'*, five-pound.]

1108 "I see through it," as the old lady said when the bottom of her wash-tub fell out.

US (Mass.), *Yankee Blade* (4 Mar. 1848). Cited in Loomis 2, p. 17; Whiting 2, p. 9.

1109 "I'd like to see you," as the blind man said to the policeman when he told him he would take him to the station house if he did not move on.

US (N.Y.), *Yankee Notions,* vol. 10 (1848), p. 60. Cited in Loomis 2, p. 10; Taylor 4, p. 290.

1110 "I see through it now," as the maid servant said when she knocked the bottom out of the pail.

US (N.Y.), *Yankee Notions,* vol. 4 (1855), p. 39. Cited in Loomis 2, p. 17. Recorded in Bryant (Ariz.).

1111 "I see through it now," as the beggar said when a stone was cast directly through the hat he was holding for alms.

US (N.Y.), *Porter's Spirit of the Times,* vol. 1 (1856), p. 243. Cited in Loomis 2, p. 18; Mieder, p. 231.

1112 "Let me see," said the blind man.

GB, CHARLES DICKENS, *Our Mutual Friend* (1864). Cited in Wilson, p. 456; Taylor 4, p. 289.

1113 "I had rather see't than hear tell o't," as blind Pate said.

GB, ALEXANDER HISLOP, *Proverbs of Scotland* (1870). Cited in Lean, p. 745.

1114 "I can see my way through," as the fly says when he's buttin' his head against the winder.
US, PALMER COX, *Squibbs of California* (1874). Cited in Loomis 2, p. 7.

1115 "I see," said the blind man, "I see plainly."
US (Kans.), c.1915–1935. Cited in Mook, p. 184. Recorded in Bryant (Kans., Pa.)

1116 "I see," said the blind man up a great big tree.
US (Kans.), c.1924–1927. Cited in Porter, p. 54.

1117 "I see through you all right," said the astronomer to his faithful telescope.
US (Calif.), *The Pelican,* vol. 31, no. 2 (1925), p. 32. Cited in Loomis 4, p. 241.

1118 "I'll see you," said our hero, as he laid down four aces in a game of strip poker.
US (Calif.), *The Pelican,* vol. 36, no. 1 (1930), p. 31. Cited in Loomis 4, p. 243.

1119 "I see," said the blind man. "You lie," said the dumb man. "Quiet!" said the deaf man.
Can. (Sask.), c.1930. Cited in Halpert 3, p. 123.

1120 "Dang it, now I'm beginning to see," as the blind feller says the time he fell in the kittle of soap.
US, 1933. Cited in Halpert 2, p. 122; Taylor 4, p. 290.

1121 "I see ahead," said the calendar.
US, c.1945–1980. Recorded in Bryant (Kans.).

1122 "I see," said the blind man as he stumbled over the log.
US, c.1945–1980. Recorded in Bryant (Oreg.).

1123 "I see," said the blind man as he walked into the river.
US, c.1945–1980. Recorded in Bryant (Ind., N.Y.).

1124 "I see," said the blind man as he was stuck with a pin.
US, c.1945–1980. Recorded in Bryant (Kans.).

1125 "I see," said the blind man, as the lame man danced.
US, c.1945–1980. Recorded in Bryant (Oreg.).

1126 "I see," said the blind man to his deaf dog.
US, c.1945–1980. Recorded in Bryant (Kans.).

1127 "I see," said the blind man to his deaf dog as they stepped off a cliff.
US, c.1945–1980. Recorded in Bryant (Kans.).

1128 "I see," said the blind man with his head cut off.
US, c.1945–1980. Recorded in Bryant (Wis.).

1129 "I see!" cried the blind man as he peeped through the hole in grandpa's wooden leg.

US (Ky.), c.1950. Cited in Halpert 2, p. 119; Taylor 4, p. 291. Recorded in Bryant (Ky., Ohio, Tenn.).

1130 "I see," said the blind man.

US (Calif.), c.1950. Cited in Halpert 2, p. 118; Taylor 4, p. 290; Whiting 6, p. 56. Recorded in Bryant (Ky., Nebr., Mich., N.Y.).

1131 "I see," said the blind man as he fell in the ditch and picked up a penny and thought he was rich.

US (Ky.), c.1950. Cited in Halpert 2, p. 118; Taylor 4, p. 290; Anon, p. 34. Recorded in Bryant (Idaho, Ill., Tenn.).

1132 "I see," said the blind man as he fell in the well.

US (Ky.), c.1950. Cited in Halpert 2, p. 119; Taylor 4, p. 290.

1133 "I see," said the blind man as he fell over the steam shovel.

US (Ky.), c.1950. Cited in Halpert 2, p. 119; Taylor 4, p. 290.

1134 "I see," said the blind man as he ran down the hill backwards.

US (Ky.), c.1950. Cited in Halpert 2, p. 119; Taylor 4, p. 290.

1135 "I see," said the blind man as he spit through the knot hole in his wooden leg.

US (Ky.), c.1950. Cited in Halpert 2, p. 119; Taylor 4, p. 291.

1136 "I see," said the blind man as he threw away his glasses.

US (Ky.), c.1950. Cited in Halpert 2, p. 119; Taylor 4, p. 290. Recorded in Bryant (Tenn.).

1137 "I see," said the blind man as he walked into the wall.

US (Ky.), c.1950. Cited in Halpert 2, p. 119; Taylor 4, p. 290.

1138 "I see," said the blind man as he was talking to the deaf and dumb woman.

US (Ky.), c.1950. Cited in Halpert 2, p. 119; Taylor 4, p. 290.

1139 "I see," said the blind man talking to his deaf sister over a disconnected telephone.

US (Ky.), c.1950. Cited in Halpert 2, p. 119; Taylor 4, p. 290.

1140 "I see," said the blind man to his deaf daughter.

US (Ky.), c.1950. Cited in Halpert 2, p. 118; Taylor 4, p. 290. Recorded in Bryant (Ohio, Tenn.).

1141 "I see," said the blind man to his deaf daughter as she turned off the television set.

US (Ky.), c.1950. Cited in Halpert 2, p. 118; Taylor 4, p. 290.

1142 "I see," said the blind man to his deaf daughter walking down a blind alley.
US (N.Y.), c.1950. Cited in Halpert 2, p. 118; Taylor 4, p. 290. Recorded in Bryant (Ky., N.Y., Tenn.).

1143 "I see," said the blind man to his deaf and dumb daughter who was knitting socks for her dead husband.
US (Ky.), c.1950. Cited in Halpert 2, p. 118; Taylor 4, p. 290.

1144 "I see," said the blind man to his deaf son; and his dumb son replied, "You're a liar!"
US (Ky.), c.1950. Cited in Halpert 2, p. 118; Taylor 4, p. 290. Recorded in Bryant (Ky.).

1145 "I see," said the blind man to his deaf wife.
US (Ky.), c.1950. Cited in Halpert 2, p. 119; Taylor 4, p. 290.

1146 "I see," said the blind man who couldn't talk.
US (Ky.), c.1950. Cited in Halpert 2, p. 118; Taylor 4, p. 290. Recorded in Bryant (Ky.).

1147 "I see," said the blind man. "You lie," says the beggar.
US (Ky.), c.1950. Cited in Halpert 2, p. 118.

1148 "I see," said the blind man. "You're a liar!" said the dumb.
US (N.Y.), c.1950. Cited in Halpert 2, p. 118; Taylor 4, p. 290.

1149 "Let me see," said the blind man when they led him across the street.
US (Tenn.), c.1950. Cited in Halpert 2, p. 119; Taylor 4, p. 290.

1150 "Now I see," says the blind man.
US (Ky.), c.1950. Cited in Halpert 2, p. 118; Taylor 4, p. 290.

1151 "Oh, I see," said the blind man after he had fallen into the ditch.
US (Ky.), c.1950. Cited in Halpert 2, p. 119; Taylor 4, p. 290.

1152 "See?" said the blind man as he stumbled over his own feet.
US (Ky.), c.1950. Cited in Halpert 2, p. 119; Taylor 4, p. 290. Recorded in Bryant (Oreg.).

1153 "I see," said the blind man, as he bumped into the light pole.
US (Kans.), 1959. Cited in Koch 2, p. 196. Recorded in Bryant (Kans.).

1154 "I see," said the blind man, as he told his deaf daughter to stick her wooden leg out the window to see if it was raining.
US (Kans.), 1959. Cited in Koch 2, p. 196. Recorded in Bryant (Kans.).

1155 "I see," said the blind man to his deaf wife, as he climbed the cherry tree to get an apple for his lame uncle.
US (Kans.), 1959. Cited in Koch 2, p. 196. Recorded in Bryant (Kans.).

1156 "I see," said the blind man, "as I never saw before."
US, 1959. Cited in Taylor 4, p. 290.

1157 "I see," said the blind man with a shake of the wooden leg, "that the price of lumber has gone up."

US, 1959. Cited in Taylor 4, p. 291.

1158 "I see," said the blind man, as he picked up his hammer and saw.

US (Kans.), 1960. Cited in Koch 2, p. 196; Taylor 4, p. 290; Simpson, p. 128; Anon, p. 34. Recorded in Bryant (Ill., Ind., Kans., Oreg.).

1159 "I see," said the blind man to his deaf daughter, as he picked up his hammer and saw.

US (Kans.), 1960. Cited in Koch 2, p. 196. Recorded in Bryant (Kans.).

1160 "I see," said the blind lady to the deaf man over the disconnected telephone.

US (Idaho), 1966. Cited in Anon, p. 238.

1161 "I see," said the blind man who couldn't see at all.

Can. (Nova Scotia), 1982. Cited in Halpert 3, p. 122.

1162 "I see," said the blind man who couldn't see at all and the man with no legs got up and walked away.

Can. (Nova Scotia), 1982. Cited in Halpert 3, p. 122.

seedy

1163 "You look too seedy," chirped the sparrow, as he turned from his meal.

US (Calif.), *The Pelican,* vol. 31, no. 1 (1925), p. 41. Cited in Loomis 4, p. 241.

seen

1164 "I don't remember having seen you before," as the lawyer said to his conscience.

US (Calif., N.Y.), *California Golden Era,* vol. 11, no. 17 (1863), p. 3; *Yankee Notions,* vol. 12 (1863), p. 147. Cited in Loomis 1, p. 304; Loomis 2, p. 18; Mieder, p. 232.

1165 "You haven't seen anything yet," said the man to his wife as she sat behind the post in the theater.

US, c.1945-1980. Recorded in Bryant (Ohio).

see red

1166 "This makes me see red," said the painter, as he was crowned with the paint pail.

US (Calif.), *The Pelican,* vol. 26, no. 8 (1921), p. 48. Cited in Loomis 4, p. 239; Mieder, p. 235.

sense

1167 "I'll take the sense of the meeting," as the man said when he passed round the hat.

US (Mass.), *Yankee Blade* (29 Jan. 1848). Cited in Loomis 2, p. 18.

service

1168 "Perfect service," murmured the defendant, as the papers were handed to him.

US (Calif.), *The Pelican,* vol. 27, no. 6 (1921), p. 8. Cited in Loomis 4, p. 239.

set

1169 "You are a 'sharp set'," as Joe said to the man at the dinner, who, for want of a chair, was seated on the edge of a shingle.

US (Pa.), *Alexander's Weekly Messenger* (1839). Cited in Tidwell 2, p. 262.

1170 "I am engaged for this set," said the hen to the rooster as she went clucking away.

US (Oreg.), *Mountain Sentinel* (6 Mar. 1880), p. 4. Cited in Hines, p. 25.

settle

1171 "Are you prepared to settle?" as the coffee said to the fish skin.

US (Mass.), *Yankee Blade* (8 Jan. 1845). Cited in Loomis 2, p. 18.

shadow

1172 "What a long shadow I cast!" hoots an owl gazing at an eclipse of the sun.

US (Wash.), *Walla Walla Union* (30 May 1874), p. 4. Cited in Hines, p. 25.

shake

1173 "Let's shake," as the ague said to the earthquake.

US (N.Y.), *Wit and Wisdom* (2 Jun. 1881), p. 16. Cited in Whiting 2, p. 10.

1174 "Shake, old man," said the chill to the feverish individual, giving him the grip.

US (Calif.), *The Pelican,* vol. 2, no. 5 (1904), p. 14. Cited in Loomis 4, p. 235.

shaken

1175 "To be shaken when taken," muttered the man while chasing the boy who was taking his fruit.

US (Mass.), *Yankee Blade* (12 Jan. 1850). Cited in Loomis 2, p. 18.

shame

1176 "Shame fa' the couple," as the cow said to her fore feet.

GB, JAMES KELLY, *Scottish Proverbs* (1721). Cited in Lean, p. 748.

1177 "Shame fa' the couple," quoth the crow to her feet.

GB, JAMES KELLY, *Scottish Proverbs* (1721). Cited in Lean, p. 748.

1178 "Shame fall the ordiner," quoth the cat to the cordiner.

GB, JAMES KELLY, *Scottish Proverbs* (1721). Cited in Lean, p. 749. [*Ordiner,* ordinary; *cordiner,* shoemaker.]

sheepish

1179 "I feel sheepish in this darned thing," muttered the Sophomore who had just bought one of those woolly angora sport sweaters.

US (Calif.), *The Pelican,* vol. 28, no. 8 (1923). Cited in Loomis 4, p. 240.

sheer

1180 "Come, sheer off," as the ram said to the man who was cutting off his wool.

US (Calif., N.Y.), *California Golden Era,* vol. 11, no. 12 (1863), p. 5; *Yankee Notions,* vol. 12 (1863), p. 101. Cited in Loomis 1, p. 304; Loomis 2, p. 18.

shine

1181 "That's where I shine," said the young man, as he showed his blue suit to the tailor.

US (Calif.), *The Pelican,* vol. 16, no. 1 (1914). Cited in Loomis 4, p. 237.

1182 "Here's where I shine," said the bootblack, as a customer hove into sight.

US (Calif.), *The Pelican,* vol. 31, no. 2 (1925), p. 13. Cited in Loomis 4, p. 241.

shot

1183 "Combination shot," murmured the lady cue artist, as she leaned too far over the billiard table.

US (Calif.), *The Pelican,* vol. 26, no. 6 (1921), p. 40. Cited in Loomis 4, p. 239.

shower

1184 "Then one afternoon came the first shower, only a little one," as the girl said of the baby.

GB, MICHAEL BURR, *A Fossicker in Anglia* (1933). Cited in Whiting 1, p. 74.

shucks

1185 "Shucks!" cried the motorist, as he skidded into the corn field.

US (Calif.), *The Pelican,* vol. 31, no. 4 (1925), p. 67. Cited in Loomis 4, p. 242.

sick

1186 "You make me sick," said the man to the germ.

US (Kans.), 1959. Cited in Koch 1, p. 180; Mieder, p. 238. Recorded in Bryant (Kans.).

sickness

1187 "Who can help sickness?" quo' the drunken wife when she fell into the gutter.

GB, THOMAS FULLER, *Gnomologia* (1732); US, 1916. Cited in Lean, p. 752; Marvin, p. 364.

side

1188 "You'll split my sides," as the oak-tree said to the lightning.
GB, *Punch,* vol. 2 (1842), p. 31. Cited in Loomis 3, p. 111.

1189 As the people said when Lady Godiva rode naked down the streets sidesaddle, "Hooray for our side."
US (Calif., N.Mex.), 1940. Cited in Hines, p. 18.

sight

1190 "Out of sight, out of mind," said the warden as the escaped lunatic disappeared over the hill.
US (Calif.), *The Pelican,* vol. 15, no. 1 (1913). Cited in Loomis 4, p. 237; Mieder, p. 235.

silence

1191 "Silence that dreadful belle," as the husband said when his wife was giving him the length of her tongue.
US (Pa.), *Alexander's Weekly Messenger* (1839). Cited in Tidwell 2, p. 262. [The reference is to a remark in Shakespeare's *Othello* (1602–1604), act 2, scene 3: "Silence that dreadful bell! it frights the isle from her propriety."]

1192 "Silence gives consent," as the man said when he kissed the dumb woman.
US (Mass.), *Yankee Blade* (27 May 1846). Cited in Loomis 2, p. 18; Mieder, p. 232. Recorded in Bryant (N.J.).

1193 "Silence that dreadful bell," as the loafer said on board the steamboat when the steward was ringing all hands up to the captain's office to settle.
US (Mass.), *Yankee Blade* (11 Oct. 1851). Cited in Loomis 2, p. 5. Recorded in Bryant (N.Y.). [See note, no. 1191.]

1194 "Silence that dreadful belle," as the lover said when he was scolded by his mistress for kissing the maid.
US (Mass.), *Yankee Blade* (11 Oct. 1851). Cited in Loomis 2, p. 5. Recorded in Bryant (N.Y.). [See note, no. 1191.]

1195 "Silence that dreadful belle," as the man said to the loud sneering miss in the Howard Athenaeum.
US (Mass.), *Ballou's Dollar Magazine,* vol. 14 (1861), p. 298. Cited in Loomis 2, p. 8. Recorded in Bryant (N.Y.). [See note, no. 1191.]

sinews

1196 "I think I know now what people mean when they talk about the sinews of war," said the soldier who was making a determined effort to masticate his first ration of army beef.
US (Calif.), *The Argonaut,* vol. 43, no. 1113 (1898), p. 16. Cited in Loomis 4, p. 235.

sinking

1197 "This is sinking pretty low," gasped the pretty girl, as she went down for the third time.

US (Calif.), *The Pelican,* vol. 26, no. 6 (1921), p. 40. Cited in Loomis 4, p. 239.

sleep

1198 "There's nothin' so refreshin' as sleep, Sir," as the servant-girl said afore she drank the egg-cup-full o' laudanum.

GB, CHARLES DICKENS, *Pickwick Papers* (1836). Cited in Maass, p. 211; Stevenson, p. 2480; Baer, p. 176.

sleeping

1199 "O lassie, are thou sleeping yet," as the owl said to the chicken one night.

US (Pa.), *Alexander's Weekly Messenger* (1839). Cited in Tidwell 2, p. 260.

slip

1200 "Here's where I slip something over on myself," said the girl, as she reached for her kimono.

US (Calif.), *The Pelican,* vol. 16, no. 4 (1914). Cited in Loomis 4, p. 237.

1201 "If I make a slip, I'm undone," cried the knot desperately.

US (Calif.), *The Pelican,* vol. 21, no. 5 (1917), p. 5. Cited in Loomis 4, p. 80.

slugs

1202 "Loaded with slugs," as the gardener said to the wall flower.

GB, *Punch,* vol. 2 (1842), p. 96; US (N.Y.), *Yankee Notions,* vol. 11 (1861), p. 25. Cited in Loomis 3, p. 111; Loomis 2, p. 18.

smart

1203 "You may think you're smart, but I think you're making some pretty bad breaks," said the tragedian, as the audience pelted him with late lamented hen fruit.

US (Calif.), *The Argonaut,* vol. 33, no. 18 (1893), p. 15. Cited in Loomis 4, p. 234. [*Hen fruit,* eggs.]

smell

1204 "My, what an offal smell!" said the maid, as she jammed on the top of the garbage can.

US (Calif.), *The Pelican,* vol. 14, no. 3 (1913). Cited in Loomis 4, p. 237.

smile

1205 "Leave me with a smile," murmured the victim, as the yegg frisked his clothes.

US (Calif.), *The Pelican,* vol. 17, no. 8 (1922), p. 21. Cited in Loomis 4, p. 240. [*Yegg,* thief, burglar.]

smoke

1206 "Do you smoke?" as the snuffers said to the candle.

US (Pa.), *Alexander's Weekly Messenger* (1839). Cited in Tidwell 2, p. 260.

1207 "This is what I call volumes of smoke," grinned the city editor as the library burned to the ground.

US (Calif.), *The Pelican*, vol. 3, no. 1 (1905), p. 9. Cited in Loomis 4, p. 236.

1208 "Holy smoke!" ejaculated the Rev. McSpivis as he inhaled his White Owl.

US (Calif.), *The Pelican*, vol. 27, no. 2 (1921), p. 18. Cited in Loomis 4, p. 239. [*White Owl*, brand of cigar.]

smoked

1209 As Joan of Arc said when she was burned at the stake, "I've never smoked more and enjoyed it less."

US (Calif.), 1959. Cited in Hines, p. 18. [A Camel cigarette advertising slogan: "Are you smoking more and enjoying it less?"]

smother

1210 "Let me kiss him for his smother," as the expiring Desdemona spoke of the jealous Moor.

US (N.Y.), *New York News* (18 Aug. 1881), p. 16. Cited in Whiting 2, p. 10.

snap

1211 "Quite a cold snap," as the fox remarked when the trap took him in.

US (Calif.), *The Argonaut*, vol. 5, no. 4 (1879), p. 4. Cited in Loomis 4, p. 231.

1212 "Snap out of it!" he yelled, ripping open a box of Zu Zus.

US (Calif.), *The Pelican*, vol. 27, no. 8 (1921), p. 26. Cited in Loomis 4, p. 240. [*Zu Zus*, probably a brand of ginger snaps.]

sneezed

1213 "Not to be sneezed at," as the loafer said ven he took a pinch of pepper, instead of snuff.

US (Pa.), *Alexander's Weekly Messenger* (1839). Cited in Tidwell 2, p. 259; Mieder, p. 230.

snuff

1214 "I'm up to snuff," as the wick said to the snuffers.

US (Pa.), *Alexander's Weekly Messenger* (1839). Cited in Tidwell 2, p. 260; Mieder, p. 231.

1215 "He's up to snuff," explained the old lady when her husband arose to take a pinch from the box which lay on the mantlepiece.

US (Calif.), *The Wasp*, vol. 3, no. 147 (1879), p. 677. Cited in Loomis 4, p. 231.

so

1216 "So what," said the monkey as the sewing machine ran over his tail.

US (Kans.), 1961. Cited in Sackett and Koch, p. 96. Recorded in Bryant (Kans.).

soap

1217 "No soap," remarked the room-mate as he washed with Sapolio.
US (Calif.), *The Pelican,* vol. 31, no. 1 (1925), p. 57. Cited in Loomis 4, p. 241.

soar

1218 "Nothing makes me soar," said the amateur aviator, as his nineteenth engine failed to get the machine off the ground.
US (Calif.), *The Pelican,* vol. 13, no. 4 (1912). Cited in Loomis 4, p. 237.

sole

1219 "I'm sole manager of this concern," as the cobbler said when engaged upon a pair of boots.
US (Mass.), *Yankee Blade* (1 Sep. 1849). Cited in Loomis 2, p. 19.

1220 "The iron has entered my sole," said the shoe to the shoemaker. "I give thee my awl, I can no more," was the reply.
US (N.Y.), *Yankee Notions,* vol. 15 (1866), p. 164. Cited in Loomis 2, p. 18. Recorded in Bryant (Ill., N.Y.).

something

1221 "There is something in it," quoth the fellow, when he drunk it, dish-clout and all.
GB, THOMAS FULLER, *Gnomologia* (1732); US, 1948. Cited in Stevenson, p. 2480.

1222 "Well, there is something in that," as the man said when he tried to put on his boot with a kitten in it.
US (Calif.), *California Spirit of the Times* (18 Mar. 1871). Cited in Loomis 2, p. 19.

1223 "Well there is something in that," as the girl said when she put on her stocking.
GB, H. R. BELWARD, *Vulgarian Atrocities* (1876). Cited in Lean, p. 751.

1224 "It would be something to one man; but for two, it is but a small portion," as Alexander said of the world.
US, 1916. Cited in Marvin, p. 357.

1225 "There's something in this," remarked the garbage man, as he lifted the can to his shoulder.
US (Calif.), *The Pelican,* vol. 32, no. 7 (1927), p. 6. Cited in Loomis 4, p. 242.

1226 "Something is better than nothing," said the wolf when he swallowed the louse.
US, 1931. Cited in Taylor 1, p. 205; Mieder, p. 223.

son

1227 "I am watching the son's raise," said the fond mother, as she gazed at her boy's mustache.
US (Calif.), *Daily Examiner,* vol. 35, no. 157 (1882), p. 4. Cited in Loomis 4, p. 232.

sorrow

1228   "I have a silent sorrow here," as the woman said whose only child was a mute.

US (Calif.), *The Argonaut,* vol. 5, no. 16 (1879), p. 5. Cited in Loomis 4, p. 231.

1229   "There's sma' sorrow at our parting," as the auld meer said to the broken cart.

GB, 1903. Cited in Lean, p. 750. [*Meer,* mare.]

sour

1230   "Sour plums," quoth the toad when he could not climb the tree.

GB, JAMES KELLY, *Scottish Proverbs* (1678); US, 1916. Cited in Lean, p. 743; Marvin, p. 359.

1231   "The grapes are sour," said the fox and couldn't reach them.

GB, 1903; US, 1948. Cited in Lean, p. 749; Taylor 2, p. 317. Recorded in Bryant (Okla.).

source

1232   "Just consider the source," said the man who was kicked by a mule.

US (Ky.), c.1950. Cited in Halpert 2, p. 118; Mieder, p. 237.

speaking

1233   "I was not speaking to you," as the chap said to the echo.

US (Mass.), *Yankee Blade* (3 Jun. 1848). Cited in Loomis 2, p. 19.

spirit

1234   "I shall hereby prevent the use of ardent spirits," as the grocer said when he watered his rum.

US (N.Y.), *Yankee Notions,* vol. 1 (1852), p. 262. Cited in Whiting 2, p. 8; Loomis 2, p. 19.

1235   "I am your father's spirit!" as the bottle of whisky said to the Glasgow weaver's boy when he found it under the bed one Saturday night.

US (Mass.), *Ballou's Dollar Magazine,* vol. 2 (1855), p. 600. Cited in Loomis 2, p. 19.

1236   "He returns in good spirits," as the British said when the body of Gen. Pakenham came home from the Battle of New Orleans in a barrel of rum.

US (N.Y.), *Yankee Notions,* vol. 8 (1859), p. 21. Cited in Loomis 2, p. 19. [Sir Edward Michael Pakenham, British major-general, was killed at New Orleans in 1815.]

1237   "The flesh is willing but the spirit is weak," as the toper said when his rum jug froze up.

US (N.Y.), *Yankee Notions,* vol. 10 (1860), p. 148. Cited in Loomis 2, p. 19.

1238 "That, sir, is the spirit of the press," said Mrs. Jinks, as she handed Nipper a glass of cider.

US (Calif.), *California Golden Era,* vol. 18, no. 5 (1869), p. 7. Cited in Loomis 1, p. 305; Loomis 2, p. 19.

1239 "I'm in the best of spirits," as the straw said to the toper.

US, PAT ROONEY, *Quaint Conundrums and Funny Gags* (1879). Cited in Browne, p. 202.

1240 "My spirits are getting low," muttered the travelling salesman, as he glanced at the gauge on the flask.

US (Calif.), *The Pelican,* vol. 12, no. 4 (1912). Cited in Loomis 4, p. 53.

1241 "I'll take it in the spirit in which it was sent," as the vicar said to the old lady who gave him brandied peaches for Christmas.

US, Stuart Palmer, *The Puzzle of the Silver Persian* (1934). Cited in Whiting 1, p. 75; Mieder, p. 236.

1242 "That's the spirit," cried the medium, as the table began to rise.

US (Calif.), *The Pelican,* vol. 45, no. 4 (1937), p. 12. Cited in Loomis 4, p. 244; Mieder, p. 235.

spit

1243 "Spit is such a horrid word," said the pig, as he was about to be barbecued.

US (Calif.), *The Pelican,* vol. 47, no. 2 (1940), p. 32. Cited in Loomis 4, p. 244.

splutter

1244 "There's an unco splutter," quoth the cow in the gutter.

GB, ALLAN CUNNINGHAM, *Glossary to Burns* (1834); US, 1916. Cited in Lean, p. 750; Marvin, p. 363. [*Unco,* uncouth, strange.]

spoils

1245 "The spoils of a victory!" screams a hardy hawk, pouncing on an elephant struck by lightning.

US (Wash.), *Walla Walla Union* (30 May 1874), p. 4. Cited in Hines, p. 25.

spotted

1246 "I sure spotted that one," he said, as he upset the punch on her dress.

US (Calif.), *The Pelican,* vol. 31, no. 5 (1926), p. 34. Cited in Loomis 4, p. 242.

spring

1247 "Come, gentle spring," says the burglar, as he picks the locks.

US (Calif.), *The Pelican,* vol. 31, no. 1 (1925), p. 57. Cited in Loomis 4, p. 241.

1248 "This is the spring of the year," exclaimed the lady, as she jumped from the peak of the Woolworth Building.

US (Calif.), *The Pelican,* vol. 31, no. 6 (1926), p. 26. Cited in Loomis 4, p. 242.

standing

1249   "You're a man of long standing in this community," said the conductor to the strap-hanger.

US (Calif.), *The Pelican,* vol. 31, no. 5 (1926), p. 10. Cited in Loomis 4, p. 242.

stars

1250   "Nice putty stars, but lord you," as the gal said to her feller, "if you could only see the bunch that's right over our front door."

US, JOHN NEAL, *Down-Easters,* vol. 1 (1833), p. 135. Cited in Whiting 2, p. 6.

stay

1251   "Nay, stay," quoth Stringer, when his neck was in the halter.

US, 1931. Cited in Taylor 1, p. 210.

steal

1252   "That is worthy of my steal," as the fellow said when he appropriated his neighbor's time piece.

US (Calif.), *California Golden Era,* vol. 14, no. 15 (1866), p. 4. Cited in Loomis 2, p. 19; Loomis 1, p. 304.

steam

1253   "Put on the steam! I am in haste," cried a snail that had crept into a railroad car.

US (Wash.), *Walla Walla Union* (30 May 1874), p. 1. Cited in Hines, p. 23; Mieder, p. 234.

steel

1254   "I come to steel," as the rat said to the trap. "And I spring to embrace you," as the steel replied to the rat.

US (Mass.), *Ballou's Dollar Magazine,* vol. 11 (1860), p. 598. Cited in Loomis 2, p. 19.

steers

1255   "Accept these steers," as the cattle-dealer said to the butcher.

US (Calif.), *The Wasp,* vol. 11, no. 383 (1882), p. 7. Cited in Loomis 4, p. 233.

step

1256   "Pray, good folk, let us not step on each other," said the cock to the horse.

GB, DANIEL DEFOE, *The Shortest Way with Dissenters* (1702); US, 1916. Cited in Taylor 1, p. 210; Marvin, p. 357; Stevenson, p. 2480. Recorded in Bryant (N.Y., Pa.).

1257   "I was not aware any such step was on foot," remarked the tramp when he was kicked into the street.

US (Calif.), *The Wasp,* vol. 17, no. 543 (1886), p. 10. Cited in Loomis 4, p. 233.

1258   The ant said to the elephant, "Let's be sports and not step on each other."
US, c.1945-1980. Recorded in Bryant (Ill.).

stew

1259   "I am all in a stew," as the shin bone said to the soup kettle.
US (Pa.), *The Casket,* vol. 5 (1830), p. 377. Cited in Loomis 5, p. 51.

stick

1260   "I'll stick to you," as the treacle said to the fly.
GB, *Punch,* vol. 2 (1842), p. 31. Cited in Loomis 3, p. 111. Recorded in Bryant (Ark.). [*Treacle,* sweet, cloying syrup; molasses.]

stiff

1261   "Shove that big stiff out of the way," said the undertaker to his assistant.
US (Calif.), *The Pelican,* vol. 38, no. 8 (1932), p. 36. Cited in Loomis 4, p. 243.

1262   "I'm bored stiff," said the dead man.
US, c.1945-1980. Recorded in Bryant (Kans.).

still life

1263   "Ah well," said the painter, preparing a fresh canvas, "while there's still life there's hope."
US (Calif.), *The Pelican,* vol. 36, no. 7 (1930), p. 22. Cited in Loomis 4, p. 243.

stock

1264   "Stocks are firm," as the rogue said when he had his feet in them.
US (Mass.), *Yankee Blade* (16 Feb. 1850). Cited in Loomis 2, p. 19.

1265   "My stock is going down!" said Solomon, as he cast his wife number 52 into the Dead Sea.
US (Calif.), *The Pelican,* vol. 27, no. 6 (1921), p. 10. Cited in Loomis 4, p. 239.

stood

1266   "I've stood as much as I can," as the bishop said to the actress.
US, LESLIE CHARTERIS, *Enter the Saint* (1930). Cited in Whiting 1, p. 73.

1267   "I've stood about enough," said the humorist, as they amputated his legs.
US (Calif.), *The Pelican,* vol. 46, no. 8 (1940), p. 27. Cited in Loomis 4, p. 244.

stork

1268   "I'm stork mad," said the father of fifteen children.
US (Calif.), *The Pelican,* vol. 44, no. 5 (1937), p. 14. Cited in Loomis 4, p. 244; Mieder, p. 235.

story

1269 "That was a pretty hard story to swallow," said the cellar when the upper part of the house fell into it.

US (Calif.), *The Argonaut,* vol. 31, no. 18 (1892), p. 15. Cited in Loomis 4, p. 234.

straightforward

1270 "I'm a straight forward man," as the toper said when he pitched into the gutter, "and nothin' else."

US (Mass.), *Yankee Blade* (6 May 1848). Cited in Loomis 2, p. 19.

1271 "Could anything be more straightforward?" as the actress said when the bishop showed her his pass-book.

US, LESLIE CHARTERIS, *Wanted for Murder* (1931). Cited in Whiting 1, p. 72.

strain

1272 "That 'strain' again," as the Poor-Law Commissioner generously said to the water-gruel sieve.

GB, *Punch,* vol. 1 (1841), p. 101. Cited in Loomis 3, p. 111.

strained

1273 "There now! It's all gut to be strained over agin!" as the old woman said when the dog peed in her milk pan.

US, JOHN NEAL, *Down-Easters,* vol. 1 (1833), p. 135. Cited in Whiting 2, p. 6; Taylor and Whiting, p. 409.

1274 "I feel strained," said the cat as he ran through the screen door.

US (Kans.), 1959. Cited in Koch 1, p. 180; Mieder, p. 237. Recorded in Bryant (Kans., Nebr.).

straps

1275 "Cut my straps and let me go to glory," as Dow Jr. exclaimed when he took his first favorite kiss.

US (Mass.), *Yankee Blade* (22 Jan. 1850). Cited in Loomis 2, p. 7.

stream

1276 "Flow out sweet stream of Jordon," as the loafer said ven he bored into the whiskey barrel.

US (Pa.), *Alexander's Weekly Messenger* (1839). Cited in Tidwell 2, p. 261.

strikes

1277 "That strikes me werry forcibly," as the chap said vot got poked over by the windmill.

US (Pa.), *Alexander's Weekly Messenger* (1839). Cited in Tidwell 2, p. 261.

striking

1278 "You have a very striking countenance," as the donkey said to the elephant when he hit him over the back with his trunk.

US (Mass.), *Ballou's Dollar Magazine,* vol. 8 (1858), p. 600. Cited in Loomis 2, p. 19.

1279 "What a striking likeness," said an ex-prizefighter on seeing Sullivan's photograph.

US (Calif.), *The Wasp,* vol. 11, no. 383 (1883), p. 7. Cited in Loomis 4, p. 233. [John L. Sullivan, American boxer, won the heavyweight championship on 7 February 1882, fighting with bare knuckles.]

stringing

1280 "Now, you quit stringing me," said Alkali Ike, as the rope tightened across the cottonwood limb.

US (Calif.), *The Pelican,* vol. 26, no. 2 (1920), p. 13. Cited in Loomis 4, p. 238.

strong

1281 "The victory is not always to the strong," as the boy said when he killed a skunk with a brickbat.

US (Mass.), *Yankee Blade* (6 May 1848). Cited in Loomis 2, p. 19; Whiting 2, p. 9. Recorded in Bryant (Ariz.).

1282 "I'm not so strong as I used to be," as the onion remarked after it was boiled.

US (Calif.), *California Golden Era,* vol. 15, no. 6 (1867), p. 2. Cited in Loomis 1, p. 304; Loomis 2, p. 19.

stubborn

1283 "He's not stubborn, he just don't give a damn," as the old man said as he built a fire under his mule and the mule still wouldn't move.

US (N.C.), c.1950. Cited in Halpert 2, p. 119.

stuck

1284 "If I am stuck up, I ain't proud," said the beetle when he was pinned to the wall.

US (N.Y.), *Yankee Notions,* vol. 2 (1853), p. 28. Cited in Loomis 2, p. 19.

1285 "It looks like I'm stuck for the drinks," moaned the penniless toper, as the bartender stabbed him through the heart.

US (Calif.), *The Pelican,* vol. 45, no. 2 (1937), p. 3. Cited in Loomis 4, p. 244.

stunt

1286 "That's a darn good stunt," said a man in the gallery when the dwarf comedian left the stage.

US (Calif.), *The Pelican,* vol. 1, no. 2 (1903), p. 7. Cited in Loomis 4, p. 235.

style

1287 "I'm sitting on the style, Mary," as the man said when he sat down on his wife's new bonnet.

US (N.Y.), *Yankee Notions,* vol. 2 (1853), p. 88. Cited in Loomis 2, p. 19.

1288 "Can't say I admire your style of acting," as the landlady said to the strolling player.

US (Calif.), *California Golden Era,* vol. 4, no. 3 (1855), p. 6. Cited in Loomis 2, p. 4.

subject

1289 "We will treat this subject from both sides," cried the king, as he walked around his faithful follower and ordered another scotch and soda.

US (Calif.), *The Pelican,* vol. 21, no. 8 (1914), p. 4. Cited in Loomis 4, p. 237.

sucker

1290 "I'm a done sucker," as the boy said when his mother weaned him.

US (Mass.), *Yankee Blade* (20 May 1848), p. 48. Cited in Loomis 2, p. 19.

sufficient

1291 "That's sufficient," as Tom Haynes said when he saw the elephant.

US, AUGUSTUS LONGSTREET, "Georgia Theatrics" (1835), in F. J. Meine, *Tall Tales of the Southwest* (1930). Cited in Whiting 2, p. 7; Stevenson, p. 2481.

suit

1292 "Won't suit me at all," as the man said to the tailor who refused him credit.

US (N.Y.), *New York News* (8 Sep. 1881), p. 5. Cited in Whiting 2, p. 11.

suite

1293 "In this suite by and by," is what the young lady sang, while contemplating apartments at a leading hotel, which she was to occupy after her marriage, a few days before the event.

US (Calif.), *The Argonaut,* vol. 2, no. 6 (1878), p. 14. Cited in Loomis 4, p. 230.

sum

1294 "I guess that's a going sum," thought the youth with a Queen, as he paid the waiter.

US (Calif.), *The Pelican,* vol. 2, no. 1 (1904), p. 15. Cited in Loomis 4, p. 235.

Sunday

1295 "Sunday is the strongest day of the week," said the boy, as he faced six week days.

US (Kans.), 1959. Cited in Koch 2, p. 196. Recorded in Bryant (Kans.).

sun struck

1296　"Be careful or you may get sun struck," as the fellow said when he squared off to his father.

US (Pa.), *Alexander's Weekly Messenger* (1830). Cited in Tidwell 2, p. 260.

support

1297　"I hope you will be able to support me," said a young lady while walking one evening with her intended, during a somewhat slippery state of the sidewalk.

US (Mass.), *Yankee Blade* (12 Jan. 1853). Cited in Loomis 2, p. 19.

1298　"I can't support you any longer," as the rotten bridge said to the elephant.

US (N.Y.), *Yankee Notions,* vol. 12 (1863), p. 221. Cited in Loomis 2, p. 19.

sure

1299　"Just to make sure," as the soldier said to Robert Bruce when he stabbed the Red Comyn in church.

GB, C.G.L. DU CANN, *Secret Hand* (1929). Cited in Whiting 1, p. 75. [Sir John Comyn the younger was stabbed by Robert Bruce (Robert I, king of Scotland) on 10 February 1306 in a church at Dumfries. Sir John, a redhead with a ruddy complexion, was called the Red Comyn to distinguish him from his father.]

surprised

1300　As the girl said to the soldier, "You'll be surprised."

US, EARL BALL, *Scarlet Fox* (1927). Cited in Whiting 1, p. 74.

suspect

1301　"I speck so," said the fly, as it lit on the wallpaper.

US (Pa.), c.1915-1935. Cited in Mook, p. 183. Recorded in Bryant (Kans., Pa.).

1302　"I speck not," said the constipated fly.

US (Tex.), 1956. Cited in Hendricks, p. 287.

1303　"I speck so," said the fly as he flew away from the garbage.

US, c.1945-1980. Recorded in Bryant (Kans., Nebr.).

suspense

1304　"I'm sorry to put you in suspense," as the hangman said to the prisoner.

US (Pa.), *Alexander's Weekly Messenger* (1839). Cited in Tidwell 2, p. 260.

1305　"What an awful state of suspense," as the fellow said when he was hanging by the neck.

US (Pa.), *Alexander's Weekly Messenger* (1839). Cited in Tidwell 2, p. 260; Hines, p. 25; Mieder, p. 234.

1306　"The suspense will kill me," as the murderer said upon the gallows.

US (Calif.), *The Wasp,* vol. 7, no. 269 (1881), p. 202. Cited in Loomis 4, p. 232.

suspicion

1307 "I am above all suspicion," chuckled the burglar in the rafters as the old lady poked under the bed with the broom.

US (Calif.), *The Pelican,* vol. 2, no. 5 (1904), p. 22. Cited in Loomis 4, p. 235.

swarm

1308 "It's 'swarm day for all of us," as the farmer remarked, as he mopped his face and found his bees ready for flight.

US (Pa.), *Philadelphia Item* (11 Aug. 1881), p. 8. Cited in Whiting 2, p. 10.

sweeping

1309 "This is a sweeping catastrophe," as the man said when his wife knocked him down with a broom.

US (Mass.), *Yankee Blade* (29 Jan. 1848). Cited in Loomis 2, p. 20.

sweet

1310 "'Tis sweet at evening hour," as the old coon said when he came down to the sugar maple to drink the sap bucket.

US (Maine), *Yankee Blade* (29 Oct. 1842). Cited in Loomis 2, p. 20.

1311 "Revenge is sweet," as the boy said who had been whipped by a grocer while he was stealing his sugar.

US (N.Y.), *Wilkes' Spirit of the Times,* vol. 6 (1862), p. 278. Cited in Loomis 2, p. 20.

1312 "Sweet are the uses of adversity," as the fly said when he fell into the molasses jug.

US (Calif.), *The Wasp,* vol. 11, no. 383 (1883), p. 7. Cited in Loomis 4, p. 233.

swells

1313 "Ah, at last I am in with the swells," quoth the social striver as she fell out of the boat.

US (Calif.), *The Pelican,* vol. 27, no. 2 (1921), p. 13. Cited in Loomis 4, p. 239.

swill

1314 "Where there's a swill there's a way," as the hog said when he rooted the back gate off its hinges to come at the kitchen swill barrel.

US (Iowa), *McGregor News* (14 Jul. 1881), p. 16. Cited in Whiting 2, p. 10.

swindler

1315 "Oh, you swindler, you've a stone inside you!" as the wasp said when he ate into the plum.

US (Wash.), *Weekly Big Bend Empire* (28 Mar. 1889), p. 3. Cited in Hines, p. 25.

sword

1316 "Ye're a fine sword," quo' the fool to the wheat braird.
GB, 1903. Cited in Lean, p. 752. [*Wheat braird,* first shoot of wheat.]

tail

1317 "This is the end of my tail," as the monkey said when he backed into the lawn-mower.
US (N.Y.), 1940. Cited in Thompson, p. 502; Stevenson, p. 2481. Recorded in Bryant (Ill.).

take

1318 "Take what you want," says God, "but pay for it."
Can., c.1945-1980. Recorded in Bryant (Ont.).

taken in

1319 "Young men taken in and done for," as the shark said to the ship's crew.
GB, *Punch,* vol. 3 (1842), p. 88. Cited in Loomis 3, p. 112.

taken up

1320 "I'm all taken up with my work," said the elevator man.
US (Calif.), *The Pelican,* vol. 31, no. 5 (1926), p. 5. Cited in Loomis 4, p. 242.

tale

1321 "Vy, sir, it's a long tale to tell," as the highvayman said ven the priest asked him an account of his crimes.
US (Pa.), *Alexander's Weekly Messenger* (1837). Cited in Tidwell 2, p. 258.

1322 "My tale is ended," as the tadpole said when he turned into a frog.
US (N.Y.), *Yankee Notions,* vol. 3 (1854), p. 5. Cited in Loomis 2, p. 20. Recorded in Bryant (Ohio).

1323 "Mine is no idle tale," said the freshman, as he leaned over for another whack.
US (Calif.), *The Pelican,* vol. 34, no. 4 (1928), p. 68. Cited in Loomis 4, p. 243.

1324 "My tale is told," said the little bear as he sat on the ice.
US (Tex.), 1956. Cited in Hendricks, p. 356; Koch 1, p. 180; Mieder, p. 237. Recorded in Bryant (Kans.).

tant mieux

1325 "Tant mieux," as the publican said when he watered the beer.
GB, *Punch,* vol. 49 (1865), p. 105. Cited in Loomis 3, p. 113. [*Tant mieux* (French), "so much the better."]

taste

1326 "What do you think of my taste?" as the fly said ven he got into the man's mouth.

US (Pa.), *Alexander's Weekly Messenger* (1839). Cited in Tidwell 2, p. 261.

1327 "We're both matters of taste," as the gingerbread said to the fine picture.

US (N.Y.), *Yankee Notions,* vol. 3 (1854), p. 142. Cited in Whiting 2, p. 4. Recorded in Bryant (Ohio).

1328 "Everyone to his taste," as Morris said when he kissed the cow.

GB, JAMES JOYCE, *Ulysses* (1922), p. 374 (1934 ed.). Cited in Whiting 6, p. 395.

1329 "Every man to his own taste," as the farmer said when he kissed the pig.

US (N.Y.), C. AIKEN, *Blue Voyage* (1927), p. 352. Cited in Whiting 6, p. 395.

1330 "Everyone to his own taste," as the farmer said when he kissed the cow.

US, V. STARRETT, *Seaports* (1928). Cited in Whiting 1, p. 73; Brewster, p. 268; Anon, p. 34; Whiting 6, p. 395; Mieder, p. 236.

1331 "Everyone to his taste," as the old lady said when she kissed the cow.

GB, STUART PALMER, *Murder on the Blackboard* (1934), p. 134; US (Ky.), c.1950. Cited in Halpert 2, p. 118; Whiting 6, p. 395. Recorded in Bryant (Ala., Ark., Ga., Ind., Miss., Nebr., Oreg., Wis.).

1332 "Everyone to her own taste," as the old lady said when she kissed the pig.

US (N.Y.), CARROLL J. DALY, *Murder from the East* (1935), p. 151. Cited in Whiting 1, p. 73; Whiting 6, p. 395.

1333 "Ev'ryone to his own taste," as the feller said when he kissed the cow.

US, PHOEBE ATWOOD TAYLOR, *Crimson Patch* (1936), p. 292. Cited in Whiting 6, p. 395.

1334 "Everyone to her own taste," as the old woman said when she kissed the cow.

US (Kans.), 1936. Cited in Porter, p. 158; Whiting 3, p. 441; Whiting 6, p. 395. Recorded in Bryant (Ark., Nebr., Ohio, W.Va.).

1335 "Every man to his taste," as the Irishman said when he kissed the cow.

US (N.Y.), 1940. Cited in Thompson, p. 501; Brookes, p. 107. Recorded in Bryant (N.Y.).

1336 "Everybody has their own taste," said the cow as she licked her calf.

US, c.1945–1980. Recorded in Bryant (Wis.).

1337 "There's no accounting for people's taste," said the cat as it licked its master's boots.

US, c.1945–1980. Recorded in Bryant (Ill.).

1338 "Everyone to his own taste," said the old maid when she kissed the cow.

US (Tenn.), c.1950. Cited in Halpert 2, p. 118.

1339 "Everyone to their own taste," as the cow said when she rolled in the pig pen.

US (Tenn.), c.1950. Cited in Halpert 2, p. 117; Mieder, p. 236.

1340 "There's no accounting for tastes," said the old maid as she kissed the cow.

US (Ky.), c.1950. Cited in Halpert 2, p. 118; Mieder, p. 237. Recorded in Bryant (Ohio, Oreg., Ind., Tenn.).

1341 For as the old maid remarked about kissing the cow, "It's all a matter of taste."

GB, ED MCBAIN, *The Mugger* (1956), p. 27. Cited in Whiting 6, p. 396.

tears

1342 "If you have tears, prepare to shed them now," as the fellow said who invited his friends into a smoky room.

US (N.Y.), *Wilkes' Spirit of the Times,* vol. 1 (1859), p. 263. Cited in Loomis 2, p. 18. [The reference is to Antony's funeral speech in Shakespeare's *Julius Caesar* (1599), act 3, scene 2.]

teeth

1343 "Teeth inserted," as the mad dog said when he bit the man.

US (Mass.), *Yankee Blade* (29 Jan. 1848). Cited in Loomis 2, p. 20.

temper

1344 "You'll put me out of temper," as the razor said to the obstinate oyster.

GB, *Punch,* vol. 2 (1842), p. 216. Cited in Loomis 3, p. 112.

temptation

1345 "Let us remove temptation from the path of youth," as the frog said when he plunged into the water upon seeing a boy pick up a stone.

US (Calif.), *California Golden Era,* vol. 19, no. 13 (1871), p. 7. Cited in Loomis 1, p. 305; Loomis 2, p. 20; Browne, p. 202; Mieder, p. 232.

thanks

1346 "I really can't express my thanks," as the boy said to the schoolmaster when he gave him a thrashing.

US (Mass.), *Ballou's Dollar Magazine,* vol. 11 (1860), p. 498. Cited in Loomis 2, p. 9.

thing

1347 "All new things sturts," quoth the goodwife when she gaed lie to the hireman.

GB, JAMES KELLY, *Scottish Proverbs* (1721). Cited in Lean, p. 741. [*Sturts,* are troublesome, contentious, vexatious.]

1348 "What pretty things men will make for money," quoth the old woman when she saw a monkey.

GB, THOMAS FULLER, *Gnomologia* (1732); US, 1948. Cited in Lean, p. 752; Taylor 2, p. 316.

1349 "Too much of a good thing," as the pismire said ven he fell into a hogshead of molasses.

US (Pa.), *Alexander's Weekly Messenger* (1839). Cited in Tidwell 2, p. 259; Loomis 2, p. 20; Mieder, p. 231. [*Pismire,* ant; *hogshead,* large cask or barrel.]

1350 "Strange things do sometimes turn up," as Tummus said when Betty the housemaid was found floating on the river.

US, THOMAS HALIBURTON, *Letter Bag of the Great Western* (1840). Cited in Taylor and Whiting, p. 369.

1351 "Too much of a good thing," as the kitten said when she fell into the milk pail.

US (N.Y.), *Wilkes' Spirit of the Times,* vol. 7 (1862), p. 206. Cited in Loomis 2, p. 20; Mieder, p. 231.

1352 "You have a nice soft thing of it here, Charley," said the gushing heiress as she fondly patted her simple young husband on the spot where his centerparted hair is.

US (Calif.), *The Argonaut,* vol. 3, no. 9 (1878), p. 11. Cited in Loomis 4, p. 230.

1353 "It was not the square thing for you to slip away from me," said the sugar-tongs to the lump in the sugar bowl.

US (Calif.), *The Wasp,* vol. 17, no. 543 (1886), p. 10. Cited in Loomis 4, p. 233.

1354 "There's a thing in't," quoth the fellow when he drank the dishclout.

GB, 1903. Cited in Lean, p. 750. [Cf. nos. 836 and 845.]

1355 "This is carrying things too far," said John Boyd, as he dropped a trunk on the third floor of Walworth.

US (Calif.), *The Pelican,* vol. 1, no. 1 (1903), p. 13. Cited in Loomis 4, p. 235.

1356 "Course one thing leads to another," as the old lady said when she pulled on her woolen stockin's.

US, MICHAEL GRAVES, *Bubblin's an' B'ilin's at the Center* (1934). Cited in Whiting 2, p. 11. Recorded in Bryant (Ky., S.C.).

1357 "Well, if it isn't one thing it's another," said the girl when her nose began to bleed.

US (Ky.), c.1950. Cited in Halpert 2, p. 117; Mieder, p. 237. Recorded in Bryant (Ky., Tenn.).

think

1358 "Don't think of me," as the man said who was on the point of being flung over the gallery into the pit, "but recollect those beneath me."

US (Mass.), *Yankee Blade* (4 Feb. 1847). Cited in Loomis 2, p. 5.

threads

1359 "Silver threads among the gold," is what the boy said when he snatched two gray hairs from the butter.

US (Calif.), *California Golden Era,* vol. 23, no. 34 (1875), p. 2. Cited in Loomis 1, p. 305; Loomis 2, p. 18.

through

1360 "Through by daylight," as the piles said to the steamboat.

US (Maine), *Yankee Blade* (22 Oct. 1842). Cited in Loomis 2, p. 20.

thumper

1361 "That's a thumper," as the mortar said to the pestle.

US (Pa.), *Alexander's Weekly Messenger* (1839). Cited in Tidwell 2, p. 262.

tick

1362 "Here's where I get one on tick," said the student as he slipped his watch to the bartender.

US (Calif.), *The Pelican,* vol. 11, no. 4 (1911). Cited in Loomis 4, p. 236.

tickle

1363 "Don't tickle me," as the rat said ven he was caught in a steel trap.

US (Pa.), *Alexander's Weekly Messenger* (1839). Cited in Tidwell 2, p. 261.

tickler

1364 "I am a tickler friend to you," as the snuff said to the nose.

GB, *Punch,* vol. 2 (1842), p. 96. Cited in Loomis 3, p. 111.

tie

1365 "I have very little respect for the ties of the world," as the chap said when the rope was around his neck.

US (Mass.), *Yankee Notions,* vol. 3 (1854), p. 122. Cited in Whiting 2, p. 7; Loomis 2, p. 20.

1366 "These are the ties which should never be severed," as the ill used wife said when she found her brute of a husband hanging in the hay loft.

US (Calif.), *California Golden Era,* vol. 14, no. 50 (1866), p. 7. Cited in Loomis 1, p. 304; Loomis 2, p. 20.

1367 "This is the tie that binds," said the goat, as he ate the cravat.

US (Calif.), *The Pelican,* vol. 31, no. 2 (1925), p. 42. Cited in Loomis 4, p. 241.

timber

1368 "Shiver my timbers!" squeaked the dance hall floor, as three hundred couples shimmied across it.

US (Calif.), *The Pelican,* vol. 26, no. 9 (1921), p. 4. Cited in Loomis 4, p. 239. ["Shiver my timbers" is a mock oath attributed in comic fiction to sailors.]

1369 "This certainly ought to add timber to my voice," remarked the opera star, as he swallowed a toothpick.

US (Calif.), *The Pelican,* vol. 31, no. 4 (1925), p. 80. Cited in Loomis 4, p. 242.

time

1370 "When you are all agreed upon the time," quoth the vicar, "I'll make it rain."

GB, THOMAS FULLER, *Gnomologia* (1732). Cited in Lean, p. 752.

1371 "Making up for lost time," as the piper of Sligo said when he ate a hail side o' mutton.

GB, WALTER SCOTT, *Woodstock* (1826). Cited in Lean, p. 747. [*Hail,* whole.]

1372 "Fine time for them as is well wropped up," as the Polar Bear said to himself, ven he was practising his skating.

GB, CHARLES DICKENS, *Pickwick Papers* (1836); US (N.Y.), 1940. Cited in Maass, p. 213; Thompson, p. 501; Stevenson, p. 2480; Baer, p. 177.

1373 "One glance satisfied me that there was no time to be lost," as Pat thought when falling from a church steeple, and exclaimed, "This would be mighty pleasant, now, if it would only last."

US, DAVID CROCKETT, *Colonel Crockett's Exploits and Adventures in Texas* (1836). Cited in Whiting 2, p. 7.

1374 "Time is money," as the man said ven he stole the patent lever watch.

US (Pa.), *Alexander's Weekly Messenger* (1839). Cited in Tidwell 2, p. 261; Mieder, p. 230. Recorded in Bryant (Pa.).

1375 "I'm trifling away your time," as the pickpocket said to the gentleman while stealing his watch.

US (Maine), *Yankee Blade* (22 Oct. 1842). Cited in Loomis 2, p. 20.

1376 "I was out on a time, marm, and I didn't care a darn whether school kept or not," as the boy said to his boss.

US (N.Y.), *Yankee Notions,* vol. 1 (1852), p. 354. Cited in Whiting 2, p. 8.

1377 "It is time to wind up," as the watchmaker said when he found that he couldn't pay his debts.

US (Mass.), *Ballou's Dollar Magazine,* vol. 3 (1856), p. 400. Cited in Loomis 2, p. 21.

1378 "You're just in time," as the watch-spring said to the flea which crept in at the key-hole.

US (Calif.), *Fireman's Journal,* vol. 4 (1857), p. 1. Cited in Loomis 4, p. 230.

1379 "Time works wonders," as the lady said when she got married after an eight years' courtship.

US (Calif.), *California Golden Era,* vol. 14, no. 9 (1866), p. 8. Cited in Loomis 2, p. 20; Loomis 3, p. 304; Loomis 5, p. 51; Hines, p. 26.

1380 "I see I was in for a lively time," as the boy said when he upset the bee hive.

US, PALMER COX, *Squibbs of California* (1874). Cited in Loomis 2, p. 13.

1381 "Now is the time to subscribe," said the cross-road's editor, as he led his wealthy bride to the marriage register and shoved a pen into her trembling hand.

US (Calif.), *The Wasp,* vol. 10, no. 351 (1883), p. 2. Cited in Loomis 4, p. 233.

1382 "Come along with me and have a fine time," remarked the policeman to a man he arrested.

US (Calif.), *The Wasp,* vol. 16, no. 5 (1885), p. 10. Cited in Loomis 4, p. 233.

1383 "Your time has come," she menaced, waving his watch on high.

US (Calif.), *The Pelican,* vol. 30, no. 1 (1924), p. 47. Cited in Loomis 4, p. 240.

1384 "Time presses," as the monkey said when the clock fell on his head.

US, FRANCIS BEEDING, *Pretty Sinister* (1929). Cited in Whiting 1, p. 74; Whiting 6, p. 629; Mieder, p. 236.

1385 "Twa'n't no time," as the old maid said when she was kissed.

US, MICHAEL GRAVES, *Bubblin's an' B'ilin's at the Center* (1934). Cited in Whiting 2, p. 11.

1386 "I've got time on my hands," said the old man as he picked up the clock.

US, c.1945-1980. Recorded in Bryant (Kans.).

1387 "Time will tell," as the monkey said when he hid the limburger in Grandpa's clock.

US (N.Y.), F. VAN WYCK MASON, *Himalayan Assignment* (1953), p. 104. Cited in Whiting 6, p. 630.

1388 "Now is the time to see my pigs," said the farmer with a sty in his eye.

US (Kans.), 1959. Cited in Koch 2, p. 196; Mieder, p. 6. Recorded in Bryant (Kans.).

1389 "Now I am in the big time," said the pigeon when it flew into the street clock.

US, 1960. Cited in Taylor 5, p. 55. Recorded in Bryant (Ohio).

1390 "How time flies," as the monkey said when it threw the clock at the missionary.

US (Tenn.), STEPHEN CHANCE, *Septimus and the Minister Ghost Mystery* (1974), p. 60. Cited in Whiting 6, p. 628.

times

1391 "These are the times that try men's soles," as the man said ven he was kicked through the streets for lying.

US (Pa.), *Alexander's Weekly Messenger* (1839). Cited in Tidwell 2, p. 259. [The reference is to a remark in Thomas Paine's *The Crisis* (1776): "These are the times that try men's souls."]

1392 "Never saw such stirring times," as the spoon said to the saucepan.

GB, *Punch,* vol. 1 (1841), p. 242; US (N.Y.), *Yankee Notions,* vol. 1 (1852), p. 67. Cited in Loomis 3, p. 111; Loomis 2, p. 19.

1393 "The times are out of joint," as the fellow said when the butcher refused any longer credit.

US (Mass.), *Yankee Blade* (4 May 1848). Cited in Loomis 2, p. 12. [The reference is to a remark in Shakespeare's *Hamlet* (1601), act 1, scene 5: "The time is out of joint."]

tit

1394 "Tit for tat," quoth the wife when she farted at the thunder.

GB, JAMES KELLY, *Scottish Proverbs* (1721). Cited in Lean, p. 751.

toast

1395 "Let the toast be, dear woman," as the boarder said when his landlady was about to remove the plate.

US (Mass.), *Yankee Blade* (2 Apr. 1849). Cited in Loomis 2, p. 20.

tobacco

1396 "That's strong tobacco," said the devil when the hunter shot off his rifle in the devil's mouth.

US, c.1945-1980. Recorded in Bryant (N.Y., Oreg.).

today

1397 "Here today and gone tomorrow," as the farmer said when he lost his piebald pig.

GB, J. LINDSAY, *Writing on the Walls* (1960), p. 71. Cited in Whiting 6, p. 634.

toenails

1398 "How sharp your toenails is," as the man said ven he cotched the hornet.

US (Mass.), *Alexander's Weekly Messenger* (1839). Cited in Loomis 2, p. 18; Tidwell 2, p. 262. [*Cotched,* caught.]

toil

1399 "I winna mak' a toil o' a pleasure," quoth the man when he carried his wife to burial.

GB, NICHOLAS BRETON, *Dialogues Full of Pith* (1603); US, GEORGE CUTLER (1820) in Emily Vanderpoel, ed., *Chronicles of a Pioneer School from 1792 to 1833* (1903). Cited in Wilson, p. 827; Whiting 5, p. 445; Lean, p. 746.

told

1400 "So I'm told," as the church bell remarked when it heard of the villager's death.

US (Calif., Wash.), *California Spirit of the Times* (8 Jun. 1872); *Walla Walla Union* (22 Jun. 1872), p. 1. Cited in Loomis 2, p. 20; Hines, p. 26; Mieder, p. 234.

top

1401 "So long, old top," said the man as his hat rolled into the sewer.

US (Calif.), *The Pelican,* vol. 32, no. 7 (1927), p. 36. Cited in Loomis 4, p. 242.

touch

1402 "Touch me not so nearly," as Shakespeel says in de play.

US, *Minstrel Gags and End Men's Hand-Book* (1875), pp. 50–51. Cited in Browne, p. 201. [The reference is to the Bible (*John* 20.17), not to Shakespeare; as literary sources, the two are commonly confused.]

1403 "One touch of nature," observed a man as he saw a mule kick a snappish dog into the next block.

US (Calif.), *The Wasp,* vol. 3, no. 134 (1879), p. 469. Cited in Loomis 4, p. 231.

touching

1404 "How touching," as the actress said to the bishop.

US, LESLIE CHARTERIS, *The Last Hero* (1930). Cited in Whiting 1, p. 72.

touchy

1405 "You are rather touchy," said the priming to the match. "Then go off with yourself," said the match, pettishly in reply.

US (Mass.), *Yankee Blade* (9 Sep. 1846). Cited in Loomis 2, p. 20.

trade

1406 "Every man to his ain trade," quoth the boy to the bishop.

GB, JAMES KELLY, *Scottish Proverbs* (1721). Cited in Lean, p. 743.

1407 "Let a' trades live," quoth the wife when she burnt her besom.

GB, ALLAN RAMSEY, *Scots Proverbs* (1737). Cited in Lean, p. 747. [*Besom,* broom.]

1408 "Every man to his ain trade," quoth the browster to the bishop.

GB, 1903. Cited in Lean, p. 743. [*Browster,* brewer.]

transported

1409 "I'm transported to see you," as the thief said to the kangeroos.

US (Mass.), *Ballou's Dollar Magazine,* vol. 15 (1862), p. 398. Cited in Loomis 1, p. 304; Loomis 2, p. 20. [From 1788 to 1852, British convicts were often "transported" (banished) to penal colonies in Australia.]

trials

1410 "I have known many trials," as the man said who had been convicted sixteen times for petty larceny.

US (N.Y.), *Yankee Notions,* vol. 14 (1865), p. 100. Cited in Loomis 2, p. 20.

trod

1411 "I won't be trod upon with impunity," as the steel trap said to the fox.

US (Mass.), *Yankee Blade* (11 Oct. 1843). Cited in Loomis 2, p. 20.

trouble

1412 "Seems to me there's trouble brewin'," said the hunter when treed by a bear.
US (Calif.), *The Wasp*, vol. 11, no. 383 (1883), p. 7. Cited in Loomis 4, p. 233.

trump

1413 "Vell, you are a trump, and no mistake," as the nobleman said ven he turned up the ace of hearts and had a violent fit of coughing at the same time.
US (Pa.), *Alexander's Weekly Messenger* (1837). Cited in Tidwell 2, p. 258.

trunk

1414 "I'll put that in my trunk," as the elephant observed to the orange.
US (N.Y.), *Wilkes' Spirit of the Times*, vol. 7 (1862), p. 206. Cited in Loomis 2, p. 20.

trunks

1415 "Bring your trunks with you," as Orpheus said to the trees when he invited a lot of them to dance at his shanty.
US (Calif.), *California Golden Era*, vol. 8, no. 52 (1860), p. 6. Cited in Loomis 2, p. 20.

truth

1416 "Truth is stranger than fiction," said the man, when told that his daughter had eloped with a negro beau.
US (Mass.), *Ballou's Dollar Magazine*, vol. 3 (1856), p. 100. Cited in Loomis 2, p. 21.

trying

1417 "This is a trying piece of work," quoth the judge, as he entered the courtroom.
US (Calif.), *The Pelican*, vol. 13, no. 1 (1912). Cited in Loomis 4, p. 236.

tug

1418 "Now comes the tug of ma," said the young woman who was lacing the maternal stays.
US (Calif.), *The Wasp*, vol. 11, no. 383 (1883), p. 7. Cited in Loomis 4, p. 233.

tumble

1419 "Do you tumble?" softly asked the meek-eyed banana peel, as the fat man sat down to think.
US (Calif.), *The Wasp*, vol. 7, no. 276 (1881), p. 311. Cited in Loomis 4, p. 232.

turn

1420 "A begun turn is half ended," quo' the good wife when she stuck the graip i' the midden.
GB, JAMES KELLY, *Scottish Proverbs* (1721); US, 1916. Cited in Lean, p. 741; Marvin, p. 351. [*Graip*, digging tool, dung fork; *midden*, dung heap.]

1421 "If you won't turn, I will," as the mill-wheel said to the stream.
GB, *Punch,* vol. 1 (1841), p. 191. Cited in Loomis 3, p. 111.

1422 "Let us have another turn," as the old ax said to the grindstone.
GB, *Punch,* vol. 2 (1842), p. 113. Cited in Loomis 3, p. 112.

1423 "You give me quite a turn," as the thief remarked when he was put upon the treadmill.
GB, *Punch,* vol. 40 (1861), p. 51. Cited in Loomis 3, p. 113.

1424 "One good turn deserves another," as the alderman said when he discharged the thief who voted for him.
US (N.Y.), *Yankee Notions,* vol. 14 (1865), p. 196. Cited in Loomis 2, p. 10; Mieder, p. 231.

1425 "Turn pikes," observed the small fish of prey to his companions when he saw the hungry shark sailing up the river.
US (Calif.), *The Wasp,* vol. 3, no. 142 (1879), p. 597. Cited in Loomis 4, p. 231.

1426 "One good turn deserves another," said the customer, as he padded the chorus girls' tights.
US (Calif.), *The Pelican,* vol. 1, no. 1 (1903), p. 15. Cited in Loomis 4, p. 235; Mieder, p. 234.

1427 "One good turn deserves another," as the dog said, chasing his tail.
GB, JOHN BENTLEY, *Mr. Marlow Stops* (1940), p. 163. Cited in Whiting 6, p. 651.

1428 "Didn't see that U turn," said the ram as he went over the cliff.
US, c.1945–1980. Recorded in Bryant (Kans.).

turn about

1429 "Turn about is fair play," as the devil said to the smoke jack.
GB, ROBERT SURTEES, *Handley Cross* (1843); US, 1916. Cited in Lean, p. 751; Marvin, p. 364.
[*Smoke jack,* device for turning a spit in a chimney.]

turned down

1430 "One or the other of us is going to be turned down tonight," muttered the young man at the flickering gaslight, as he awaited his beloved in the front parlor.
US (Calif.), *The Argonaut,* vol. 37, no. 21 (1895), p. 16. Cited in Loomis 4, p. 234.

twig

1431 "Twig that," as the old bird said to the younger one, when she pointed to a knot hole and wanted to learn him to make a nest.
US (Maine), *Yankee Blade* (17 Dec. 1842). Cited in Loomis 2, p. 21.

two

1432 "Two of a kind again," remarked a young hopeful whose wife had presented him with twins for the fifth time.
US (Calif.), *The Argonaut,* vol. 4, no. 4 (1879), p. 12. Cited in Loomis 4, p. 231.

udder

1433   "Just an udder day," said the cow, as she rolled over for the night.

US (Calif.), *The Pelican,* vol. 36, no. 5 (1930), p. 2. Cited in Loomis 4, p. 243.

unequal

1434   "It's unekal," as my father used to say ven his grog warn't made half-and-half.

GB, CHARLES DICKENS, *Pickwick Papers* (1836). Cited in Maass, p. 210; Baer, p. 177.

union

1435   "In union there is strength," as the landlady said when she mixed lard with butter for her boarders.

US (Calif.), *California Golden Era,* vol. 8, no. 12 (1860), p. 6. Cited in Loomis 2, p. 21.

1436   "Union is not always strength," as the sailor said when he saw the purser mixing his rum with water.

US (N.Y.), *Wilkes' Spirit of the Times,* vol. 2 (1860), p. 6. Cited in Loomis 2, p. 21.

united

1437   "United we fall, divided we stand," as the temperance man said to the glass of liquor.

US (Mass.), *Yankee Blade* (21 Jul. 1847). Cited in Loomis 2, p. 21.

unsung

1438   "Much remains unsung," as the tom-cat said to the brickbat when it abruptly cut short his serenade.

US (N.Y.), *Yankee Notions,* vol. 8 (1858), p. 356. Cited in Loomis 2, p. 17.

up against

1439   "I'm up against it now," he said, as he faced the firing squad.

US (Calif.), *The Pelican,* vol. 30, no. 4 (1924), p. 42. Cited in Loomis 4, p. 241.

use

1440   "To such base uses we may come at last," as the yarn said when it was being wound into a ball for the use of a ball club.

US (N.Y.), *Yankee Notions,* vol. 12 (1863), p. 9. Cited in Loomis 2, p. 4. Recorded in Bryant (N.Y.).

1441   "What's the use?" said the rooster, "Just an egg yesterday and a feather duster tomorrow."

US, c.1945-1980. Recorded in Bryant (Miss.).

vagabond

1442   "It's not every vagabond that snuffs up his nose at me," as the polecat said ven he caught the nigger in the woods.

US (Pa.), *Alexander's Weekly Messenger* (1839). Cited in Tidwell 2, p. 259.

valet

1443 "I'm going through the dark valet," said the highwayman as he robbed the colored coachman.

US (Calif.), *The Wasp,* vol. 9, no. 319 (1882), p. 566. Cited in Loomis 4, p. 232.

vane

1444 "How vane are all things here below," as the swallow said, when he perched upon the weather cock.

US (Mass.), *Ballou's Dollar Magazine,* vol. 15 (1862), p. 598. Cited in Loomis 2, p. 21.

vanities

1445 "I am not fond of such vanities," as the hog said when his owner put a ring in his snout.

US (Mass.), *Yankee Blade* (22 Aug. 1843). Cited in Loomis 2, p. 21.

variety

1446 "Variety is the spice of life," as the shoemaker said when he was chewing wax, leather, and tobacco, all at once.

US (Mass.), *Yankee Blade* (30 Jul. 1845). Cited in Loomis 2, p. 21; Mieder, p. 232.

veal

1447 "Veal," quoth the Dutchman. Is not "veal" a calf?

GB, WILLIAM SHAKESPEARE, *Love's Labour's Lost* (1595), act 5, scene 2. Cited in Lean, p. 751. [The line is spoken by Katherine, making an elaborate pun on *veal,* as a Dutch pronunciation of *well* and as a synonym of *calf* (imbecile); on *veil* (face); and on *ville,* part of her wooer's name, Longueville.]

vein

1448 "I'm not i' the vein," as the lancet said when the unskilled practitioner stuck it in the artery.

US (N.Y.), *Yankee Notions,* vol. 14 (1865), p. 201. Cited in Loomis 2, p. 21. [*Lancet,* small, pointed surgical knife.]

victim

1449 "I think he's the wictim o' connubiality," as Blue Beard's domestic chaplain said, with a tear of pity, ven he buried him.

GB, CHARLES DICKENS, *Pickwick Papers* (1836). Cited in Maass, p. 209; Stevenson, p. 2480; Baer, p. 178.

1450 "I'm a victim of an artificial state society," as the monkey said when they put trousers on him.

US (N.Y.), *Yankee Notions,* vol. 1 (1852), p. 9. Cited in Whiting 2, p. 7; Loomis 2, p. 4.

virtue

1451 "Virtue is its own reward," as the gentleman said to the little sweep at the crossing when he held out his hand for a penny.

US (Mass.), *Ballou's Dollar Magazine,* vol. 5 (1857), p. 500. Cited in Loomis 2, p. 21.

1452 "Virtue in the middle," as the man said, when sitting between two lawyers.

US, *Hokey Pokey Joke Book* (1870). Cited in Browne, p. 202; Mieder, p. 233.

1453 "Virtue in the middle," said the Devil and sat between two old harlots.

US, 1931. Cited in Taylor 1, p. 207.

1454 "Virtue in the middle," said the Devil and seated himself between two priests.

US, 1931. Cited in Taylor 1, p. 217.

visits

1455 "Short visits are the best," as the fly said when he lit on the hot stove.

US (N.Y.), *Yankee Notions,* vol. 1 (1852), p. 29. Cited in Whiting 2, p. 8; Loomis 2, p. 18; Loomis 1, p. 304. Recorded in Bryant (N.J.).

void

1456 "He has left a void that cannot be easily filled," as the banker touchingly remarked of the absconding cashier.

US (Calif.), *California Golden Era,* vol. 22, no. 24 (1874), p. 2. Cited in Loomis 1, p. 305; Loomis 2, p. 21.

wagging

1457 As the little dog said when the train cut off his tail, "That ruined my waggin'."

US (Ky.), c.1950. Cited in Halpert 2, p. 117.

wahoo

1458 "Wahoo, wahoo," said the Indian squaw.

US (Pa.), c.1915–1935. Cited in Mook, p. 183.

walk

1459 "Please to walk in," as the snake said ven he swallowed the toad.

US (Pa.), *Alexander's Weekly Messenger* (1839). Cited in Tidwell 2, p. 262.

1460 "I can hardly walk," said the feeble old woman as she ran out of the house from a mouse.

US (Tenn.), c.1950. Cited in Halpert 2, p. 120; Mieder, p. 237.

wants

1461 "He wants you particklar; and no one else'll do," as the Devil's private secretary said ven he fetched avay Doctor Faustus.

GB, CHARLES DICKENS, *Pickwick Papers* (1836). Cited in Maass, p. 210; Williams, p. 94; Baer, p. 175.

war

1462 "In short, sir," as the Irishman said, "in short, sir—there is policy in war."

GB, JOHN NEAL, *Brother Jonathan,* vol. 2 (1825), p. 97. Cited in Whiting 2, p. 6.

wash

1463 "It'll all come out in the wash," as the feller said about the tomato soup.

US, PHOEBE ATWOOD TAYLOR, *The Mystery of Cape Cod Tavern* (1933). Cited in Whiting 1, p. 73; Mieder, p. 236.

watches

1464 "I love the silent watches of the night," as the nocturnal thief said when he was robbing the jeweller's shop.

US (N.Y.), *Porter's Spirit of the Times,* vol. 1 (1857), p. 306. Cited in Loomis 2, p. 21.

water

1465 "It's of the first water," as the milkman said ven his customers asked him if his milk was good.

US (Pa.), *Alexander's Weekly Messenger* (1839). Cited in Tidwell 2, p. 260.

1466 "The water will tell you," said the guide when the travelers asked him how deep the river was.

US, 1931. Cited in Taylor 1, p. 203.

way

1467 "It's a great deal more in your way than mine," as the gen'l'm'n on the right side o' the garden vall said to the man on the wrong 'un, ven the mad bull wos a comin' up the lane.

GB, CHARLES DICKENS, *Pickwick Papers* (1836). Cited in Maass, p. 211; Baer, p. 178.

1468 "There is a right way and a wrong way in doing everything," as the Frenchman said who wrote a book on the best way of blowing out a candle.

US (Mass.), *Ballou's Dollar Magazine,* vol. 5 (1857), p. 100. Cited in Loomis 2, p. 17.

1469 "Things are coming my way tonight," remarked the cat, as he gazed pensively on the heap of old boots, lumps of coal, tin-cans, etc. with which he had been presented.

US (Calif.), *The Argonaut,* vol. 28, no. 8 (1891), p. 15. Cited in Loomis 4, p. 234.

1470 "On his way," as the actress said of the bishop.

US, LESLIE CHARTERIS, *Wanted for Murder* (1931). Cited in Whiting 1, p. 72.

1471 "It's this way, and that way," as the country bumpkin said when he lost his spotted pig.

US, 1948. Cited in Stevenson, p. 2481.

weaker

1472 "Getting weaker and weaker," as the rabbit said when the dog was eating it.

US, J. L. MITCHELL, *Three Go Back* (1932). Cited in Whiting 1, p. 74; Mieder, p. 236.

weakness

1473 "You know what the counsel said, Sammy," as defended the gen'l'm'n as beat his wife with the poker venever he got jolly. "And arter all my lord," says he, "It's an amiable weakness."

GB, CHARLES DICKENS, *Pickwick Papers* (1836). Cited in Maass, p. 209; Bailey, p. 338; Stevenson, p. 2488; Baer, p. 178.

wear out

1474 "Better wear out than rust out," as the whetstone said to the old knife.

US (Mass.), *Yankee Blade* (7 Jan. 1846). Cited in Loomis 2, p. 21; Mieder, p. 232.

1475 "One consolation, here's something I can't wear out," said the co-ed as she put on her kimono.

US (Calif.), *The Pelican*, vol. 25, no. 7 (1920), p. 47. Cited in Loomis 4, p. 238.

weather

1476 "Changeable weather," quoth Molly Hogg, "rain every day."

GB, MICHAEL DENHAM, *Folk-lore of the North* (1858). Cited in Lean, p. 742.

week

1477 "The week is beginning well," said one who was to be hanged on Monday.

US, 1931. Cited in Taylor 1, p. 219.

weigh

1478 "Don't give me a weigh," as the fat woman said when asked to get upon the scales.

US (Calif.), *The Argonaut*, vol. 4, no. 5 (1879), p. 3. Cited in Loomis 4, p. 231.

1479 "How do you get that weigh?" queried the customer indignantly, as the crafty grocer manipulated his trick scales.

US (Calif.), *The Pelican*, vol. 28, no. 5 (1923), p. 46. Cited in Loomis 4, p. 240.

weight

1480 "Weight for the wagon," observed the farmer, as he helped his 300-pound wife to a seat in the vehicle.

US (Calif.), *Daily Examiner,* vol. 35, no. 45 (1882), p. 4. Cited in Loomis 4, p. 232.

welcome

1481 "You're welcome," as the actress said to the bishop on a particular auspicious occasion.

US, LESLIE CHARTERIS, *Last Hero* (1930). Cited in Whiting 1, p. 72.

1482 "You're intirely welcome, sor!" as the widdy-woman said when the circus clown kissed her.

US (Ky.), c.1950. Cited in Halpert 2, p. 120. [*Widdy-woman,* widow.]

1483 "We ain't got much, but you're welcome to what there is of it," as the little boy said to the schoolteacher.

US (Kans.), 1958. Cited in Porter, p. 160.

well

1484 "All's well that ends well," said the monkey contemplating the kinks in his tail.

US (N.Y.), *Yankee Notions,* vol. 11 (1862), p. 53. Cited in Loomis 2, p. 9; Mieder, p. 238. Recorded in Bryant (Kans.).

1485 "All's well as ends well," as the actress used to say.

US, LESLIE CHARTERIS, *The Last Hero* (1930). Cited in Whiting 1, p. 72.

1486 "All's well that ends well," said the peacock when he looked at his tail.

US, 1931. Cited in Taylor 1, p. 210; Mieder, p. 223.

1487 "Well, well," said the old man of England when he swallowed the broad ax and picked up the smoothing iron.

US (Ky.), c.1950. Cited in Halpert 2, p. 119.

1488 "All's well that ends well," said the monkey as the lawn mower ran over his tail.

US (Kans.), 1959. Cited in Koch 1, p. 180; Mieder, p. 238.

Westinghouse

1489 "This is my westin' house," said the rabbit sitting in the Westinghouse refrigerator.

US, c.1945–1980. Recorded in Bryant (Kans.).

wether

1490 "Postponed on account of the wether," as the boy said when the ram chased him out of the orchard.

US (Calif.), *The Wasp*, vol. 3, no. 131 (1879), p. 458. Cited in Loomis 4, p. 231. [*Wether*, a castrated male sheep.]

whale

1491 "Very like a whale," as the schoolmaster said when he examined the boy's back after severely flogging him.

GB, *Punch*, vol. 1 (1841), p. 25. Cited in Loomis 3, p. 110.

1492 "This is very like a whale," as the schoolboy said when he received a merited castigation from the teacher.

US (N.J.), *Somerville Journal* (24 Mar. 1881), p. 16. Cited in Whiting 2, p. 9.

whalebone

1493 "Whalebone is whalebone," says the dressmaker, as she bones her customers.

US (Calif.), *The Wasp*, vol. 17, no. 543 (1886), p. 10. Cited in Loomis 4, p. 233. [*Bones*, puts stays in a garment.]

wheamow

1494 "I am very wheamow," quoth the old woman when she stepped into a milk bowl.

GB, JOHN RAY, *English Proverbs* (1678). Cited in Lean, p. 745; Wilson, p. 882. [*Wheamow*, nimble.]

whistle

1495 "I paid very dear for my whistle," as the steam-engine said to the railroad.

GB, *Punch*, vol. 1 (1841), p. 191. Cited in Loomis 3, p. 111.

1496 "Mair whistle than woo," quoth the souter when he sheared the sow.

GB, 1904; US, 1916; US (N.Y.), 1940. Cited in Lean, p. 747; Marvin, p. 357; Thompson, p. 502. [*Mair*, more; *woo*, wool; *souter*, shoemaker.]

white

1497 "That is mighty white of you," said the maid, as the grocer delivered a case of Ivory soap.

US (Calif.), *The Pelican*, vol. 31, no. 7 (1926), p. 82. Cited in Loomis 4, p. 242.

whole

1498 "I see the whole of your disorder," as the cobbler said to the boot that was worn out and wanted patching.

US (N.Y.), *Yankee Notions*, vol. 3 (1854), p. 142. Cited in Whiting 2, p. 4. Recorded in Bryant (Ariz.).

wife

1499 "Wife is just one sham thing after another," thought the husband, as his spouse placed her teeth, hair, shape, and complexion on the bureau.
US (Calif.), *The Pelican,* vol. 17, no. 4 (1914), p. 2. Cited in Loomis 4, p. 237; Mieder, p. 235.

will

1500 "Give her her will or she'll burst," quoth the goodman when his wife was dinging him.
GB, JAMES KELLY. *Scottish Proverbs* (1721); US, 1916. Cited in Lean, p. 744; Marvin, p. 353; Taylor 1, p. 217. [*Dinging,* beating, striking.]

1501 "Where there's a will there's a whey," as the nurse said when she put the saucepan of pure Orange County milk on the fire.
US (N.Y.), *Yankee Notions,* vol. 5, (1856), p. 106. Cited in Whiting 2, p. 9.

1502 "I go against my Will," murmured she sweetly, as she fondly leaned on William's arm, as they wandered to the theater.
US (Calif.), *Daily Examiner,* vol. 34, no. 65 (1882), p. 4. Cited in Loomis 4, p. 232.

1503 "Your will's law," quo' the tailor to the clockin hen when she picked out his twa een and cam for his nose.
GB, 1903. Cited in Lean, p. 752. [*Clockin,* clucking; *twa een,* two eyes.]

1504 "Thy will be done," said the lawyer as he handed it to his client to sign.
US (Calif.), *The Pelican,* vol. 13, no. 1 (1912). Cited in Loomis 4, p. 236.

winches

1505 "Man the winches," cried the captain, as he dismissed the crew for shore leave.
US (Calif.), *The Pelican,* vol. 35, no. 7 (1930), p. 18. Cited in Loomis 4, p. 243.

wiser

1506 "As men grow older they grow weisser," said the saloon keeper, when his grandfather called for a glass of Berlin beer.
US (N.Y.), *New York News* (24 Mar. 1881), p. 16. Cited in Whiting 2, p. 9.

wit

1507 "Great wits jump," says the poet, and hit his head against the post.
US, BENJAMIN FRANKLIN, *Poor Richard's Almanack* (August 1735). Cited in Stevenson, p. 2549; Loomis 5, p. 51. Recorded in Bryant (N.Y.).

1508 "I'm at my wit's end," said the king, as he trod on the jester's toe.
US (Calif.), *The Pelican,* vol. 12, no. 1 (1912). Cited in Loomis 4, p. 236; Mieder, p. 235.

without

1509 "I'm better off without you," as the thief said when he broke jail.

US (Maine), *Yankee Blade* (13 Aug. 1842). Cited in Loomis 2, p. 21. Recorded in Bryant (N.Y.).

wood

1510 "Wood is the thing, after all," as the man with the real leg said when the mad-dog bit it.

US (N.Y.), *Yankee Notions,* vol. 1 (1852), p. 313. Cited in Loomis 1, p. 305; Loomis 2, p. 21.

1511 "Don't halloo til you're out of the woods," as the ale-bottler said when he heard the strong malt liquor singing in the cask.

US (N.Y.), *Yankee Notions,* vol. 13 (1864), p. 105. Cited in Loomis 2, p. 21.

worn

1512 "Velvet sacks are very much worn," as the young lady remarked on discovering a hole in the sleeve of her "Sunday best."

US (Calif.), *California Golden Era,* vol. 18, no. 9 (1870), p. 7. Cited in Loomis 1, p. 305; Loomis 2, p. 21. [*Sacks,* short, loose-fitting coats for women and children.]

worst

1513 "But no matter, dear Pete," as the man said of the sausages, "Hope for the best, but be prepared for the worst."

US, JONATHAN KELLY, *Humors of Falconbridge* (1856). Cited in Taylor and Whiting, p. 236.

wrongs

1514 "Two wrongs don't make a right," said Vernon J. Veritas, the old truth-teller.

US (Mass.), *Boston Herald* (16 Feb. 1958), p. 5A. Cited in Whiting 6, p. 706.

wurst

1515 "The wurst is yet to come," cried the Frosh, after ordering another Coney Island.

US (Calif.), *The Pelican,* vol. 31, no. 1 (1925), p. 45. Cited in Loomis 4, p. 241. [*Frosh,* high-school or college freshman; *Coney Island,* short for *Coney Island Red Hot,* sandwich of frankfurter sausage and chili or sauerkraut on a roll, invented around 1910 at Coney Island, a pleasure resort in Brooklyn, New York.]

yoke

1516 "Dat bane gude yoke on me," said the old Swede, as he spilled the egg on his vest.

US (Calif.), *The Pelican,* vol. 31, no. 3 (1925), p. 5. Cited in Loomis 4, p. 242. [*Bane,* be, is; *gude,* good.]

LIST OF SOURCES

Anon   Anonymous. "Some Wellerisms from Idaho." *Western Folklore* 25 (1966): 34.

Baer   Florence E. Baer. "Wellerisms in *The Pickwick Papers*." *Folklore* (London) 94 (1983): 173-183.

Bailey   Sir William H. Bailey. "Wellerisms and Wit." *The Dickensian* 1 (1905): 31-34.

Brewster   Paul Brewster. "Folk Sayings in Indiana." *American Speech* 14 (1939): 261-268.

Brookes   Stella B. Brookes. *Joel Chandler Harris, Folklorist, 107*. Athens: University of Georgia Press, 1950.

Browne   Ray B. Browne. "Wellerisms in Negro Minstrelsy and Vaudeville." *Western Folklore* 20 (1961): 201-202.

Bryant   Margaret M. Bryant, comp. Collection of the Committee on Proverbial Sayings of the American Dialect Society (c.1945-1980). Archives of the University of Missouri–Columbia.

Halpert 1   Herbert Halpert. "Folktale and 'Wellerism': A Note." *Southern Folklore Quarterly* 7 (1943): 75.

Halpert 2   Herbert Halpert. "Some Wellerisms from Kentucky and Tennessee." *Journal of American Folklore* 69 (1956): 115-121.

Halpert 3   Kathleen E. Young and Elizabeth L. Mapplebeck. "Proverbial Sayings." In *A Folklore Sampler from the Maritimes*, edited by Herbert Halpert, pp. 119-123. St. John's: Memorial University of Newfoundland, 1982.

Hendricks   George D. Hendricks. "Texas Wellerisms." *Journal of American Folklore* 69 (1956): 356.

Hines   Donald M. Hines. "Wry Wit and Frontier Humor: The Wellerism in the Inland Pacific Northwest." *Southern Folklore Quarterly* 35 (1971): 15-26.

Jones   Joseph Jones. "Wellerisms: Some Further Evidence." *American Speech* 20 (1945): 235-236.

Kent   Charles Kent. *Wellerisms from "Pickwick" and "Master Humphrey's Clock."* London: George Redway, 1886.

Koch 1   William E. Koch. "Wellerisms from Kansas." *Western Folklore* 18 (1959): 180.

Koch 2   William E. Koch. "More Wellerisms from Kansas." *Western Folklore* 19 (1960): 196.

Lean	Vincent Stuckey Lean. "Proverbial Witticisms and Other Sayings." In *Lean's Collectanea*, vol. 2, pp. 739-752. Bristol: J.W. Arrowsmith, 1903. Reprint, Detroit: Gale Research Company, 1969.
Loomis 1	C. Grant Loomis. "American Wellerisms in the *Golden Era*." *American Speech* 20 (1945): 304-305.
Loomis 2	C. Grant Loomis. "Traditional American Wordplay: Wellerisms or Yankeeisms." *Western Folklore* 8 (1949): 1-21.
Loomis 3	C. Grant Loomis. "Wellerisms in Punch." *Western Folklore* 14 (1955): 110-113.
Loomis 4	C. Grant Loomis. "Wellerisms in California Sources." *Western Folklore* 14 (1955): 229-245.
Loomis 5	C. Grant Loomis. "American Pre-Weller Wellerisms." *Western Folklore* 16 (1957): 51-52.
Maass	M. Maass. "39 Odd Similes aus den *Pickwick Papers* von Charles Dickens," *Archiv für das Studium der neueren Sprachen und Literaturen* 41 (1867): 207-215.
Marvin	Dwight Edwards Marvin. *Curiosities in Proverbs*, vol. 2, pp. 351-364. New York: G.P. Putnam's Sons, 1916. Reprint, Darby, Pa.: Folcraft Library Editions, 1980.
Mieder	Wolfgang Mieder. "Wellerisms." In *American Proverbs: A Study of Texts and Contexts*, pp. 223-238. Bern: Peter Lang, 1989.
Mook	Maurice A. Mook. "Northwestern Pennsylvania Wellerisms." *Journal of American Folklore* 70 (1957): 183-184.
Porter	Kenneth Porter. "Some Central Kansas Wellerisms." *Midwest Folklore* 8 (1958): 158-160.
Sackett and Koch	Samuel J. Sackett and William E. Koch, eds. "Proverbs and Riddles." In *Kansas Folklore*, pp. 95-98. Lincoln: University of Nebraska Press, 1961.
Simpson	John A. Simpson, ed. *The Concise Oxford Dictionary of Proverbs.* Oxford: Oxford University Press, 1982.
Stevenson	Burton Stevenson. "Wellerisms." In *The Macmillan (Home) Book of Proverbs, Maxims and Familiar Phrases*, pp. 2480-2481. New York: Macmillan, 1948.
Taylor 1	Archer Taylor. "Wellerisms." In *The Proverb*, pp. 201-220. Cambridge, Mass.: Harvard University Press, 1931. Reprint, Hatboro, Pa.: Folklore Associates, 1962. Reprint, with an introduction and bibliography by Wolfgang Mieder, Bern: Peter Lang, 1985.
Taylor 2	Archer Taylor. "Review of *Apologische Spreekwoorden* by C. Kruyskamp." *Western Folklore* 7 (1948): 316-317.
Taylor 3	Archer Taylor. "Shakespeare's Wellerisms." *Southern Folklore Quarterly* 15 (1951): 170.
Taylor 4	Archer Taylor. "The Use of Proper Names in Wellerisms and Folktales." *Western Folklore* 18 (1959): 287-293.
Taylor 5	Archer Taylor. "Wellerisms and Riddles." *Western Folklore* 19 (1960): 55.
Taylor 6	Archer Taylor. "'Hell,' said the Duchess." *Proverbium*, no. 2 (1965): 32.

Taylor and Whiting	Archer Taylor and Bartlett Jere Whiting. *A Dictionary of American Proverbs and Proverbial Phrases, 1820–1880.* Cambridge, Mass.: Harvard University Press, 1958.
Thompson	Harold W. Thompson. "Proverbs." In *Body, Boots & Britches*, pp. 481-504. Philadelphia: J.B. Lippincott Company, 1940.
Tidwell 1	James N. Tidwell. "Wellerisms of '82." *Western Folklore* 11 (1952): 216.
Tidwell 2	James N. Tidwell. "Wellerisms in *Alexander's Weekly Messenger*, 1837-1839." *Western Folklore* 9 (1959): 257-262.
Whiting 1	Bartlett Jere Whiting. "A Handful of Recent Wellerisms." *Archiv für das Studium der neueren Sprachen und Literaturen* 169 (1936): 71-75.
Whiting 2	Bartlett Jere Whiting. "American Wellerisms of the Golden Age." *American Speech* 20 (1945): 3-11.
Whiting 3	Bartlett Jere Whiting. "Proverbs and Proverbial Sayings from North Carolina." In *The Frank C. Brown Collection of North Carolina Folklore*, edited by Newman Ivey White, vol. 1, pp. 329-501. Durham: Duke University Press, 1952.
Whiting 4	Bartlett Jere Whiting. "The Earliest Recorded English Wellerism." *Philological Quarterly* 15 (1960): 310-311.
Whiting 5	Bartlett Jere Whiting. *Early American Proverbs and Proverbial Phrases.* Cambridge, Mass.: Harvard University Press, 1977.
Whiting 6	Bartlett Jere Whiting. *Modern Proverbs and Proverbial Sayings.* Cambridge, Mass.: Harvard University Press, 1989.
Williams	Gwenllian Williams. "Sam Weller." *Trivium* 1 (1966): 88-101.
Wilson	F. P. Wilson, ed. *The Oxford Dictionary of English Proverbs.* Oxford: Clarendon Press, 1970.
Wright	Elizabeth Mary Wright. *Rustic Speech and Folklore.* New York: Oxford University Press, 1913. Reprint, Detroit: Gale Research Company, 1968.

BIBLIOGRAPHY

This comprehensive bibliography includes collections of wellerisms as well as scholarship that deals with this verbal folklore. Anglo-American publications contained in the "List of Sources" of this book are not repeated here. For annotations of these works on wellerisms, see Wolfgang Mieder, *International Proverb Scholarship: An Annotated Bibliography*, 3 vols. (New York: Garland Publishing, 1982, 1990, and 1993).

Abrahams, Roger D. "Proverbs and Proverbial Expressions." In *Folklore and Folklife*, edited by Richard M. Dorson, 117-127. Chicago: University of Chicago Press, 1972.

Almqvist, Bo. "Siúl an phortáin: Friotalfhocal aqus fabhalscéal (AT276)." *Sinsear*, no volume given (1982-1983): 35-62.

Alster, Bendt. "Paradoxical Proverbs and Satire in Sumerian Literature." *Journal of Cuneiform Studies* 27 (1975): 201-230.

Barley, Nigel. "A Structural Approach to the Proverb and Maxim with Special Reference to the Anglo-Saxon Corpus." *Proverbium*, no. 20 (1972): 737-750.

Bartels, Paul. "Das apologische Sprichwort im Niederdeutschen und Dänischen." *Niederdeutsche Zeitschrift für Volkskunde* 8 (1930): 223-250.

Bausinger, Hermann. "Redensart und Sprichwort." In *Formen der "Volkspoesie,"* 95-112. Berlin: Erich Schmidt, 1980.

Bede, Cuthbert. "Sam Vale and Sam Weller." *Notes and Queries*, 6th series, 5 (May 20, 1882): 388-389.

Beintema, T. *Wiere wurden, sprekwurden an zei-siswizen.* Ljouwert: Osinga, 1983.

Bergenthal, Marie Theres. "Verkehrte Welt—Sprichwörter." In *Elemente der Drolerie und ihre Beziehungen zur Literatur*, 146-158. Berlin: Hohmann, 1934.

Bergfors, Georg. *Ordspråk, talesätt och härm pa ytterlännäsmål.* Sollefteå: Dahlberg, 1981.

Berthold, Luise. "Beispielssprichworte in Hessen und Nassau." *Hessische Blätter für Volkskunde* 23 (1924): 113-115.

Blehr, Otto. "What is a Proverb?" *Fabula* 14 (1973): 243-246.

Brunvand, Jan Harold. "Proverbs and Proverbial Phrases." In *The Study of American Folklore: An Introduction*, 38-47. New York: W. W. Norton, 1968.

Bryan, George B., and Wolfgang Mieder. "As Sam Weller Said, When Finding Himself on the Stage: Wellerisms in Contemporary Dramatizations of Charles Dickens' *The Pickwick Papers*." *Proverbium* 11 (1994): forthcoming.

Büld, Heinrich. *Niederdeutsche Schwanksprüche zwischen Ems und Issel.* Münster: Aschendorff, 1981.

Bykova, A. A. "Semioticheskaia struktura velerizmov." In *Paremiologicheskie issledovania,* edited by Grigorii L'vovich Permiakov, 274-293. Moscow: Nauka, 1984; also published in French translation as "La structure sémiotique des wellérismes." In *Tel grain tel pain. Poétique de la sagesse populaire,* edited by Grigorii L'vovich Permiakov, 332-356. Moscow: Editions du Progré, 1988.

Casares, Julio. "La frase proverbial y el refrán." *Universidad Pontificia Bolivariana* 27 (1964): 36-49.

Casares, Julio. "La locucción, la frase proverbial, el refrán y el modismo." In *Introducción a las lexicografía moderna,* 165-242. Madrid: S. Aguirre Torre, 1950.

Castillo de Lucas, Antonio. "'Wellerismos' espaoñles de aplicación médica (refranes personificados)." *Clinica y Laboratorio* 61 (1956): 69-72.

Cederschiöld, Gustav. *Om ordstäv och andra ämnen,* 5-33. Lund: Gleerup, 1923.

Chaves, Luis. "Velerismos: 'Come diceba' . . . 'Comme dit' . . . 'Como diz' ou 'como disse' . . ." *Revista de Etnografia* 7, no. 1 (1966): 67-85.

Christiansen, Reider Thoralf. *Gamle visdomsord: norske ordsprog i utvalg,* 83-87. Oslo: Steenske Forlag, 1928.

Cirese, Alberto M. "Wellérismes et micro-récits." *Proverbium,* no. 14 (1969): 384-390; published in Italian translation as "Wellerismi et micro-récits." *Lingua e stile* 5 (1970): 283-292.

Clough, Wilson O. "A Neglected American Myth-Man ['as the feller says']." *California Folklore Quarterly* 2 (1943): 85-88.

Colajanni, Antonio. "Intorno a Proverbio e 'Cultura'." *Problemi,* no. 9 (1968): 419-423.

Cornette, James C. "Luther's Attitude toward Wellerisms." *Southern Folklore Quarterly* 9 (1945): 127-144.

Corso, G. "Wellerismi e locuzioni di Troia." *Folklore* (Napoli) 3, nos. 1-2 (1948): 68-70.

Corso, Raffaele. "Wellerismi italiani." *Folklore* (Napoli) 2, nos. 3-4 (1947-1948): 3-26.

Cray, Ed. "Wellerisms in Riddle Form." *Western Folklore* 23 (1964): 114-116.

D'Aloi, Antonio. "Wellerismi del nicoterese." *Folklore della Calabria* 1 (1956): 22-29.

Davidson, Levette J. "Folk Speech and Folk Sayings." In *A Guide to American Folklore,* 42-52. Denver: University of Denver Press, 1951.

de Beul, Daniel. *Zei-spreuken.* Ranst bij Antwerpen: D. de Beul, 1978.

de Caro, Frank A. "Riddles and Proverbs." In *Folk Groups and Folklore Genres. An Introduction,* edited by Elliott Oring, 175-197. Logan: Utah State University Press, 1986.

Dundes, Alan. "Seeing is Believing." *Natural History,* no. 5 (May 1972): 8-14 and 86; reprinted in *Interpreting Folklore,* 86-92. Bloomington: Indiana University Press, 1980.

Dundes, Alan. "Some Yoruba Wellerisms, Dialogue Proverbs, and Tongue-Twisters." *Folklore* (London) 75 (1964): 113-120.

Emenanjo, E. Nolue. "Are Igbo Wellerisms Proverbs?" *Anu: Journal of Igbo Culture,* no. 5 (1989): 62-77.

Englisch, Paul. "Skatologische Sprichwörter." In *Das skatologische Element in Literatur, Kunst und Volksleben*, 129-137. Stuttgart: Julius Püttmann, 1928.

Fendl, Josef. *Nix wie lauter Sprüch*. Pfaffenhofen: W. Ludwig, 1975.

Fleischer, Wolfgang. *Phraseologie der deutschen Gegenwartssprache*, 80- 86. Leipzig: VEB Bibliographisches Institut, 1982.

Frank, Ernst. *Lebensweisheiten des Alltags, Redewendungen und Aussprüche. Sag Trin—Sagte Katharina. In Niederrheinischer Mundart und Hochdeutsch*. Duisburg: Walter Braun, 1983.

Frijlink, H. "Samwelleriana." *Het Leeskabinet*, no. 2 (1859): 155-158; and no. 2 (1863): 139-141.

Gennep, Arnold van. "Wellérismes français." *Mercure de France*, no. 248 (15 December 1933): 700-704; reprinted in *Le Folklore Brabançon* 13 (1933-1934): 331-333.

Gennep, Arnold van. "Wellérismes français." *Mercure de France*, no. 253 (1 July 1934): 209-215.

Gennep, Arnold van. "Wellérismes français et flamands." *Mercure de France*, no. 270 (15 September 1936): 645-648; reprinted in *Le Folklore Brabançon* 16 (1936-1937): 291-294.

Gordon, Edmund I. "Sumerian Animal Proverbs and Fables: Collection Five." *Journal of Cuneiform Studies* 12 (1958): 1-21 and 43-75.

Grambo, Ronald. "Paremiological Aspects." *Folklore Forum* 5, no. 3 (1972): 100-105.

Greenway, John. "The Literature of Language: Riddles and Proverbs." In *The Primitive Reader. An Anthology of Myths, Tales, Songs, Riddles and Proverbs of Aboriginal Peoples around the World*, 148-170. Hatboro, Pennsylvania: Folklore Associates, 1965.

Grzybek, Peter. "Kulturelle Stereotype und stereotype Texte." In *Natürlichkeit der Sprache und der Kultur*, edited by Walter A. Koch, 300-327. Bochum: Norbert Brockmeyer, 1990.

Hain, Mathilde. "Das Sprichwort." *Deutschunterricht* 15, no. 2 (1963): 36-50; reprinted in *Ergebnisse der Sprichwörterforschung*, edited by Wolfgang Mieder, 13-25. Bern: Peter Lang, 1978.

Hain, Mathilde. "Sprichwort und Rätsel." In *Deutsche Philologie im Aufriss*, edited by Wolfgang Stammler (vol. 3), 2727-2754. Berlin: Erich Schmidt, 1962.

Halpert, Herbert. "Folktale and 'Wellerism'—A Note." *Southern Folklore Quarterly* 7 (1943): 75-76.

Hassell, J. Woodrow. "A Wellerism in the Tales of Des Périers." *Romance Notes* 5 (1963): 66-71.

Haupt, Moriz. "Anglicis plurimis utitur vel unus ille Dickensii Samuel Wellerus." In *Opuscula* (vol. 2), 395-406. Leipzig: Salomon Hirzel, 1876.

Henssen, Gottfried. "Hundert Schwanksprüche des Münsterlandes." In *Volk erzählt. Münsterländische Sagen, Märchen und Schwänke*, 357-362. Münster: Aschendorff, 1954.

Herzog, Heinrich. *Beispielssprichwörter gesammelt für Alt und Jung*. Aarau: Sauerländer, 1882.

Hines, Donald M. *Frontier Folksay. Proverbial Lore of the Inland Pacific Northwest Frontier*. Norwood, Pennsylvania: Norwood Editions, 1977.

Hoefer, Albert. "Über Apologische oder Beispiels-Sprichwörter im Niederdeutschen." *Germania* 4 (1844): 95-106.

Hoefer, Edmund. *Wie das Volk spricht. Sprichwörtliche Redensarten.* Stuttgart: Kröner, 1855 (10th ed. 1898).

Hofmann, Winfried. *Das rheinische Sagwort. Ein Beitrag zur Sprichwörterkunde.* Siegburg, Germany: F. Schmitt, 1959.

Holmström, G. *Sa' han och Sa' hon. Ordstäfsbok innehållande öfver 1200 ordstäf.* Stockholm: no publisher given, 1876.

Hoyos Sancho, Nieves de. "Wellerismos agricolas de España." *Folklore* (Napoli) 9, nos. 1-2 (1954): 57-62.

Jacob, Arthur. "De duivel-zeispreuken bij Guido Gezelle." *Wetenschappelijke Tijdingen* 24 (1965): 289-308.

Jacob, Arthur. "Enkele beschouwingen over de 'zeispreuk' en het 'Sagwort'." *Spieghel Historiael van de Bond van Gentse Germanisten* 2, no. 4 (1960): 73-96.

Jacob, Arthur. "Quelques remarques sur les 'Wellerismi Italiani' ou 'comme-dit'." *Le Folklore Brabançon*, no. 170 (1966): 225-230.

Jacob, Arthur. "Wellerismen-Forschung." *Proverbium*, no. 16 (1971): 595.

Järviö-Nieminen, Iris. *Suomalaiset sanomukset. Finnish Wellerisms.* Helsinki: Suomalaisen Kirjallisuuden Seura, 1959.

Jente, Richard. "El refrán." *Folklore Americas* 7, nos. 1-2 (1947): 1-11; reprinted in *Folklore* (Lima) 2, no. 19 (1948): 520-532; reprinted in shortened form in *Revista de la Universidad* (Tegucigalpa) 14, no. 2 (1950): 82-85.

Jente, Richard. "The Untilled Field of Proverbs." In *Studies in Language and Literature,* edited by George R. Coffman, 112-119. Chapel Hill: University of North Carolina Press, 1945.

Jones, Joseph. "Wellerisms: Some Further Evidence." *American Speech* 20 (1945): 235-236.

Kainis, Dr. *Die Derbheiten im Reden des Volkes.* Leipzig: Literatur-Bureau, 1872.

Kalén, Johan. "Några utbyggda ordstäv från Halland." *Folkminnen och Folktankar* 12, no. 2 (1925): 27-38.

Kirchberger, J. "Gegensatz-Sprüche." *Unser Egerland. Monatsschrift für Heimaterkundung und Heimatpflege* 27, nos. 11-12 (1923): 116-121.

Kjaer, Iver. "Wellerisms in Earlier Danish Tradition." *Proverbium*, no. 16 (1971): 579-582.

Klimová, Dagmar. "Vztah prislovi a prozaického folklóru." *Slovensky Národopis* 29, no. 4 (1981): 543-549.

Kramer, Wolfgang. "Über Phraseologismen in Artikeln des *Niedersächsischen Wörterbuchs.*" In *Niedersächsisches Wörterbuch. Berichte und Mitteilungen aus der Arbeitsstelle,* edited by Dieter Stellmacher, 33-51. Göttingen: Vandenhoeck & Ruprecht, 1990.

Krappe, Alexander Haggerty. "The Proverb." In *The Science of Folklore,* 143-152. New York: The Dial Press, 1929.

Kristensen, Evald Tang. *Danske Ordsprog og Mundheld,* 633-650. Copenhagen: Gyldendal, 1890.

Kruyskamp, C. *Apologische Spreekwoorden.* s'Gravenhage: Martinus Nijhoff, 1947 (3rd ed. 1965).

Kunze, Horst. *Irren ist menschlich, sagte der Igel* . . . *Alte und neue Beispielsprichwörter*. Berlin: Eulenspiegel Verlag, 1972; 2nd ed. with the new title of *Spaß muß sein! Eine Blütenlese von alten und neuen Beispielsprichwörtern*. Berlin: Eulenspiegel Verlag, 1976.

Kuusi, Matti. "Wellerismit." In *Sananlaskut ja puheenparret*, 143–146. Helsinki: Suomalaisen Kirjallisuuden Seura, 1954.

Kuusi, Matti. "Sananparret ja arvoitukset." *Oma maa* 11 (1962): 164–175.

Lapucci, Carlo. *Come disse* . . . *dizionario delle facezie proverbiali della lingua italiana*. Florence: Valmartina, 1978.

Laukkanen, Kari. "Savolainen pirusanomus." *Kotiseutu*, no volume given (1961): 178–183.

Laukkanen, Kari. "Se on mun, sano Eenokki akkaansa." *Kotiseuta*, no volume given (1964): 144–148.

Lauri, Achille. "Wellerismi della media Valle del Liri." *Folklore* (Napoli) 3, nos. 3–4 (1948–1949): 107–113; 4, nos. 1–2 (1949): 109–118; and 6, nos. 1–2 (1951): 58–67.

Leino, Pentti. "Comments [on Wellerisms]." *Proverbium*, no. 9 (1967): 196–197.

Leino, Pentti. "Dialogsprichwort oder Replikenanekdote." *Proverbium*, no. 23 (1974): 904–908.

Leistner, Ernst. *Witz und Spott, Scherz und Laune in Sprichwörtern und Volksredensarten*. Lahr, Germany: Schauenberg, 1879.

Lindfors, Bernth, and Oyekan Owomoyela. "Yoruba Wordplay: A Tongue Twister, a Tone Twister and a Wellerism." *Southern Folklore Quarterly* 39 (1975): 167–170.

Lindow, Wolfgang. "Das Sagwort als Sonderform des Sprichwortes." In *Volkstümliches Sprachgut in der neuniederdeutschen Dialektdichtung* (vol. 1), 139–214; (vol. 2), 8–13. Ph.D. Diss., University of Kiel, 1960.

Loukatos, Demetrios S. "'Citations proverbiales' plutôt que 'wellérismes latents'." *Proverbium*, no. 20 (1972): 759.

Loukatos, Demetrios S. "Wellérismes 'latents'." *Proverbium*, no. 9 (1967): 193–196.

Luomala, Katherine. "'Drowning the Otter': Comment on a Danish Wellerism." *Proverbium*, no. 17 (1971): 630.

Luomala, Katherine. "The Narrative Source of a Hawaiian Proverb and Related Problems." *Proverbium*, no. 21 (1973): 783–787.

Mango, Achille. "Wellerismi e farsa cavaiola." *Problemi*, no. 9 (1968): 425–427.

Melo, Verissimo de. "Wellerism." *Tradición: Revista peruana de cultura* 2, no. 3 (1951): 31–37.

Meyer, Annemarie. "Rund um das Sprichwort: 'Viel Geschrei und wenig Wolle'." *Schweizerisches Archiv für Volkskunde* 41 (1944): 37–42.

Miccolis, P. M. "Wellerismi salentini." *Lares* 32, nos. 1–2 (1966): 51–58.

Mieder, Wolfgang. *Antisprichwörter*. 3 vols. Wiesbaden: Gesellschaft für deutsche Sprache, 1982 and 1985; Wiesbaden: Quelle & Meyer, 1989.

Mieder, Wolfgang. "Das Sprichwort im humoristischen Kaleidoskop der Illustrierten." *Sprachspiegel* 30 (1974): 68–74; reprinted in *Das Sprichwort in unserer Zeit*, 23–30. Frauenfeld, Switzerland: Huber, 1975.

Mieder, Wolfgang. "Dingsbums (Wellerismen)." In *Deutsche Sprichwörter und Redensarten*, 157–160. Stuttgart: Philipp Reclam, 1979.

Mieder, Wolfgang. "'Eulenspiegel macht seine Mitbürger durch Schaden klug'. Sprichwörtliches im *Dil Ulenspiegel* von 1515." *Eulenspiegel-Jahrbuch* 29 (1989): 27-50.

Mieder, Wolfgang. "'Gedankensplitter, die ins Auge gehen'. Zu den sprichwörtlichen Aphorismen von Gabriel Laub." *Wirkendes Wort* 41 (1991): 228-239.

Mieder, Wolfgang. "Sexual Content of German Wellerisms." *Maledicta* 6 (1982): 215-223.

Mieder, Wolfgang. "'Spaß muß sein', sagte der Spaßmacher, aber . . . Zu den Sagwörtern von Markus M. Ronner." *Sprachspiegel* 42 (1986): 162-170.

Mieder, Wolfgang. "Sprichwörter im modernen Sprachgebrauch." *Muttersprache* 85 (1975): 65-88; reprinted in *Deutsche Sprichwörter in Literatur, Politik, Presse und Werbung*, 53-76. Hamburg: Helmut Buske, 1983.

Mieder, Wolfgang. "Sprichwörtliche Schwundstufen des Märchens. Zum 200. Geburtstag der Brüder Grimm." *Proverbium: Yearbook of International Proverb Scholarship* 3 (1986): 257-271.

Mieder, Wolfgang. "'Wahrheiten: Phantasmen aus Logik und Alltag'. Zu den sprichwörtlichen Aphorismen von Werner Mitsch." *Muttersprache* 98 (1988): 121-132.

Mieder, Wolfgang. "'Wenige jedoch rudern gegen den Strom': Zu den sprichwörtlichen Aphorismen von Hans Leopold Davi." *Sprachspiegel* 46 (1990): 97-104.

Mino, Calogero di. "Wellerismi, distici o motti?" *Folklore* (Napoli) 3, nos. 1-2 (1948): 20-40.

Mittelstädt, Hartmut. "Die isländischen Sprichwörter—Quellen, Bildgehalt, Klassifikation, Funktion im Text." *Nordeuropa Studien* 14 (special issue, 1981): 85-94.

Moll, Otto. "Parömiologische Fachausdrücke und Definitionen." *Proverbium*, no. 10 (1968): 249-250.

Monye, Ambrose. "Devices of Indirection in Aniocha Proverb Usage." *Proverbium: Yearbook of International Proverb Scholarship* 4 (1987): 111-126.

Moretti, P. "Wellerismi sardi." *Rivista di Etnografia* 19 (1965): 72-91.

Moser, Dietz-Rüdiger. "'Die wellt wil meister klueglin bleiben . . .' Martin Luther und das deutsche Sprichwort." *Muttersprache* 90 (1980): 151-166.

Negreanu, Constantin. "Din istoricul încercarilor de clasificare si definire a proverbelor." *Mehedinti. Istorie si cultura* 3 (1981): 273-278.

Nelson, Timothy. "Die Fabel und das Sagwort." In *"O du armer Luther . . ." Sprichwörtliches in der antilutherischen Polemik des Johannes Nas (1534–1590)*, 121-153. Bern: Peter Lang, 1992.

Neumann, Siegfried. "Aspekte der Wellerismen-Forschung." *Proverbium*, no. 6 (1966): 131-137.

Neumann, Siegfried. "Das Sagwort in Mecklenburg um die Mitte des 19. Jahrhunderts im Spiegel der Mundartdichtungen Reuters und Brinckmans." *Deutsches Jahrbuch für Volkskunde* 12 (1966): 50-66.

Neumann, Siegfried. "'Dat seggt man, wenn . . .' Sagwörter im Munde eines alten mecklenburgischen Maurers." *Kikut. Plattdütsch gistern un hüt*, no. 12 (1987): 55-61.

Neumann, Siegfried. "John Brinckman und das mecklenburgische Sprichwort." *Wissenschaftliche Zeitschrift des Pädagogischen Instituts Güstrow* 2 (1963-1964): 23-24; reprinted in *Festschrift zum 150. Geburtstag von John Brinckman*, edited by Hans-Jürgen Klug, 21-25. Güstrow, Germany: Stadt Güstrow, 1964.

Neumann, Siegfried. "Sagwörter im Schwank—Schwankstoffe im Sagwort." In *Volksüberlieferung. Festschrift für Kurt Ranke*, edited by Fritz Harkort, Karel C. Peeters, and Robert Wildhaber, 249-266. Göttingen: Schwartz, 1968.

Neumann, Siegfried. "Sagwort und Schwank." *Letopis. Jahresschrift des Instituts für sorbische Volksforschung*, series C, nos. 11-12 (1968-1969): 147-158.

Ojoade, J. Olowo. "Some Ilaje Wellerisms." *Folklore* (London), 91 (1980): 63-71.

Opata, Damian U. "Characterization in Animal-Derived Wellerisms: Some Selected Igbo Examples." *Proverbium: Yearbook of International Proverb Scholarship* 7 (1990): 217-231.

Opata, Damian U. "Personal Attribution in Wellerisms." *International Folklore Review* 6 (1988): 39-41.

Paducheva, E. V. "O semanticheskikh sviaziakh mezhdu basnei i ee moral'iu (na materiale basen ezopa)." In *Paremiologicheskie issledovaniia*, edited by Grigorii L'vovich Permiakov, 223-251. Moscow: Nauka, 1984; published in French translation as "Liens sémantiques entre la fable et sa morale." In *Tel grain tel pain. Poétique de la sagesse populaire*, edited by Grigorii L'vovich Permiakov, 168-206. Moscow: Éditions du Progrès, 1988.

Pérez de Castro, J. L. "Dialogismos en el refranero asturiano." *Revista de dialectologia y tradiciones populares* 19, nos. 1-3 (1963), 116-138.

Permiakov, Grigorii L'vovich. *Paremiologicheskie eksperiment. Materialy dlia paremiologicheskogo minimuma*. Moscow: Nauka, 1971.

Perusini, Gaetano. "Wellerismi friulani." *Rivista di Etnografia* 2, no. 4 (1948): 12-23.

Petsch, Robert. "'Geflügelte Worte' und Verwandtes. Aus der Formenwelt der menschlichen Rede." In *Deutsche Literaturwissenschaft. Aufsätze zur Begründung der Methode*, 230-238. Berlin: Emil Ebering, 1940.

Petsch, Robert. "Das Volkssprichwort." In *Spruchdichtung des Volkes. Vor- und Frühformen der Volksdichtung*, 103-125. Halle: Max Niemeyer, 1938.

Pettenati, Gastone. "Per la definizione del wellerismo." *Problemi*, no. 9 (1968): 423-425.

Pilz, Klaus Dieter. "Wellerismen (Sagwörter) und Dialogsprichwörter." In *Phraseologie. Versuch einer interdisziplinären Abgrenzung, Begriffsbestimmung und Systematisierung unter besonderer Berücksichtigung der deutschen Gegenwartssprache* (vol. 2), 667-673. Göppingen, Germany: Alfred Kümmerle, 1978.

Predota, Stanislaw. "Zur niederländischen Sprichwörterlexikographie im 20. Jahrhundert." *Acta Universitatis Wratislaviensis*, no. 942 (1986): 103-119.

Prümer, Karl. *Westfälische Volksweisheit. Plattdeutsche Sprichwörter, Redensarten, Volkslieder, Reime und Kinderlieder*, 3-23. Bremen: Möllenhoff, 1881.

Redlich, Friedrich. "Sprichwort." In *Deutsche Volksdichtung. Eine Einführung*, edited by Hermann Strobach, 221-240, 392-393 (notes). Leipzig: Reclam, 1979.

Rehbein, Detlev. *Spaß muß sein, sagte der Kater . . . : Sagwörter aus europäischen Sprachen*. Leipzig: Bibliographisches Institut, 1990.

Rehbein, Detlev. *Viel Geschrei und wenig Wolle . . . Deutsche Sagwörter*. Berlin: Eulenspiegel Verlag, 1991.

Rodegem, Francis M. "La parole proverbiale." In *Richesse du proverbe*, edited by François Suard and Claude Buridant (vol. 2), 121-135. Lille: Université de Lille, 1984.

Rodegem, Francis M. "Une forme d'humour contestataire au Burundi: les wellérismes." *Cahiers d'études africaines* 14 (1974): 521-542.

Rodegem, Francis M. "Un problème de terminologie: Les locutions sentencieuses." *Cahiers de l'institut de linguistique* 1, no. 5 (1972): 677-703.

Rodegem, Francis M., and P. Van Brussel. "Proverbes et pseudo-proverbes. La logique des parémies." In *Europhras 88. Phraséologie contrastive. Actes du colloque international Klingenthal-Strasbourg, 12-16 mai 1988*, edited by Gertrud Gréciano, 349-356. Strasbourg: Université des Sciences Humaines, 1989.

Roderich, Albert. "Glossierte Sprichwörter." In *Gedankensplitter. Gesammelt aus den "Fliegenden Blättern,"* 281-286. Munich: Braun & Schneider, 1885.

Röhrich, Lutz. "Die Parodie." In *Der Witz. Figuren, Formen, Funktionen*, 65-73. Stuttgart: Metzler, 1977.

Röhrich, Lutz. "Sprichwörtliche Redensarten aus Volkserzählungen." In *Volk, Sprache, Dichtung. Festgabe für Kurt Wagner*, edited by Karl Bischoff and Lutz Röhrich, 247-275. Gießen: Wilhelm Schmitz, 1960; reprinted in *Ergebnisse der Sprichwörterforschung*, edited by Wolfgang Mieder, 121-141. Bern: Peter Lang, 1978.

Röhrich, Lutz. "Sprichwort, Wellerismus und Redensart." In *Gebärde- Metapher-Parodie. Studien zur Sprache und Volksdichtung*, 181-214. Düsseldorf: Schwann, 1967.

Röhrich, Lutz, and Wolfgang Mieder. "Wellerismus (Sagwort, Beispielsprichwort)." In *Sprichwort*, 11-14. Stuttgart: Metzler, 1977.

Ronner, Markus M. *Moment mal!* Bern: Benteli, 1977.

Rooth, Anna Birgitta. "Den epigrammatiska formen." In *Folklig diktning. Form och teknik*, 87-101. Uppsala: Almqvist & Wiksell, 1965.

Rudeck, Wilhelm. "Die Sprichwörter." In *Geschichte der öffentlichen Sittlichkeit von Deutschland*, 133-138. Berlin: H. Barsdorf, 1905.

Rupprecht, Karl. "Paroimia." In *Realencyclopädie der classischen Altertumswissenschaft* (vol. 18, part 4), 1707-1735. Stuttgart: Metzler, 1949.

Russo, Antonio. "Gli studi sul wellerismo in Italia." *Archivio per l'antropologia e l'etnologia* 97 (1967): 101-107.

Sacchetti, Alfredo. "Dicette 'a luciola' . . ." *Uomini e idee* 6, no. 1 (1964): 60-62.

Sallinen, Pirkko. "Skandinavische Entsprechungen finnischer Wellerismen." *Proverbium*, no. 14 (1969): 390-395; and 15 (1970): 522-525.

Salveit, Laurits. "Beobachtungen zu einem Sonderfall der Parataxe in deutschen Sprichwörtern." In *Aspekte der Germanistik. Festschrift für Hans-Friedrich Rosenfeld*, edited by Walter Tauber, 657-670. Göppingen: Alfred Kümmerle, 1989.

Sánchez y Escribano, F. "Dialogismos paremiológicos castellanos." *Revista de Filologia Española* 23 (1936): 275-291.

Schellbach-Kopra, Ingrid. *Finnisch-Deutsches Sprichwörterbuch*, 9-33. Bonn: Rudolf Habelt, 1980.

Schultz, Johan Gustaf. *Sex hundra svenska ordstäv*. Stockholm: no publisher, 1870.

Schütze, Johann Friedrich. "Apologische Sprüchwörter der niedersächsisch-holsteinischen Volkssprache." *Neuer Teutscher Merkur* 3 (October 1800): 112-115.

Seiler, Friedrich. *Deutsche Sprichwörterkunde*, 429-431. Munich: C. H. Beck, 1922 (reprint 1967).

Seiler, Friedrich. "Ein 'alter Reim' bei Goethe." *Zeitschrift für deutschen Unterricht* 33 (1919): 383-386.

Seiler, Friedrich. "Ursprung, Verbreitung, Sammlungen und inhaltliche Gruppierung des Sagworts." In *Das deutsche Lehnsprichwort*, 1-53, 166-172 (word index). Halle: Verlag der Buchhandlung des Waisenhauses, 1924 (*Die Entwicklung der deutschen Kultur im Spiegel des deutschen Lehnworts*, vol. 8).

Simon, Irmgard. *Sagwörter. Plattdeutsche Sprichwörter aus Westfalen.* Münster: Aschendorff, 1988.

Simon, Irmgard. "Zum Aufbau eines Sprichwortarchivs: Das Westfälische Sprichwortarchiv bei der Kommission für Mundart- und Namenforschung." In *Sprichwörter und Redensarten im interkulturellen Vergleich*, edited by Annette Sabban and Jan Wirrer, 13-27. Opladen, Germany: Westdeutscher Verlag, 1991.

Singer, Samuel. "Schweizerische Sagsprichwörter." *Schweizerisches Archiv für Volkskunde* 38 (1941): 129-139; and 39 (1941-1942): 137-139.

Singer, Samuel. "'Viel Geschrei und wenig Wolle'. Nachtrag." *Schweizerisches Archiv für Volkskunde* 41 (1944): 159-160.

Speroni, Charles. "Five Italian Wellerisms [Collected in California]." *Western Folklore* 7 (1948): 54-55.

Speroni, Charles. *The Italian Wellerism to the End of the Seventeenth Century.* Berkeley: University of California Press, 1953.

Speroni, Charles. "Wellerismi tolti dai proverbi inediti di Francesco Serdonati." *Folklore* (Napoli) 4, nos. 1-2 (1949): 12-31.

Ström, Fredrik. *Svenska ordstäv*, 5-39. Stockholm: Bonnier, 1939.

Sutermeister, Otto. *Die schweizerischen Sprichwörter der Gegenwart*, 39-47. Aarau, Switzerland: J. J. Christea, 1869.

Swierczynska, Dobroslawa. "O kilku gatunkach przyslow. Welleryzmy, dialogi, priamele." *Literatura ludowa* 18, nos. 4-5 (1974): 29-35.

Tabarcea, Cezar. "Proverbul si speciile inrudite. Proverb si zicatoare." *Analele Universitatii Bucuresti* 29 (1980): 95-103.

Tamony, Peter. "To See the Elephant." *Pacific Historian* 12 (Winter 1968): 23-29.

Taylor, Archer. "A Bibliographical Note on Wellerisms." *Journal of American Folklore* 65 (1952): 420-421.

Taylor, Archer. "Names in Folktales [and Proverbs]." In *Märchen, Mythos, Dichtung. Festschrift zum 90. Geburtstag Friedrich von der Leyens*, edited by Hugo Kuhn and Kurt Schier, 31-34. Munich: C.H. Beck, 1963.

Taylor, Archer. "Problems in the Study of Proverbs." *Journal of American Folklore* 47 (1934): 1-21; reprinted in *Selected Writings on Proverbs by Archer Taylor*, edited by Wolfgang Mieder, 15-39. Helsinki: Suomalainen Tiedeakatemia, 1975.

Taylor, Archer. "The Collection and Study of Proverbs." *Proverbium*, no. 8 (1967): 161-177; reprinted in *Selected Writings on Proverbs by Archer Taylor*, edited by Wolfgang Mieder, 84-100. Helsinki: Suomalainen Tiedeakatemia, 1975.

Taylor, Archer. "The Wisdom of Many and the Wit of One." *Swarthmore College Bulletin* 59 (1962): 4-7; reprinted in *Selected Writings on Proverbs by Archer Taylor*, edited by Wolfgang Mieder, 68-73. Helsinki: Suomalainen Tiedeakatemia, 1975.

Taylor, Archer, F. W. Bradley, Richard Jente, Morris Palmer Tilley, and Bartlett Jere Whiting. "The Study of Proverbs." *Modern Language Forum* 24 (1939): 57-83; reprinted in *Selected Writings on Proverbs by Archer Taylor*, edited by Wolfgang Mieder, 40-67. Helsinki: Suomalainen Tiedeakatemia, 1975.

Tillhagen, Carl-Herman. "Die Sprichwörterfrequenz in einigen nordschwedischen Dörfern." *Proverbium*, no. 15 (1970): 538-540.

Tillhagen, Carl-Herman. *Folklig ordakonst.* Stockholm: LTs förlag, 1980.

Tucci, Giovanni. "250 wellerismi della Campania." *Dicette Pulicenella . . . Inchiesta die antropologia culturale sulla Campania,* 21-304. Milan: Silva Editore, 1966.

Tucci, Giovanni. "Inchiesta sui wellerismi della Campania." *Rivista di Etnografia* 16 (1962): 3-51.

Tucci, Giovanni. "Saggio sul wellerismo. Storia, nome e definizione, forma e classificazione." *Revista de Etnografia* (Lima) 11, no. 2 (1968): 293-316.

Tucci, Giovanni. "Studi e ricerche sui wellerismi." *Rivista di Etnografia* 20 (1966): 109-121.

Tucci, Giovanni. "Studi e ricerche sui wellerismi in Italia." In *Atti del congresso internazionale di linguistica e tradizioni popolari,* edited by Giacomo Devoto, 293-309. Udine: Società filologica friulana, 1969; also published in *Rivista di Etnografia* 23 (1969): 3-25.

Tucci, Giovanni. "Valore dei wellerismi nello studio della cultura popolare." In *La religiosità popolare nella Valle Padana. Atti del II convegno di studi sul folklore padano,* no editor given, 419-430. Florence: Leo Olschki, 1966.

Tucci, Giovanni. "Wellerismi della Campania." *Rivista di Etnografia* 17 (1963): 3-50.

Wander, Karl Friedrich Wilhelm. "Das apologische oder Beispielssprichwort." *Blätter für literarische Unterhaltung,* no. 8 (18 February 1864): 148- 149.

Wander, Karl Friedrich Wilhelm. *Deutsches Sprichwörter-Lexikon,* 5 vols. Leipzig: F. A. Brockhaus, 1867-1880; reprint, Darmstadt: Wissenschaftliche Buchgesellschaft, 1964.

Woeste, Friedrich. "Apologische Sprichwörter in Mundarten des märkischen Süderlandes." *Die deutschen Mundarten* 3 (1856): 253-264.

Woods, Barbara Allen. "Unfamiliar Quotations in Brecht's Plays." *Germanic Review* 46 (1971): 26-42.

INDEX OF SPEAKERS

INDEX OF SITUATIONS

bid friend good night during thunderstorm, 313

big tall man steal kiss, 605

bind up offspring's finger, 583

bishop show actress pass-book, 1271

bishop tell actress she reminds him of Aspasia, 860

bite anchor, 556

bite cock's head off, 1005

bite man, 1343

bite piece out of man's arm, 446

bleed boy to death, 861

blow block off, 383

blow steamboat sky high, 144

blow up ministers, 190

body of Gen. Packenham in barrel of rum, 1236

bone customers, 1493

bore into whiskey barrel, 1276

bottom of washtub fall out, 1108

box of specie go to bottom of river, 482

box young man's jaw, 935

boy come in with wet feet, 304

boy pinch tail, 417

boy pull goose through hole by tail, 277

boy rob old crow's nest, 180

boy run by himself, 500

brand steer's leg, 623

bray and drag cart, 854

break bottle of oil over Brown's head, 905

break jail, 1509

break out of enclosure and run off, 942

bridge fall down, 293

brush lapels of coat, 752

bugger porcupine, 959

build fire under mule, 1283

bull come up lane, 1467

bump into light pole, 1153

burn at stake, 1209

burn body in quick lime, 117

bury Blue Beard, 1449

bury quack doctor, 477

bury seventh husband and look anxiously for another, 618

butcher refuse credit, 1393

butcher's dog snap teeth through loafer's leg, 946

butler flog young gentleman, 136

butt head against window, 1114

buy angora sweater, 1179

buy handsome print of houses of parliament, 661

buy wife pair of five-dollar spectacles, 391

buzz along in trail of comet, 897

cabbage neighbor's half-bushel, 811

Caesar stab Shakapeel in House of Representatives, 603

calf swallow grindlestone, 638

call for glass of water, 372

called cuckold by wife, 834

can't reach grapes, 1231

can't see at all, 1161

can't talk, 1146

cannon ball smash sailor's skull, 568

cannot climb tree, 1230

cannot recite lesson, 128

canter along road with bulldog sampling coat tails, 923

capsize rider in mud, 700

carry gentleman to Tyburn, 710

carry wife to burial, 1399

cast wife into Dead Sea, 1265

cat peep down rat's hole, 771

catch dog trying to kill sheep, 152

catch family physician kissing wife, 91

catch hornet, 1398

catch nigger in woods, 1442

catch tail in lawn mower, 758, 904

caterpillar gaze up at butterfly, 495

caught by dog, 1039

caught in steel trap, 1363

charge passengers double price, 407

charge two cents more a pound for beef, 1046

chase boy taking fruit, 1175

chase tail, 1427

chased by journalist's dog, 210

chew carpenter's glue, 1082

chew wax, leather, and tobacco, 1446

chickens pass on street, 474

chloroform St. Vitus patient, 275

circus clown kiss widow, 1482

clear for Texas, 764

click shears on frosh, 572

climb cherry tree to get apple, 1155

climb into barber's chair, 761

clip elephant's ears, 83

clock fall on head, 1384

cock say to horse, 1256

coffin fall out of car, 1026

collide with sidewalk, 327

come across man eating dinner, 95

come down from roof of five-story mansion, 300

come to a mud puddle, 646

come to sugar maple to drink sap bucket, 1310

constable call "Stop thief!", 38

constable catch thief, 564